T0156776

Also by Donna Underwood

Non-fiction:
Original Loss
Original Loss Revisited
Grief Works

Fiction: All of the following are mystery novels;
The Support Group
The Divorce Group
The Prisoner's Group
Salt and Pepper Detective Agency

Coming next....
Salt and Pepper Detective Agency and The Dream
Team

Salt and Pepper Detective Agency

A MYSTERY NOVEL

Donna Underwood

abbott press

Abbott Press books may be ordered through booksellers or by contacting:

Abbott Press
1663 Liberty Drive
Bloomington, IN 47403
www.abbottpress.com
Phone: 1 (866) 697-5310

Because of the dynamic nature of the Internet, any web addresses or
links contained in this book may have changed since publication and
may no longer be valid. The views expressed in this work are solely those
of the author and do not necessarily reflect the views of the publisher,
and the publisher hereby disclaims any responsibility for them.

Any people depicted in stock imagery provided by Getty Images are
models, and such images are being used for illustrative purposes only.
Certain stock imagery © Getty Images.

ISBN: 978-1-4582-2180-3 (sc)
ISBN: 978-1-4582-2179-7 (hc)
ISBN: 978-1-4582-2178-0 (e)

Library of Congress Control Number: 2018907200

Print information available on the last page.

Abbott Press rev. date: 6/19/2018

DEDICATED TO...

To all who experienced cruelty, chaos, neglect, abuse, abandonment.

To all who were not taught to recognize their own self-worth or potential.

To all who have spent time in juvenile hall, jail or prison.

To all who despite their painful childhoods have grown to be kind and loving adults.

When you know better, you do better.
Maya Angelou (1928-2014)

IN APPRECIATION...

To my husband, Wayne, for his unfailing encouragement. His enjoyment of this writing was demonstrated by his laughter and tears.

To my editor and friend Patty Clark, for her patience and suggestions.

To Sergeant Ken Lattin of the Kennewick Police Department, for reading parts of my manuscript. He was kind enough to help me legitimize said parts.

To Jennifer Dansberry for generously offering to be my second editor. My high school English teacher would have been horrified to read my manuscript before Wayne, Patty, and Jennifer came to my grammatical rescue.

MAIN CHARACTERS

Houston Hayfield, recently released from prison and now has opened a Detective Agency with her friend, Wilamina.

Wilamina Robinson, recently released from prison is working with Houston as a private detective-investigator for their own agency.

Detective Sark Lorenzo works in the Homicide Division in the Whitefall Police Department.

Monte Jacks, nickname Stoney. He works for Luke Jones Landscaping Co. part time doing stone work, patios, paths, fire pits......hence the name Stoney.

Detective Sasha Voss worked undercover in Lancer's Prison, now works as a Homicide Detective in the Whitefall Police Department.

Sammy Lincoln, will be released from prison and is friends with Houston and Wilamina.

MORE CHARACTERS

Dr. Blackmore, veterinarian.

Lacona Monroe, manager of an animal rescue shelter. Partner of Sammy Lincoln.

The Grief Clinic: the social workers, Brooksie, Lucinda, Rachael and Anita.

Luke, husband of Brooksie.

Tony, husband of Lucinda.

Roco, attorney and husband of Rachael.

The inmate Dr. Sharon Primm. The psychologist who had worked at the Grief Clinic prior to her imprisonment. She authored the program that helped to set Houston and Wilamina free.

Hunt Rickels, a private investigator in Seattle, WA.

Jessie Rickels, a private investigator, Hunt's wife.

Jason Spade, an insurance fraud investigator.

**"What's done to children,
they will do to society."**
Karl Menninger (1893-1990)

PROLOGUE

"We've got him!" shrieked Houston, muffling her voice with her hands.

At that very moment her cell phone started to play fairly loud music and both women froze in place.

"What the hell is that?" whispered Wilamina. As her head flinched back slightly.

"The f.....g cell phone." Houston grabbed the phone and rammed it down into her bra in an attempt to stifle the sound. She peaked out the window and saw Mr. Germain looking up at the same window. He quickly jumped down from the ladder and ran into his house.

"My God, Willy, I think he heard us. What if he comes looking over here?" Houston grabbed her friend and said, "Let's go out the back door and hide behind the garage."

They raced down the stairs as Wilamina prayed out loud to Jesus. They went out the door and had just enough room to squeeze between the garage and the neighbor's fence. There were a few tall bushes and several trash cans to get around. They both squeezed in and squatted down just as Mr. Germain came running to the back door of the empty house. They could hear him opening the door apparently he went inside. Both frightened detectives were holding their breath. They couldn't see what he was doing or where he was. After what seemed like hours to them they heard his footsteps, on the gravel driveway, coming toward them.

As he walked toward the garage he verbally threatened, "If you damn kids are lurking around here again, You're going to get more than you bargained for. I'm not calling the police this time 'cause I got a better plan. They'd probably just arrest you. My plan for you is far more painful."

Everything was deathly quiet for a second or two and then the two terrified investigators hear footsteps moving further away down the driveway. They waited breathlessly for what seemed like an eternity. Then slowly Houston inched her way through the bushes, walking sideways because of the tight fit. She was able to get close to the edge of the garage and peak out. She didn't see him. Wilamina was right behind holding onto Houston's pant's pocket.

INTRODUCTION

The year is 2017 and the place is Whitefall, Washington. Whitefall is located approximately one hour from downtown Seattle. Houston Hayfield, nicknamed Tex, has been released recently from Lancer's Women's Prison. Houston was incarcerated for the killing of her mother's boyfriend. He'd attempted to strangulate her mother. Houston was able to beat him off by using her fists and a nearby trophy. He died from the beating that same day. Her mother was a long time alcoholic and didn't even remember that her boyfriend was trying to choke her to death, despite the bruises and the handprints on her neck. She testified against her daughter in court. The court appointed defender did a lousy job and Houston was falsely found guilty of manslaughter. She spent several years in prison until an attorney named Roco Lagunta was made aware of the unfairness of her imprisonment and took on her case pro bono and won her release.

Wilamina Robinson is still waiting to be released from Lancer's Prison. Willy, her prison nickname, defended her brother Royal from her then boyfriend Armon. The boyfriend was a long time body builder and Royal had a much smaller physique. The fight was over drug money that Royal supposedly owed Armon. Armon was enraged and beat her brother until he was unconscious. He continued to kick and pound on Royal with both fists. In her attempt to stop the beating of her brother, Willy hit her boyfriend over and over. Then he turned his rage to her. She continued to fight back with a frying pan. Armon died in the hospital from the blows to his head. She was arrested, and like Houston was assigned a very incompetent lawyer. She was also found guilty of manslaughter of her brother's attacker. A few years after her incarceration, Mr. Lagunta took on her case and successfully had the conviction reversed. He also proved she killed only self defense and to save her brother. She was to be released from prison soon after Houston was granted her freedom.

While Houston and Wilamina were in prison, they had enrolled in a pilot program written by Dr. Sharon Primm, a psychologist and also an inmate. Sharon was incarcerated at Lancer's Prison for the killing of her sister, Maureen. She discovered her sister had already murdered two men and was planning to kill again. Sharon made the heart-breaking choice to take her sister's life in order to prevent her sister from murdering anyone else. She tried for years to get treatments for Maureen, but all attempts had failed. Sharon decided to make the best use of her imprisonment by writing books and programs that would hopefully better the lives of the inmates and reduce the recidivism rate.

Four social workers from the Grief Clinic volunteered to be the facilitators for Sharon's program. They became friends while Sharon was working at the Grief Clinic as a psychologist and they remained close after she was sent to prison. Sharon discovered how common and deeply imbeded the lack of self-worthiness and overwhelming sense of hopelessness that most of the women prisoners had. She found it imperative to write a program to teach the women self-respect, produce hope, and possibly help the inmates to make constructive choices, in and out of prison. Her friends from the clinic offered their free services to get the program started.

Houston and Willamina signed up for the six month program. During those six months they became friends. They eventually decided that when they were released, they would like to go into business together.

The Salt and Pepper Detective Agency was formed. So named because of the color of their skin.

CHAPTER ONE

Houston talked with Willy by phone. She discussed the town of Whitefall and the business opportunities there. She described the small town and it's close proximity to Seattle and the potential for clients.

"Our truck was donated by Luke Jones and Tony Padilla. They are the husbands of Brooksie and Lucinda, our two favorite social workers. The truck is older, not much to look at, but it runs great. So Willy, we got wheels. Tony and Luke are both pretty good mechanics. I'm looking at working as a waitress in a coffee shop. The place is called The Table Talk Cafe. Brooksie and Lucinda, told me to go there and apply. I think the owners liked me and are going to give me a chance. There may be a job for you, too. That's if you want it?"

"Yes, yes I want it! I don't know why so much good has come into our lives Tex, but sure as hell we'll pay everyone back, somehow, someday."

"My brother said he wants to help us get started in our agency and he can afford to do that," stated Houston. "He opened a bank account for me and put in five thousand dollars for seed money for us. I'm gonna start scouting for an office after I find out about licenses we may need for our investigative work. There's much to be done. I'm so excited I'm about to pee on myself. Can't wait for you to get out. Two of us can get more done than just one. How's it going for you?"

"I'm gettin' restless as a cat in heat. The days go by slow, but I'm keeping busy reading the detective book you loaned me. Bye partner, my phone time is up. Later."

"Bye Willy, see you soon. Don't get careless in there. Be sure to watch your back."

CHAPTER TWO

Six weeks later..........

A group of well wishers were excitedly milling around the prison's parking lot awaiting for the gate to open and Wilamina Robinson to appear. The four social workers from the Grief Clinic, Dr. James, the warden of the prison, Dr. Gibran the prison's M.D. on the night shift, her nurse Mela Washington and Royal, Wilamina's brother were all standing together at the gate. Her lawyer, Roco Lagunta, had just parked his car and quickly joined the others. They were holding balloons and flowers for Wilamina.

They could hear Willy before they could see her. She was belting out "Amazing Grace."

When Wilamina caught site of her welcoming committee she started to wail, sounding like a wounded animal. She ran into her brother's arms and grabbed Houston and as many friends as she could and tried to hug everyone at the same time.

"Oh my God! You all came for me? I can't believe this is happening. Thank you Jesus, and thank you everyone."

Houston said, "Welcome to your new life which this time includes true friends."

Mela Washington, one of the prison's night nurses, stood back from the rest of the group. She kept wiping her nose. Her wet cheeks were glistening in the sunlight. "Your freedom makes my heart filled with hope for other innocent inmates." She handed

Willy a card and asked her not to open it 'til later. "It's from Dr. Gibran, Warden James, Sharon and me." The outside of the envelope read, 'Our wish is for the success of the Salt and Pepper Detective Agency. May the bad dudes beware of the two street-wise warriors. With love from Florence, Mela and Sharon.'

After some time passed, and many hugs, tears and tons of happy talk, the group filed off to their cars and left to go home or to work. Houston's brother, Lee, had just pulled into the parking area. He drove his Suburban because it could seat more people. Houston, Wilamina, and Royal all piled in and headed for Lee's house. Everyone was previously informed about a party that was planned for Houston and Wilamina for next Saturday. It was to be held at the Table Talk Cafe at 5 p.m.

The Table Talk Cafe..........

With help from the Grief Clinic social workers and the cafe staff they decorated the back meeting room for the happy occasion. The guests included all those that had been a part of the welcoming committee who had gathered at the gates of the prison. Dr. Blackmore, the veterinarian who befriended Sammy, was also present. Sammy was still an inmate at Lancer's, with hopes of being released in the near future. She had become friends with Wilamina and Houston. She was enrolled in the same workshop.

There was one surprise guest standing near the back of the room. Sasha was an inmate at Lancer's the same time as Houston and Wilamina. She had been also in the same pilot program. She was quietly observing the celebration when Houston spotted her.

"What the hell. How'd you get here, Sasha? Shit, how'd you even get out?"

Sasha smiled and stood up slowly to show Houston and Wilamina what she was wearing.

Wilamina's eyes became as big as saucers. She exclaimed, "What the hey, you got on a police uniform, badge and gun. What's going on here?"

The warden was also grinning ear to ear. She said, "Willy and Tex, I'd like to introduce you to Sasha Voss, our hard working undercover police woman. Better known to you as 'Sasha the ho.'"

"No way! Is this a damn trick?" challenged Houston.

"Yes, Tex," responded Sasha. "I was undercover, but now I'm a homicide detective. I've been on the force for the last ten years."

"Did you know all along, Warden?" asked Houston.

"No, Tex. I was just as fooled as you were. We got her out of Lancer's right after Wilamina was released under the pretense that she was hospitalized for some terrible ailment."

"I've just gotta hug me a born again ho," said Wilamina. Everyone laughed. Sasha laughed the loudest. She returned the bear hug with enthusiasm. A meal of fried and baked chicken, mashed potatoes, green beans, okra, biscuits and honey was laid out on a big table. There were three different kinds of pies and one beautifully decorated cake with "Salt and Pepper" spelled out in black and white frosting.

Animated conversations, happy chatter and laughter could be heard for the next two hours.

Brooksie announced, "Time to open a few gifts, ladies." Lucinda carried several wrapped boxes and some envelopes over to the two guests of honor.

Wilamina was already turning on the tear faucet and Houston's face was flushed.

"I ain't ever had me a birthday party. Tex, you have to open them things up. I'm shaking too hard."

Houston picked the boxes first. The biggest one held a computer. It was from Dr. Blackmore. "It's not new, but it's got many years left of service. I hope you can use it for your new business," he said.

"How are we gonna learn to use it?" cried out Wilamina. Lee, Houston's brother said, "No problem. I can teach you easily and I can set you up for business, taxes and just about everything else you want to keep records for."

The next gift was a printer, also from Dr. Blackmore. Other gifts included a set of pans, dishes and cleaning supplies. The card from the warden, Sharon, Dr. Gibran and Mela held a gift certificate for the department store in the amount of $3,000.00. Warden James said, "The three of us thought you will need most everything for your apartment or wherever else you decide to live. The local department store has just about everything you can think of."

The Grief Clinic staff also gave them two gift certificates from two dress shops. Mr. Lagunta's gift was for one year paid insurance on their used truck.

Tony and Luke reminded them that they were the official mechanics for them, if they needed help with their older truck.

Wilamina and Houston were both so overwhelmed they looked to be in shock. "What can we say? How can we ever thank you? I don't know if Willy is ever gonna be able to stop blubbering; and I'm speechless."

Brooksie stood up and said, "You owe nothing to any one of us for your gifts, except maybe to be the best darn investigators of all time. That would be your payback."

Cheers, handshakes, hugs and of course more tears followed for the next half hour. The gifts were placed in their "new" truck. With Houston at the controls, she told the others the next step was to find an apartment and an office. "You're all invited to our apartment as soon as we find one. We'll throw a real Texas kind of party. Thanks a thousand times over for everything. Willy would thank you too, if she could stop her sniveling." As they drove off, the group heard Willy's powerful voice yell out, "Bless you all!"

CHAPTER THREE

Houston and Wilamina were temporarily living at Lee's home. Every day they would look at apartments and offices. One of their friends suggested they try a certain real estate agency. Houston made an appointment to meet with Mrs. Marshall, the owner. They dressed up in their newly bought clothes. "We don't look so bad for two ex-cons," stated Houston.

Houston was thirty-five years old, blond, 5'8", trim and firm. She had religiously worked out when she was incarcerated. Her face was heart-shaped and her eyes were a robin blue. Wilamina was thirty-three years old, black hair cut short and close to the head. She was 5'6", well-rounded in the bust and buttocks. She was always struggling to keep her weight down. Her mother was a black woman and her dad was bi-racial. She had high cheek bones and the most expressive eyes. They looked soft and as endearing as a doe's eyes.

They drove up and parked in front of the Marshall Real Estate building. Houston admiringly looked back at their 2010 Ford Truck. "I still can't get over our good fortune. It scares the shit out of me. There's got to be some real bad crap showing up one of these days. When it does, this time we're gonna be ready. Some fine people have our backs. Tony and Luke are two great guys. So glad that Brooksie and Lucinda married such fine, generous husbands."

They walked into the agency and introduced themselves to the receptionist. "Please sit down Ms. Hayfield and Ms. Robinson. Mrs. Marshall is expecting you and will be right with you."

Within minutes, the agent emerged from her office and greeted the customers. "So nice to meet the two of you. You both have been highly recommended by a number of people. I want to show you what is available in your price range for a two bedroom, two bath apartment and a two person office close by."

They followed the agent into her office and sat down. Wilamia asked, "If you don't mind me saying, you're one tall, healthy, looking woman. How tall are you?"

"I'm 5'10" barefooted. I'm flattered you see me as healthy. Now, may I show you on the computer the places I found that I think you might find interesting?"

A half hour later Houston asked if they could see one of the places in person. It was an office on the first floor and the apartment on the second floor. It had three bedrooms and two baths. There were two parking spaces in the back and parking available in the front of the building. It was located on Greenleaf Ave., five blocks from the center of town.

Mrs. Marshall drove them down to the office on Greenleaf Ave. and pointed out other businesses on the way. Houston commented the office looked good from the outside and was in a good location. They went inside and looked over the office and the apartment. The ex-cons smiled at each other. Houston's face was practically aglow and she said, "This is better than I ever expected. What'a you think Willy?"

"I love it. It seems so big. Can we afford it?"

Mrs. Marshall answered, "Let's go back to my office and talk terms. I'm sure we can work something out. You have some good friends by the way. They gave me a sterling report on both of you. They've paid a portion of your first year's rent. The rent price will increase for you the second year. Your friends believe you will be successful with your new agency and will be able to pay more for the office and apartment within one year. It seems they have great faith in both of you."

Houston asked, "Can you give me the names of the folks that are helping us and have said such nice things about us?"

"They want to remain anonymous for now," responded Mrs. Marshall.

The three returned to the real estate office and signed the necessary papers. Mrs. Marshall received a check from Houston. Houston commented as she handed over the check, "This is the first check I've written in many years and I promise this check won't bounce like a basketball. Seems strange to be legit, but I gotta say, it feels pretty good."

Mrs. Marshall replied, "I'm not worried about you one bit. Not after your friends expounded on your virtues. You may have seen some of the darker sides of life, but now you are back standing in the sunlight. Don't sell yourselves short and no one else will." She put two sets of keys into Houston's hands and offered instructions as to how to get the utilities turned on.

"You mean we can move in right away?" asked Wilamina with her eyes wide and glowing.

"Absolutely. And I wish you both success with your new adventure and business enterprise."

CHAPTER FOUR

Moving day..........

A group of supporters of the soon-to-be investigators gathered at 2010 Greenleaf Ave., the small town's main street. They all had eagerly volunteered to help with the move into the apartment and office.

Luke and Tony already picked up two desks and chairs from the warden's home and Dr. Blackmore's office. The used computer and new printer were set up upon a larger desk. That was to be Wilamina's work station since she had discovered she had a knack for numbers and computers.

A day earlier Lee and Royal, the ex-cons' brothers, took their sisters to a used furniture store and to Goodwill. They picked out two beds, two dressers, a kitchen table with four chairs and one couch.

Lucinda brought several lamps, bedding, towels and bathroom supplies.

Everyone was busy carrying things into the new space. Passers-by took a double take at all the people carrying things into the place. It looked like a beehive of activity. In a few hours the apartment and the office were ready for the excited occupants.

"Looks like a real office and home. I never had anything this nice before. Tex, can you believe this is really our own? I gotta' hug somebody before I explode." She grabbed the nearest person on the sidewalk and gave him a bear hug, much to the surprise of both of them!

"Thanks for the powerful hug lady, but I don't know you. I'm not complaining, just surprised." said the stranger.

"Oh my God! Sorry sir. I just get too full of gratefulness and can't stop myself. My name is Wilamina and this here place is now home and our new office. My friend, Tex, and me are investigators. If you got problems we can help."

"My name is Raul and I am the owner of The Hot Tamale Restaurant right down the street. I'll be sure to send you customers if they need your kind of help. You got a pretty good set of strong arms. I'm sure you won't be needing any handcuffs. Come in for lunch, on me, after you and your friend get settled, adios."

Raul could be heard chuckling as he walked toward his restaurant.

Houston walked over to her partner and said, "Willy, you got to quit fooling around and frightening strangers."

"He ain't no stranger anymore. His name is Raul and he owns the Mexican restaurant down the street. He said we could come for a free lunch one of these days. My loving arms always makes friends."

Standing in the middle of the office, Wilamina announced, "This here looks like a real office and our apartment is one fine livin' place. Can't believe only a short time ago I was sitting in a stinkin' cell." Her eyes began to water.

"Now don't start your sniveling and praying, partner. We have much to do about starting up our business!" bellowed out Houston.

"Time for a break," announced Lucinda. "We have coffee and Tony's fantastic cinnamon buns and maple coffee cake." Lucinda winked at her husband.

The group gathered in the kitchen area of the upstairs. While they stuffed their mouths with the goodies, they joked, laughed and got to know each other a little better. Sasha agreed she had never had so much fun moving. While everyone was enjoying Tony's baked contribution, the phone rang.

"Oh my heavens, is that our phone?" cried Wilamina.

"Yes it is, so get a grip Willy and answer it."

"What do I say?"

"Salt and Pepper Detective Agency," responded Houston.

Wilamina answered the phone with the suggested greeting then immediately covered the mouthpiece and started to giggle uncontrollably. Houston grabbed the phone and listened to the caller.

"Hello. This is Rachael Satori from the Grief Clinic and the pilot program at Lancer's Prison. I believe I may have an appropriate client for your agency."

"Hi Rachael, I'm Houston." she swallowed several times to clear her throat.

"Hello, Houston. I'm facilitating a divorce group and one of the participants would like to meet with you and your partner. Can I put her on the phone? Her name is Rosalyn."

"Yes, yes, please put her on and thank you for giving her our names."

"Hello, I'm Rosalyn and wonder if I could make an appointment?"

"Absolutely. Would tomorrow morning or afternoon be convenient?"

They made an appointment for the next afternoon. Houston gave her the address. Good-byes were said. By the time Houston finished the conversation and put down the phone, her hands were noticeably shaking. She grabbed Willy's hands and started to dance around the room. She yelled, "Our first client, partner!

We're really in business. Luckily we have off tomorrow from our jobs at Table Talk. We still owe them two weeks of morning shifts. Actually I think they'll be glad to have us finish. We both suck as waitresses, but we're not too bad doing the clean-up jobs."

True to her usual ways, Wilamiina began to wail and bless everyone plus every stick of furniture in the room.

Lee asked, "What are you going to charge for your services?"

"Damn! I have no idea. Willy and I haven't even talked about that. What do you all think we should charge?"

Their attorney said they could check with other investigators as to what the going rate was. In the meantime maybe they could start with $50.00 per hour plus expenses. He explained what out-of-pocket expenses were such as gas and film. "You will learn more as you go along."

Brooksie added, "I did a little research on Google and it looks like the prices vary. I'd say for you just starting out, start low. The $50.00 per hour sounds reasonable plus expenses. You must keep complete records of everything you spend for each client. Keep written records in your car and in the office. For example, if you have to go out of town for client business, you would keep track of gas, plane, hotel, food, rental car, parking fee and so forth. I imagine you received some information from the Licensing Board regarding permission forms for your clients to sign and other necessary documents?"

"Yes. We have a booklet of information. I haven't looked it over completely 'cause I wasn't expecting to have a client so soon. Willy, we have to get started immediately reading up on all this stuff. God I hope we don't mess up with our first case.

"We've already given our notice to Table Talk Cafe. They were great to let us work for almost four weeks, especially since we weren't very good at our waitressing jobs. Willy talked too much to the customers and I was too impatient. We were good at clean-up because we had plenty experience cleaning up at our last address. Thor, and his wife, Antoya were so kind and patient. They gave us our first job without really knowing us. They only knew about our time in Lancer's prison."

Wilamina added, "I never believed there were so many kind and trusting folks around. Lordy, Lordy, thank you, Jesus. My heart is gonna bust right out of my generous bosom."

"Would you like Tony and me to stay and help you get the paper work in order?" asked Lucinda. " Mr. Lagunta, would you also be able to stick around a short time and help them with some legal questions?"

"I'll be glad to, if you would all please call me Roco."

"Thanks, Roco," said Tony and Lucinda in unison.

The rest of the working crew hugged the two novice investigators and left the five to get to work on the details. "What if we can't do this? I don't know nothing about keeping records and stuff like that," lamented Wilamina.

"Listen, sister," snapped Houston. "We know a lot about the dark side of living and we managed to survive. We got more experience than most folks when it comes to the dirt bags of this world. Our friends believe in us and we're not gonna let them down. We just got some learning to do. Let's get started right now."

CHAPTER FIVE

Next day..........

"I'm so excited Tex. I'm about to wet my pants. You'd better do all the talking. I don't want to screw up our first case."

"Willy, you're gonna do just fine. Be yourself. Don't be worrying about every move. Remember we are now helping others. I think we're gonna be damn good at it 'cause we've been plenty beaten down before. We know how shitty that feels and now we can fight back. This time we stand up for strangers who haven't yet learned how to fight back for themselves."

Just at that moment, a young woman walked hesitantly through the office door. She was wearing a gray pant suit and her long hair was pulled back from her face and pinned neatly at the sides with barrettes.

Houston quickly moved around her desk and walked up to the young woman. "Hello, you must be Rosalyn Moore. I'm Houston Hayfield and this here is my partner, Wilamina Robinson."

"Thanks for seeing me so soon." She hesitated, took a deep breath and continued, "I'm not sure I'm doing the right thing. I'm really nervous."

"Please sit down Miss Rosalyn. Would you like a cup of coffee or a glass of water?" asked Wilamina. "Honey, you don't have to be nervous with us." *I'm nervous enough for the both of us,* thought Wilamina to herself.

"No, thank you. What information do you want me to give you?"

Houston pulled her chair up next to the client and Wilamina followed her partner's lead. "Maybe you can tell us about the troubles you're having with your husband. Are you afraid of him?"

"Oh no! Nothing like that. I love him. It's just that he has changed in the last six months or so. Maybe longer than that even. He's real quiet now. We used to talk about everything, every day. Now, when he leaves in the morning, he doesn't kiss me good-bye. He says nothing. He just waves and closes the door and leaves for work. We've been married fifteen years and he has always been extremely affectionate." She looked down at the floor and whispered, "He doesn't even touch me anymore. You understand what I'm saying?"

Houston answered, "I think you are saying he doesn't have sex with you anymore. You don't need to be embarrassed about anything with us. We've both been around the block lots of times."

"I'll try. I don't understand what's happened to us. He never used to criticize my cooking or how I looked, but some days he's terribly cranky. I can't seem to please him anymore. My friend Lottie told me he might be having an affair. She said when her husband was cheating on her, he acted the same way." At this point Rosalyn choked up, rummaged through her purse looking for something. Wilamina handed her a box of tissues.

"This friend of yours, Lottie, how long have you been friends?" asked Houston.

"Thanks for the tissue, Miss Robinson. I'm sorry I'm such a mess, but I love him and I can't believe he has someone else in his life. You would agree with me if you knew him. To answer your question about Lottie, Craig and I moved next door to her and her husband five years ago. I liked Lottie right off from the start. She's very different from me. She's outgoing, spontaneous and fun. I'm more reserved. Her husband is more like her and Craig is more like me. I don't think my husband ever really felt comfortable around Royal cause he gets pretty loud and too friendly at times. He likes his cocktail hour. Craig says the guy is a phony."

"I'm confused. Why are you going to a divorce group at the Grief Clinic? Your sure don't sound like you want a divorce," inquired Wilamina.

"Lottie suggested I go. She attended a group a while back and learned a lot about herself. She said the group work helped her to work through the problems she and her husband were having. The group is not just for people already divorced but for those considering the option of divorce. I can't afford individual counseling and the group is cheaper. I'm willing to try anything to save us. I can't believe I'm really going to hire you to spy for me. I'm so ashamed, but I'm desperate. Can you help me? Please."

"We will need some information to start with," said Houston. "You'll need to sign a few papers and then my partner and I will sit down and discuss a plan of action. How can we get in touch with you? I don't think you want your husband to know he is being checked up on so we need a way to talk to you or see you without his knowledge. Would you be willing to write down his regular schedule, days and times? To help us, we will need addresses of places he visits regularly, a picture of him, the make and model of his car and his driver's license."

"I have my own cell phone. You can also get in touch with my friend Lottie and she will give me your message. I will call you back as soon as I can. Will that work? Do you want me to write this all down right now? I have a picture of Craig with me and I could leave it with you. I would like to have it back."

"That will work fine. And of course you will get the picture back."

Rosalyn asked, "How much do you charge? I'm not rich, but I'm not poor. I have a full time job and have my own money."

Houston responded with the fifty dollars an hour fee and she would also give her a itemized bill once a week or every two weeks. The three settled down to getting pertinent information about addresses, work schedules, usual haunts of the husband, hobbies and so forth. The novices asked for everything they could possibly think of to help them find out what the husband was up to.

Rosalyn Moore shook hands with both and made an appointment for two weeks later. She again blew her nose and wiped away the mascara from under her eyes."Thank you both. I hope I'm doing the right thing."

"Thank you, Mrs. Moore. We'll do our very best for you, and don't you be losing any sleep over payment of our bill. We'll work fast as we can to keep the hours down."

CHAPTER SIX

As soon as the client left the office, Houston and Wilamina sat down in front of their desks. "Where the hell to begin?" moaned Houston. "We are so unprepared for this. You know what Willy, I think our first trip needs to be to the police department. After that, we need to talk with those people at the private detective agency in Seattle. They have been investigators for a long time and maybe they would be willing to help us with some guidelines. What'a you think?"

"I think you've gotta good idea there. Let's just do it. First the police and then on to Seattle."

Later same day.....

They spent a productive hour with Sergeant Lathy at the local police station. She introduced them to several officers who were standing around in the break room. Officer Joe Bennet welcomed them and offered them some coffee. He remarked, "We can definitely use some woman power in the field. Maybe you can help us with the domestic crap that takes up so much of our time. Personally I think everyone should have to enroll in a year-long class before getting hitched. I know I wish I had."

"Shut up, Joe" bellowed Sergeant Lathy. "Don't be airing your dirty laundry in front of these ladies. They've just opened their new investigative business and they're trying to learn the ropes."

"Sorry ladies," responded officer Joe. "I wish you lots of luck. Glad to have such good looking investigators to call upon. I'll be glad to help anytime, just give me a whistle and I'll come running."

"Thanks Officer Bennet, 'cause we'll be grateful for any help you can spare," said Houston.

"Call me, Joe."

"Okay Joe, and you can call me Tex, and my partner here is Willy."

After an hour or so of asking questions, getting a heads up of procedures and what to look out for, the ladies thanked the officers and headed out for Seattle. Sergeant Lathy had suggested a particular detective agency that they may find useful. He gave them the Seattle address.

Once in the car, Wilamina shared her thoughts on the visit. "They sure were nice to us, especially the Sergeant and Officer Bennet. The Sergeant had some sad eyes. Maybe she's seen too much bad. I pray my eyes don't turn that way."

"If you didn't get sad eyes while in prison, then you don't have to worry about that now, Willy."

"I saw that look Officer Joe had for you, Tex. He seemed pretty eager to help us, or more like help YOU. You already itching to get hooked up with a man?" Wilamina snickered.

"Don't be fixing me up with anybody in that head of yours. I'm not looking for no man. I never was good at picking them and I don't plan to start making stupid choices now. In fact, you had your problems with your pickin's as well as I did."

"You're right, Sister, I picked'm for outside looks, not the inside stuff. I'm smarter now and so are you," confirmed Wilamina.

They pulled up in front of the address the sergeant gave them and saw the sign over the door which read, 'Rickel's Detective Agency.'

"Now that we are here, what are we going to talk about?" asked Wilamina.

"We're gonna introduce ourselves and hope they start the conversation," answered Houston. "Maybe we should've brought some goodies?"

"That's a great idea," responded Wilamina. "I saw a bakery sign at the beginning of this block. Let's go back there and buy something."

They did just that. After their purchase of some baked goods, they returned to Rickel's Agency. They parked the car and carried their sweet smelling gift inside.

"Hello there ladies. And what can I do for you?" asked a fairly tall man with graying sideburns.

"My name is Houston Hayfield and this is my business partner, Wilamina Robinson. We have just opened our own private detective agency in Whitefall this very week. We came to introduce ourselves and brought you some goodies from the bakery down the street."

"Well I'll be damned, competition bringing bribes and calories. That's mighty nice of you. My name is Hunt Rickles and my partner is my wife, Jessie Rickels. She is out on a job today. Please sit yourselves down. How about we have some coffee and get into that pastry box?"

"Sure thing Mr. Rickels, but I don't think of us as competition. You're here working in the big city and we are an hour away. We would really appreciate anything you can tell us about investigating in general. You see, we both were recently released from Lancer's Women's Prison and this is our first business venture, first legitimate one, that is."

"The hell you say. You were really inmates at that prison? For how long?"

"Both of us spent several years until a saint of an attorney got our verdict thrown out and our sentence was revoked and here we are today. Now we plan to help others who also got a bad rap. Our goal is to put the real scumbags where they belong."

Mr. Rickels scratched his head and took a sip of coffee and said, "I've got to chew on this for a while. I'll be damned if I'm not pleased to meet you two fine ladies and offer any help you might need to get started. Please call me Hunt, sounds friendlier and I bet you we become good friends real quick. I can't wait to tell Jessie about you two. She loves gutsy women. She's one herself. As soon as I tell her about you two, she's going to want to invite you to one of her special ladies' lunches. She knows more about investigating than me. She started this agency. Then we had our two babies. She worked from home until they both entered first grade. They're both in college now. Two great kids, thanks to Jessie."

"Your wife sounds very interesting and we'd love to get together with her. Please give her our phone number."

The three settled down, drank coffee, ate pastries and generally got acquainted. Mr. Rickels gave them a list of resources and said he would put together a longer more completed list and send it to their office. They talked about surveillance, picture taking, and how to access info from the computer and conduct library research. He also talked highly about a Detective Lorenzo of the Whitefall Police Department and suggested they make a point of getting in to see him and his partner, Detective Voss. She's really something. The two of them are known as the Dynamic Duo."

The exchange of information continued for the better part of two hours. Finally, the new investigators said their thanks and good-byes and made an appointment for more questions and answers the next month.

Back in Whitefall.....

Wilamina took her turn driving back to their office. She commented, "He's a pretty nice guy. He made me feel right at home. I really hope we get to meet the wife and her friends."

"Yep, he did. He seemed to know his business pretty well and wanted to help us all he could. His wife may also help us out. Hope she calls us soon. What do you think about us making an appointment with Detective Lorenzo? Sasha is already helping us"

"Sounds good to me, Tex."

Houston stared out the window in silence as the miles went by. Then snapped her fingers and announced, "We need to make a plan. What exactly are we going to do to find out what Rosalyn's husband is up to? Today is a good day to start our surveillance of Mr. Moore. We have time to go by the building where he works. It'll be close to the time he could be leaving. That's only half an hour from now. I have Rosalyn's chart with me and we have all the addresses and times she thought we might need. She wrote it all down for us. We've got the description of his car and the license plate number. She even told us where he usually parks."

"Sounds like a good start. I hope we find out that he's a good guy and not into something shitty. His wife is a sweet lady and I hate to have to give her any ugly news," bemoaned Wilamina.

"I'm with you, Willy. Guess we're gonna have to get used to handing out bad news some times. We're no strangers to the nasty sides of people."

As soon as Wilamina drove up to Mr. Moore's office building and located his car, she parked down the road a short distance away from his car. They had a clear view of his car and the front of the building. While they were watching and waiting, Houston read what Rosalyn had written about her husband's schedule. 'Every Monday and Friday he leaves for work at 7:30 a.m. and to lunch at Italian restaurant on Apple Street, a block from his office..The other days he takes his lunch to work. Leaves work a little after 5 p.m. and usually heads home. Some days he stops at the cleaners or grocery store for me. For the last three or four months he doesn't come right home, Sometimes he gets home at 6 or 7 p.m. He says he just ran an errand. Lately he gets angry if I ask him anything about what he does after work.'

Houston excitedly yelled, "Start the engine Willy and get ready to follow him! There he is coming from the building and looks like he's headed for his car."

"Are you sure that's him?" asked Wilamina. "You know all you whites look alike," she snorted and then giggled.

"Yeah! And all you blacks look the same to me," responded Houston with a grin. "He looks just like the picture she gave us. That's him. Follow him, but don't get too close."

Wilamina started the engine and the two newbies gave each other the high five. They were off on their very first assignment.

Surveillance.......

Mr. Moore drove a few blocks, stopped, parked and walked into the town cleaners. Wilamina quickly parked a few cars behind him, turned off the engine and nervously waited. The wait was short and Mr. Moore came out carrying some clothes on hangers covered in plastic, got into his car and drove off with Wilamina not far behind.

"I feel like some P.I. in the movies. The problem is I have to pee and the movies actors never seem to need a pit stop," said Wilamina frowning.

"Damn it! So do I. What sort of detectives are we going to be if every time we start spying we both have to pee?" She began to laugh and so did Willy. "Shit. Laughing is only gonna make it harder to keep from wettin' myself."

Just then, Mr. Moore's car pulled into a neighborhood and a block or so later he drove up into a driveway. The garage door opened and he parked his car inside.

"We managed to follow him home. What great detectives we're turning out to be. Willy, keep driving. Let's get out of here, back to our office and to the bathroom. We must start keeping records on what we did today. Everyone has told us how important it is to keep good daily records for each client. I'll admit I'm eager to put our daily activities into our new record book. You're in charge of keeping the hours and dates for billing purposes. Hell, I'm really pumped up. I sound kinda silly, don't I Willy?"

"No, my friend. You sound excited and happy. Me too."

"Not too sure how successful we're going to be with this surveillance crap. We both have weak bladders and I don't suppose the suspects are going to be very accommodating and wait while we find a restroom," expressed Houston.

"Maybe we can wear those diaper like things," chuckled Wilamina.

"They're called Depends, you ninny." Both women began to howl with laughter and Houston crossed her legs in an attempt to hold back the dam.

Wilamina, still laughing uncontrollably, managed to say, "No fair. I'm driving and can't cross my legs. Next time you drive." She started to chant, "I can make it, I can make it."

CHAPTER SEVEN

Next morning, Houston and Wilamina rose early, had breakfast and were out the door by 7:30 a.m. They had decided the night before to follow Mr. Moore from morning till night.

Rosalyn had told them that on Tuesdays he often arrived home late. So they decided today being Tuesday, they would stick to him like glue.

Houston suggested, "We'd better go directly to his office and make sure he shows up. Then watch to see if he leaves for lunch, where he goes and when he returns. We need to be back at this office at least by 4:30 and see where he goes after that."

Wilamina affirmed the plans and added, "I'm not drinking much of anything today. I'm not gonna torture my bladder anymore."

They arrived at Mr. Moore's place of employment and parked. Mr. Moore arrived ten minutes before 8 a.m. They watched him enter through the office door and decided they had enough time to run few errands. They were back in front of his office at 11 a.m. A few minutes before noon, Mr. Moore appeared and he walked down to the Hot Tamale Restaurant and there he remained until ten minutes before 1 p.m. After which he walked back to his office.

Wilamina suggested they return to their home, have lunch and return around 4 p.m. to Mr. Moore's office, which they did. He appeared at 5:05 p.m. and this time he drove off in the opposite direction away from his home.

"Here we go, Willy. Let's hope he's not another creep playing footsie with some big breasted bimbo."

"Are you calling me a bimbo 'cause I have a great set of girls?" She flashed a smile at her friend. "That wouldn't be envy raising it's ugly face, now would it?"

"Listen pal," countered Houston, "You're the one who complains of backaches from the heavy load you carry up front. Mine are just the perfect size for the right hands. Well lookie here, he's turning onto Raintree St. That's near the hospital."

Mr. Moore drove into the parking area, parked and got out of his car. He hesitated a moment, looked at the building and walked in through the front door of the building marked "A."

"I'm parking here. Let's split up. You stay near the front door, I'll go in and see where he's off to," stated Houston.

Before Houston could walk through the door of building A, Mr. Moore practically ran into her. He didn't look at her, but walked straight from Building A to Building B. As soon as he entered that building, Houston was right behind him and saw him enter the empty elevator. She had quickly placed a large hat on her head. It covered her hair and a portion of her face, and she whipped on her oversized sunglasses. Unfortunately for her, Mr. Moore was a gentleman and called to her from the opened elevator door, "Miss, can I wait for you?" She purposely dropped her purse, turned around and knelt down to retrieve her possessions. "No thank you, please go on."

He let the door close and she watched, her hands shaking, to see at which floor the elevator stopped. The light above the elevator showed floor three. She quickly looked at the names listed on the wall and noticed Dr. Webster - Oncology Department. It was the only name listed. She fumbled around in her purse, finally came up with a pen and small notebook in which she wrote Dr. Webster, Oncology and the address. This she would give to Rosalyn. She looked out the door and witnessed her partner tippy-toeing from one bush to another. She whispered to herself, "If this is her idea of keeping a low profile, an elephant would be better hidden."

She raced out the door, grabbed Wilamina and told her they should wait in the car to see where Mr. Moore goes next.

While they were waiting for Mr. Moore to reappear, Houston related the events at the elevator. "I felt like a deer caught in the head lights. He was the only person in the lobby and was waiting for the elevator. Then I raced in, and too late, realized there was only the two of us. He had to be the gentleman and offered to hold the elevator for me. I dropped my purse, actually I threw it down, and my stuff scattered everywhere. I got down on my knees and started to pick up stuff. I could hardly find my voice. I felt like a Keystone Cop. I wanted to laugh. I said, "No thank you," and he closed the door. I watched to see at what floor the elevator stopped. Now we'll see where he's going next.

"I admit I'm a ridiculous spy. I either want to laugh or pee. Speaking of ridiculous, you going from bush to bush as if no one would notice a good looking, well endowed woman, wearing oversized sun glasses and a huge hot-pink hat. A blind man would have seen you. We both stand out like two ladies of the night, in the middle of Catholic convention of nuns. You couldn't have attracted more attention to yourself even if you had been stark naked." They stared at each other for a minute exchanging knowing looks, before turning away and bursting out in laughter.

"We've got to become better sneaks. Maybe Sasha can give us some tips?"

"You're right, Tex. Sure hope she can teach us somethin' helpful. She has lots of experience as an undercover cop. I can't believe how many people she fooled, even the warden didn't catch on. When do we let Rosalyn know about the doctor visit?"

"Better wait 'til tomorrow after the mister leaves for work. I'm not sure if we are giving her good or bad news. The doc is a cancer doctor. I wonder if she knows about any visits of her husband to that doctor."

One hour later Mr. Moore surfaced, got into his car and drove off. He was followed by one older, used truck. They were able to keep three to four cars between them. They soon realized he was on his way home and they turned and aimed for home themselves.

Back at their home/office.....

"Hello, Sasha. This is Houston Hayfield. Willy and I need to see you as soon as you have some free time. We desperately need some help with undercover work. We are more like two clowns, not two professional investigators!"

Sasha agreed to meet them on the coming Saturday at their home/office. She added she would bring a few disguises and a make-up kit. They visited for a while longer, shared some laughs and agreed on the time on Saturday.

Next morning..............

Houston hesitated before dialing Rosalyn. "I'm not so good with bad news calls. You better be the one to tell her about the doctor visit. You're better with the emotional stuff."

"Go ahead Tex, dial and I'll talk with her." She dialed and handed the phone to her partner.

"Hello Rosalyn, this is Wilamina. Do you have a minute to talk?"

"Yes, of course. Do you have some information already?"

"Yes we do. Not sure what it means, but yesterday we followed your husband after work and he drove to a Dr. Webster's office.

This is the address." Wilamina then added practically in a whisper," Dr. Webster seems to be a cancer doctor. Do you know anything about this doctor or why your husband would see him?"

Rosalyn was silent forever, or so it seemed to the other two waiting on the other end of the line. "No. I don't know why he would be seeing that kind of doctor. I don't know what to think. Can I come to your office this morning? I can be there in one hour."

Wilamina responded, "We'll be waiting with the coffee on. See you soon."

Less than one hour later............

Rosalyn arrived fifteen minutes early. "Hope I'm not here too soon, but I'm so anxious to hear anything, even if I'm afraid of the news."

"Miss Rosalyn we followed your husband, after he left from work, to a medical building." relayed Wilamina. Houston handed her the address and name of the doctor. "Mr. Moore came out of the building one hour later and we followed him back to your house."

Rosalyn sat quiet, staring down at the floor. She was holding her hands so tightly her knuckles were white.

"What do I do now?" she cried.

Wilamina responded, "You've told us how much you love Mr. Moore and how good he's always been to you. If he's sick, you need to know so you can help him. You've got to find out why he went to see that doctor. What do you want to do next?"

"I want to hold him and tell him I love him no matter what. What if he hates me because I had him investigated?"

Houston asked, "Have you been honest with each other for most of your married life?"

"Yes. Only the past six months have been so different."

"What if you ask him, in your own loving way, 'are you sick?' See what he says. You may never have to tell him about us. My mama always said, 'Truth is so much easier, lies are harder to remember,'" quoted Wilamina.

Wilamina pulled her chair in front of Rosalyn and took hold of both her tight fisted hands and softly said, "love is strong. If your husband is sick, you can do what you need to for him. Remember you don't know why he is seeing a doctor."

Tears slowly rolled down Rosalyn's cheeks and landed on her blouse. "If this is all about him being ill and not some sordid affair, what does this say about me? I've been thinking the worst, an affair, when maybe he has been simply trying to protect me. I'm a terrible wife," she blurted out.

"You're a caring and brave wife," responded Houston. "You're not one of those cowardly women who stick their heads in the sand. You've got guts. I hope you will let us know what you decide to do. We won't do anymore checking on Mr. Moore unless you ask us to."

"I'm okay now and I'll call you soon when I know something. Do I pay you now?"

"No. We will print out a statement. It's not that much 'cause we didn't spend a lot of time. We can mail it to you or have it here and you can pick it up, your choice. Please let us know how you're doing 'cause we will be thinking about you and your husband."

They said their good-byes and after Rosalyn drove off they started to, walk to the cafe for breakfast.

CHAPTER EIGHT

Rosalyn Moore decided to do nothing until the following Tuesday, and then to follow her husband to Dr. Webster's office. When her husband emerged from the medical building she was waiting for him.

"What the hell are you doing here, Rosalyn?" he shouted, wiping perspiration off his forehead.

"I followed you from your office. I knew something has been terribly wrong between us for a long time. Craig, I love you and want to be of some help to you, but I can't if you keep secrets from me. Please tell me what's going on. Are you sick, my dear?"

He immediately put his arms around her and crushed her to his chest. "Yes." he sobbed. "I'm so afraid of leaving you and I couldn't bear the thought of you grieving and being on your own. I know that eventually you'd be okay. You're strong and smart, but I thought if you could hate me, my death would be easier for you, You could get over your grief sooner if you were already disgusted with me."

"Your death! My God what are you saying. Do you have cancer?" Her voice choked with tears and she placed a shaky hand to her forehead.

"I have bladder cancer. The treatments seem to be working. I was going to tell you as soon as the doctor could give me a clean bill of health. I haven't felt very good for a few months and I was afraid to see a doctor. I saw blood in the toilet months back. I told my office buddy Armin and he told me I needed to see a doctor. He gave me Dr. Webster's name and I made an appointment. That was the beginning of the end, at least that is what I thought.

"Dr. Webster told me today that the treatments are working. I'm embarrassed to say I broke down right there in that office." Craig dropped his chin to his chest, "I won't blame you if you never forgive me. I was so stupid and so very disappointed in myself. I do love you so much and I wouldn't blame you if your feelings for me have changed. Will you ever be able to trust me again?"

She gently took his face into her hands, wiped his eyes with her fingers and kissed him on both cheeks. "I could never hate you no matter what. Death will come for both of us someday. Who will go first is unknown. You have brought love, joy, interest, laughter and hope into my life. If you died first, I'd grieve until I joined you, but I will be thankful every day for every moment we've shared."

They stayed a long time holding each others' hands, crying, laughing and remembering wonderful past moments they had together.

"When is our next appointment with Dr. Webster?" asked Rosalyn.

"Not for six more weeks and I'm so happy to have you go with me."

"No more secrets, between us Craig. Promise me."

"You've got my word, my love."

"Okay then. Now I need to tell you my secret." For the next fifteen minutes Rosalyn explained that she had hired Houston and Wilamina, two private investigators to follow him and report back to her. "I'm not sorry in the least. They helped us both, more than they may ever know."

"I'd like to thank your detectives for their good work. Could I go with you and meet them?"

"Absolutely, dear, and while we are at their office you can take care of their bill."

They both laughed heartily and agreed, since they were in two cars, to meet at the Hot Tamale Restaurant for a celebration meal later that day.

CHAPTER NINE

"We just got a call from Rosalyn." said Wilamina. " She is coming in this morning around 10 a.m. and has a surprise for us."

Houston replied, "Hope it's good news. Bad news is never good, but if it comes in the morning it can ruin the rest of the day."

The phone rang. Wilamina answered, "Salt and Pepper Detective Agency." She winked at her friend who was sitting across from her. The caller talked for a couple of minutes. Wilamina smiled and put her hand in the air showing the okay sign with her fingers. "1 p.m. will be just fine. Do you need directions. Okay then, see you this afternoon, Mr. Spade."

"What's happening this afternoon?" asked Houston.

"Our second case is coming in today. Mr. Spade works for the Reliable Insurance Company. His office is on the next block. He asked to come in and discuss a possible fraud case. He will give us all the details in person. Tex, do we know what the heck we're doing? I don't know beans about insurance. I ain't never had any."

Houston answered, "We have car insurance now my friend, and when we can afford it we're going to look at some health insurance. Right now we've got to get us a bill made up for Rosalyn. My brother told me to call it a statement. He's pretty smart about such things. He said to make three copies, one for the client, one for tax purposes and one for our office records."

Together they looked through their almost blank journal for the exact date and hours spent working for Rosalyn. Houston said, "Everyone has been telling us how important it is for us to keep good records, a folder for each case. We've got to include all hours and every expense. I can keep the hours and you could record the money we spend for our spy work. Also we have to keep all receipts by month and year. This business stuff gets pretty complicated. Lee offered to help us anytime. Mr. Lagunta and Rachael also offered their assistance. Folks sure have been fantastic."

They looked through their time keeping ledger and added the hours. "We didn't spend much time looking after Mr. Moore," said Wilamina.

They read over their notes and agreed they'd only traveled about ten miles altogether at twenty-five cents a mile on the first day, and spent one and one half hour, second day about three hours. All time and gas added up to one hundred and fifty-two dollars.

"What'd you think Willy, too much, too little?"

"Looks fair to me. We know she is a working woman and is not loaded."

Wilamina typed up the statement, made a few copies and placed the original in an envelope and set it down on her partner's desk.

Houston, looked at the envelope and remarked to her partner, "So does this mean you want me to be the one to give her the bill?"

"I hate asking for money or anything, Tex. Am I letting you down?"

"No my friend. We are both trying to do what we feel comfortable doing. You're great with the emotional stuff and secretary work and I'm okay asking for what we need and planning our sneaking around. Sounds like we make a good team."

10 a.m...........

Mr. & Mrs. Moore walked briskly through the office door holding hands. They looked at each other. Rosalyn spoke first, "Hello ladies. I want you to meet the best husband in the world."

Houston let out a noticeable sigh and Wilamina greeted the couple with her all encompassing hug.

"Thank heavens you are both smiling. I've got to admit we were worried about you both," said Wilamina.

"This is Craig, my rock. Craig, this is Houston and Wilamina. They are the angels who cleared up our mystery."

Everyone sat down and Rosalyn shared the story of her husband's cancer and the fact that he kept it a secret from her and why.

Wilamina wiped her nose and sniffed loudly. Houston sat very straight in her chair, appeared to inhale deeply several times. It was a way for her to keep her emotions in check.

Mr. Moore waited for a lull in the conversation then asked for the billing statement. Houston handed him an envelope, he opened it and read it over. He placed his already written check and note inside and handed it back to Houston. "It's close to lunch time and my wife and I would like to take you to lunch, if you have the time," offered Mr. Moore.

The two investigators looked at each other and said simultaneously, "We'd like that very much!"

It was agreed for all to meet at the Table Talk Cafe at 11:30 a.m. The united couple left the office and Houston opened the envelope and exclaimed, "Wow! Willy, this check is for five hundred dollars. The note reads 'Please accept our deepest gratitude. We will never forget what you have done for us.' They both signed their names."

"Lordy Lordy! Can you believe that? Never thought I'd be getting thanks **and** money for helping. This may be the best day of my life."

"Willy, we're gonna have lots of best days from now on. I have to keep pinching myself making sure I'm awake. Can you believe we're really gonna make a difference, in a good way? I could sing your favorite hymn if I had any kind of a voice." Didn't take another word from her ex-prison mate for Willy to belt out Amazing Grace. Her partner joined in, although painfully off-key. It didn't matter much 'cause Wilamina's powerful voice drowned out the other happy singer.

1 p.m..........

A slightly overweight man, unshaven, his hair uncombed, came racing through their front office door, breathing heavily.

"Sorry if I've kept you ladies waiting. Lack of sleep the past two days and I never hit the pillow last night at all. Please excuse my miserable appearance. I'm Jason Spade. I talked with you earlier. I'm the insurance investigator."

"Happy to meet you, Mr. Spade. Can we give you some coffee or soda?"

"Black coffee would be much appreciated. I'll get right to my problem and hopefully you will be able to help me out. A Mr. Germain has filed an insurance claim for a home accident, or so he says. He claimed he fell off the roof of the house he's renting, attempting to rescue some stray cat. By trade he is a plumber. He is forty years old, divorced and has two older children. It seems he's never paid child support and hasn't even seen them in over ten years or more.

"The records I've been able to uncover in the last week or so, show this is his fourth claim in the last six or seven years. He moved around quite a bit, didn't stay in one place for more than a year or so.

"This supposed accident took place in the evening, no witnesses, not even a cat. He was found by the next door neighbor who was coming home from shift work and he heard Mr. Germain yelling for help. The neighbor, a male nurse, called for an ambulance. Mr. Germain supposedly received a blow to the head, back and wrist injury. He claims he cannot return to his plumbing career and that the constant back pain is debilitating.

"I think he's as phony as hell, excuse my French ladies, but I'm exhausted from lack of sleep trying to watch the bastard twenty-four hours a day. I can show you more of what I've found out about him, back at my office. Most of it looks mighty suspicious to me.

"Is this something you'd be willing to help me with? The hours of surveillance can be long and boring, but the pay is good. I figure with the three of us watching him, on and off, he will slip up and do something that will prove he's a fraud. You'd be paid every two weeks for surveillance hours, gas, meals and film. You must keep thorough records in triplicate."

Houston told Mr. Spade that she and Wilamina work as a team for safety reasons. "Willy and I need to talk over your interesting offer. Can we get back to you this afternoon by phone? By the way what brand of camera do you use? We need to buy a second one. Do you know that we just opened up our business last week? So we are playing catch up with purchasing items we need. If we agree to work with you when would you want us to start?"

"If I had my preference you would begin today, but I do need to give you more information you will need. If you say yes to my proposal this afternoon, you could come by my office tomorrow so I can catch you up with Mr. Germain's routines, addresses and such.

"I'll be on my way now and hopefully I will get an affirmative answer this afternoon from you. I want to add, I'm glad you have opened up this office. This town and surrounding areas are growing rapidly and have need for more investigators. Good-day ladies."

The two women sat silently staring at the closed front door. "What the hell just happened here?" exclaimed Houston. "What have we gotten ourselves into? On the one hand I'm excited and on the other hand I'm terrified. What are you thinking, Willy?"

"I'm not thinking, I'm numb. I was mighty close to laughing and had to hold my breath to keep from losing it. Do you really think we can do the job and catch Mr. Germain doing something he shouldn't be doing?"

Houston tilted her head and paused a moment. "If we're gonna make a name for ourselves we just got to jump in with both feet. I say yes, let's call Mr. Spade and say yes and go to his office tomorrow for more details. Mr. Spade knows we're new at this and I kinda got the feeling he'd be glad to help us. What do you say, partner?"

"We're a team, you and me, Tex. Let's call him."

Houston dialed the number with shaky hands and advised Mr. Spade that they would see him the next morning, and get all the details and thanked him for asking for their help.

CHAPTER TEN

Wilamina was busy making a breakfast of biscuits and gravy, sausage and eggs, the Southern way.

"Willy, you've got to quit with all this great cooking. My pants are getting so tight that I have to lie on the bed just to get the zipper to close. I'm not complaining about your delicious meals only about my expanding middle."

"I know you're right. I've been blaming the washing machine for shrinking my pants. It's just that I'm having so much fun cooking in the good old way of my mama, and the food is worth eatin'. That stuff they served us in prison was nothin' but jail house rot.

"Today we're eatin' good 'cause Miss Sasha is coming and I want to show off."

The office door bell rang, Houston offered, "I'll go let her in while you cook up another masterpiece."

"Hi Sasha, good thing you're a little early 'cause Willy has whipped up her specialty, a real southern style breakfast. It's a waist killer. The sort of meal that makes your pants tight. Let me help you carry those suitcases upstairs."

After the three had polished off a football player's sized meal, Sasha opened up one of the suitcases. It was filled with an assortment of wigs, hats and other paraphernalia.

"Since you guys told me your suspect is a white man I figured he will have trouble remembering Willy's features. I'm not trying to insult anyone here, but I've done undercover work for many years and I learned some of the tricks.

"Hope you don't mind if I make a few suggestions. When you need to physically follow your fraud suspect, I think one of you will need to be a man. Willy, you would be better disguised as a man because you have short hair which can be covered easily with different wigs, hats or caps and your body can be concealed in a suit or something else that covers your great shape.

"Tex, you can also use an assortment of wigs and ill fitting clothes, dark glasses or a variety of other tinted glasses."

Sasha laid wigs, clothes and accessories on the floor for her friends to inspect.

"Wait a minute here," said Wilamina. "You saying I'm the man 'cause Mr. Germain is a white man. You wouldn't be referring to that shit that all blacks look alike would you?"

"Willy don't get your feathers all ruffled up. Yeah, all blacks look alike to some white people and all whites look alike to some blacks. You even told me yourself one time in Lancer's that you had a hard time telling some of us white folks apart. Remember?

"Okay ladies before the hair starts flying, I suggest that for most of the time if the suspect is white, Willy sometimes will dress like the man and if the suspect is black, then Tex puts on the male disguise. You will be changing your disguises frequently. You will have to learn your own styles and what works best. There are no set rules. Successful surveillance takes imagination and flexibility and lots of perseverance."

The two women agreed that taking turns sounded fair and then Houston laughed, snorted and gasped for air. They all exchanged looks and burst out into uproarious laughter, holding their sides and trying to wipe their noses at the same time.

"I bet I'm gonna be the best looking man ever! You two better not get any ideas," teased Wilamina.

The teasing and laughter continued throughout the morning while Sasha had them practice using make up and different outfits. Willy decked herself out in anticipation for their first surveillance of Mr. Spade.

She was in her room alone trying on suits, hats and glasses. When she finally emerged she was wearing a dark brown shirt with a tan suit coat. The trousers were chocolate brown. Her head was covered with an old style hat. She limped slightly as she came through her bedroom door.

"Wow! Willy you look great! Middle aged even. Where the hell did your boobs go?" asked Houston, staring at her partner's chest.

"No bra, a tight T shirt, two scarves and the shirt and coat does the rest."

"You've got the hang of it Willy," said Sasha displaying a wide grin. "You could be successful with undercover work in a heartbeat. Your turn to practice, Houston."

"Okay but don't expect too much. Willy has more imagination than me." Houston tried on all the different colored wigs, some short haired and others long haired. She modeled wearing a house dress, then a form fitting knit dress and lastly Levis with a clinging T shirt.

"First off, I say get rid of the seductive T shirt," advised Sasha. "If you look too sexy you will easily be remembered unless of course you are wanting to be a distraction.

"Your disguises need to fit the circumstances and personality of the suspect. Call me anytime if you have any questions about what to wear. I sort of feel like your mentor or maybe even your mother. You guys are really something special and I'm proud to be associated with you."

Houston added, "You're the pro, Sasha. You had an entire prison convinced you were a happy ho. The warden still talks about what a great actress you were."

"Thanks for the compliment my friends. Actually the prison pilot program taught me the importance of respect and many other things about myself. I hate to admit this, but truthfully I thought I was better than most of the inmates. When I started working undercover at Lancer's I had a superiority complex but hearing their stories really changed me and I believe I'm a better person for it."

"Sasha, I haven't talked this over with Willy, but I bet she feels the same way and would be okay with me asking you to be part of our surveillance team once in a while. We'd pay you of course." She glanced over at her partner who was smiling and shaking her head up and down with enthusiasm.

"I'll have to think about that. My first inclination is to say yes, but often times I work long hours and can be called back in without a moment's notice. I might be able to be of assistance once in a while. That would please me. Thanks for asking! So I guess what I'm saying is yes, if it doesn't interfere with my job."

"I've got to give you a hug, Sasha, that's my way." Willy wrapped her strong arms around Sasha and pulled Houston into a group hug.

"Don't squeeze too hard Willy, I'm full like a stuffed sausage after your great breakfast."

They said their thanks and good-byes and Sasha walked out the office door.

"We got ourselves another real friend, a cop! Can you believe that?" said Houston thoughtfully.

CHAPTER ELEVEN

Sunday.....

Houston awakened earlier than usual. She showered, picked up her room, took the linens off the bed, gathered all her dirty laundry and placed it on top of the washing machine. The washer and dryer were conveniently located in her bathroom. She called to Willy, "Wake up detective. We've got plans to make and I'm getting ready to throw some stuff into the washer. You got anything you want washed?"

"Yeah. Just give me a minute. This is Sunday, a day of rest. Does this mean you're going to church with me? You're gonna get some religion at last. The music will stir your soul, Tex. How about it?"

"I'm stirred up enough. Thanks for the offer though, maybe some other Sunday. I'll vacuum the apartment and the office if you'll make breakfast. I can finish up the laundry while you're singing your heart out at church."

"Good plan, Tex. Being Sunday, I'm gonna whip up my special eggs and fried grits. Okay if I take the truck to church?"

"The truck belongs to the both of us. No permission needed. I've been thinking that we're gonna need a second vehicle soon. How about we talk to Tony and Luke and our brothers to see what they all suggest. I'll see if I can get someone on the phone this morning while you're at church and maybe later go car shopping with you."

Wilamina said, "Now that we have all this spying to do, we really could use another car. Don't bother calling our brothers. Remember we're meeting them both at the Hot Tamale Restaurant tonight. We can ask them first about ideas and tomorrow ask Tony and Luke."

"Good plan. I had forgotten about our dinner date."

After breakfast was finished, they went to work going over the plans for tomorrow. First appointment for Monday was with Mr. Spade who was to give them more information on Mr. Germain and to work out a schedule for surveillance. They had already agreed by phone to follow Mr. Germain on Tuesday, Thursday and Saturday. Mr. Spade would take Monday, Wednesday and Friday.

Wilamina left for church and Houston began her household chores. She whistled "The Yellow Rose of Texas" while she worked.

Monday.....

Mr. Spade arrived exactly on time at the Salt and Pepper Agency. Wilamina had baked some great smelling cinnamon buns and Houston put out the coffee cups and plates.

"Welcome, Mr. Spade," announced both ladies at the same time.

"How about we use our first names, sounds friendlier. I'm Jason."

"I'm Houston and this here is Wilamina. "

Taking in some deep breaths, Jason said, "Sure smells good in here, ladies. I've got to tell you I'm excited to have you join me to put this Germain sleazebag away. I was sure burning out from so many hours sitting and staring out the car window. Let's hope he does something stupid real soon and gives himself away.

Germain has gone to the Safeway the last two Thursdays around 10 a.m. Then he stops for lunch at the Table Talk Cafe and the next Thursday at the Hot Tamale restaurant. Both times he took about an hour and then he went on home. I checked at 4 p.m. 7 and 10 p.m. and his car was in his car port each time.

"At noon on both Tuesdays, the gardener cut the grass in front and back. Germain's car was in the carport. This guy sure seems to love his yard. That's surprising to me, him being such a crook.

"He went to Ringo's Bar both Saturday nights and returned home at midnight. I've only been watching him for two weeks so I don't really know much about his routine. Yet I figured with the three of us following him, we should be able to get a better handle on what he does with his time. I'll start again this evening and you guys can start tomorrow. At the end of two weeks we will meet again and compare notes.

"I really appreciate you gals working with me. Call me anytime day or night if you have any problems or questions."

Mr. Spade handed them a small notebook with the addresses of all the places Mr. Germain had visited in the last two weeks: the doctor's office, the gym, the massage therapist, bars and so forth. He handed them a folder and said, "Inside this folder is all the background information I've collected up until now.

"Please keep detailed records and collect all receipts. The American Insurance Co. will send you a check every two weeks, as soon as they receive your bill, and receipts plus dates and times of surveillance. Thanks again. Great buns, Wilamina."

Wilamina looked startled and stared hard at Jason.

"I'm speaking about your baking skills, Wilamina. The best darn cinnamon buns ever." He displayed a wide grin and gave Wilamina a slight nudge. Talk with you soon."

"Good-bye Jason. Glad you like my baking talents. The rest of me ain't so bad either." She had a broad smile that showed off all her pearly white teeth. Jason and Houston both were laughing as he went out the door.

Tuesday.....

At 9 a.m., the two investigators were parked one block down from Mr. Germain's house. They were both drinking coffee and munching on rolls. Houston was in the driver's seat. She looked over at her partner who was decked out in sun glasses, a short light--brown wig covered with a black baseball cap. Houston said, "You remember Mr. Spade said Mr. Germain's house was being painted last week. There is only one paint store in town and they may have referred the suspect to a certain painter. We could ask them if they refer people to painters and do they remember Mr. Germain. We can also go to Ringo's Bar Saturday night and keep our eyes open. We'd have to wear disguises though."

Wilamina added, "I'm praying like crazy that we can pull this disguise stuff off. Too bad we're not two short, fat, old women 'cause then we wouldn't need any disguises. No one looks at old women, fat or skinny."

"I'm grateful we're not," chuckled Houston. "We are two good-looking broads and men do look as us when we pass by them. We need a second vehicle so we can take turns following these creeps sometimes. At least we could separate during the day. Night surveillance is another thing and I believe we should always be together for safety reasons.

"I just had another thought, if Mr. Germain goes to a gym, one of our brothers could do a little spying for us. They could pretend to be interested in joining the club and maybe even go a few times to work-out like they're trying out the club. They could take pictures of Mr. Germain to see what he does there. We could get lucky by catching him doing more than he pretends he can do."

The ladies remained in place until noon when the gardener showed up. A few minutes after he started to mow the front lawn, Mr. Germain came out of his house and started talking to the gardener. Houston watched them through a pair of borrowed binoculars. The suspect was pointing to his flowers and waving his arms angrily. The gardener just shook his head and Mr. Germain seemed less upset and less agitated. He was wearing a back brace thing and a cast on his left wrist. Houston finished describing what she witnessed to Wilamina and added, "He didn't seem to be in much pain waving his arms around."

Wilamina responded, "His yard looks mighty pretty, especially his flower garden. He must really care about his yard if he pays someone to come every week to help him keep it up."

"I think we better leave now." said Houston. "Someone is gonna wonder why we've parked here so long. Let's go have lunch and drive back just to look for his car. We can drive around the corner and one of us can walk back to look for it. We've been told constantly to change our routine. Let's call Sasha and Sargeant Lathy and see if they can give us more background information on this man."

"That's sounds good to me," answered Wilamina. "We can stop at the paint store on the way back home. I'll call Royal and see if he has time to go to the gym and spy on the suspect."

CHAPTER TWELVE

It was decided that Wilamina would walk into the Rainbow Paint Store since she was already somewhat disguised. The clerk responded to Wilamina's request for a recommendation and gave her the names of two house painters and their phone numbers. She then told the clerk that she lived on Rose St. and noticed one of her neighbors just had his house painted and it looked great. As she spoke she kept her head down, trying to hide her face from the clerk.

"As a matter of fact, ma'am, I know that Pete Lowe painted Mr. Germain's house on Rose Street about two weeks ago. I'll just write down his name and phone on our business card for you."

"You have a mighty good memory young man. Do you know Mr. Germain?"

"Not really. He comes in here once and a while to purchase paint. He is quite particular and demanding, but that's probably 'cause of his injuries. Do you want to look at paints today?"

"Not today, but when it's time I'll be back and buy what I need from you. Thanks again for your help."

Back in the car, Wilamina shared the information from the clerk. "Are we gonna call the painter right away or what?"

"I think the first thing will be to look over the folder from Spade and then make the call to the painter."

Back at the office......

Houston began reading the contents of the folder on Mr. Germain out loud. "In 1999, George Germain filed a claim against Farmers Ins., New York City, for five hundred thousand dollars. He was twenty-eight years old, married, with two small children. He collected two hundred thousand dollars. He had been working for a plumbing company and was injured on the job. (Head injury, broken leg and ankle and back injuries.) He spent two weeks in a hospital. He obtained a divorce same year. In 2012 he filed a claim with Richards Ins. Co. Chicago, Ill. for seven hundred fifty thousand dollars and collected five hundred thousand. He claimed he had mostly the same injuries as in 1999, no witnesses. In year 2014, Richie's Ins. Co. of Kansas he filed for two hundred fifty thousand and collected one hundred thousand. Same type of injuries, no witnesses. Interesting note, the same doctor signed the report both times. Seems the doctor moved to the same state as Mr. Germain. Up until now, I haven't been able to find any information on the so-called Dr. Lightfoot. Now in 2017, Reliable Ins. Co. of Seattle, Germain has filed for five hundred thousand dollars, similar injuries."

Houston stopped to finish off her coffee and take a bite of toast. She continued reading, "Background info. Parents dead, lived in up- state N.Y. They had left the landscape business to their only child, George. He tried to keep the business going, but had trouble keeping employees. It seems he was often rude, demanding and quick tempered. The injuries listed: torn ligaments of ankles, shoulder, severe sprains, fractures of two vertebrae, head concussions, vision problems, blackouts, nightmares, referred to a psychologist. There were never any witnesses to the different sort of accidents that the client claimed, except for the first accident. Work background listed was from working his own nursery and working as an employee in landscaping with another company. Also worked as a plumber and other construction type jobs and now this last job, working from home for a collection company."

Wilamina asked, "Are there any doctors besides Dr. Lightfoot listed on hospital reports in the folder?"

"I don't see any. Guess we need to ask Jason about those reports. You know Willy, I've been thinking. This Germain guy seems to care a whole lot about his flowers. I had a thought that if we're gonna catch him, we need to see what he is actually doing in his backyard. He may do some real yard work there, maybe at night.

"We've got to figure out how to take pictures of him moving around more, like on his knees or climbing ladders and not wearing his back thing-a- majig."

Wilamina offered a suggestion that maybe they could get up on his garage roof or the neighbor's roof to take pictures.

"How the hell are we gonna do that in the day time and him not seeing or hearing us? If we do it at night then how can we take pictures in the dark?"

"Well Miss pale face," retorted Wilamina, "I've been reading some of the detective books and they talk about cameras that will take night pictures. Maybe Sasha would know about that. Maybe we could even ask at a camera shop. We gotta try something."

"Not bad, Willy. Maybe you got a good idea there. Let's drive by his house tonight after dark, park in the next block and walk back by his house. We could, or one of us could pretend walking is our exercise. We could even borrow a dog from one of our friends. Seems more natural to go walking with a dog, don't you think?"

"I didn't see any street lights on that road. You know I'm not black black, more like carmel color. If I wear the blond wig, that should confuse the hell out of anyone I come across. My skin color don't show up so much in the dark."

"Okay we got a plan. I'll call Brooksie or Luke and see about borrowing one of their dogs so you can look like you're actually walking your dog with the goal of exercise for the both of you."

CHAPTER THIRTEEN

After dark that night Houston and Wilamina drove by the suspect's house. They had Sugar, one of Brooksie's dogs, riding look-out with them. The dog wasn't thrilled about walking on a leash and acting tough. She was used to running amuck in her owner's large back yard and simply clowning around. It took some serious convincing that this new routine was any fun. Sugar was a thirty-five pound mix of Scottie and whatever male had visited her mother. She had a curly, light brown coat with charcoal-colored eyes. The only thing she would ever attack was her food dish and an occasional butterfly or two.

"This here mutt is such a friendly little girl. She wouldn't scare a mouse, but she's awful sweet. I could get used to having a pet like her," said Wilamina.

"I want a pet too, but we have no yard. A dog needs a good-sized yard to run around. How about we foster some small dogs or even cats until we get our own home and yard. Brooksie said her Aunt Tilly can hook us up as foster parents. We keep the animals until someone offers a forever home. What'da think of the idea, Willy?" Just then they arrived at their destination.

"Here we are. Look, there's a light on downstairs and I see some light coming from the back of the house. Damn we've got to find out what he's doing back there. How about you and Sugar getting out of the car and walk quietly up to his fence and try to hear something. I'll drive around the block and then pick you up."

"Okay," said Wilamina. "I'll be as quiet as a thieving skunk sneakin' around the chicken coop looking for dinner."

Wilamina tippy-toed, holding on to Sugar's leach tightly. She got in position and listened for a short time before she saw her friend's car slowly coming down the street. She scurried back to the car, placed the dog in the back seat, who immediately jumped up front, got on her lap and started licking her face in the hopes of receiving a treat for a job well done. At least in Sugar's mind.

"Did you hear anything?" asked Houston.

"Yes, it sounded like a drill or something with a motor. I couldn't see over the fence, but there was definitely someone working back there."

Houston excitedly shared, "I noticed something that may be very helpful when I was coming back to get you. The house on his left is for sale. If it's empty, we can sneak inside and watch out the windows to see what he is up to. From the second floor we could get pictures of him working in the backyard, if that's what he's doing. Let's come back here tomorrow night with our camera. I could also call the real estate office located on that sign over there and ask to see the house. I'll tell'm I'm interested in buying a house and then we'll know for certain the house is empty."

"Are we gonna break in?" asked Wilamina with her eyes wide opened and her blond wig sitting lopsided on her head.

Houston glanced over at her business partner and laughed out loud. "Willy, you gotta get more practice wearing a wig and keeping it on straight. If we fail as detectives we might have to switch to a comedy act."

They drove back to Brooksie's house to give back their "borrowed walking prop," then return to their own place. In their nearly blank record book, Wilamina took care of writing the date, and time spent on the job. "You know Tex, I kinda like keeping the records. Makes me feel smart and useful."

"You are smart and useful, Willy. I already knew that. You've listened to the wrong people in your life. They were worthless and wanted you to be the same as them. Guess I sort of did the same thing.

"I'll call the real estate company tomorrow. I'm gonna hit the hay my friend. I'm bushed. See you in the morning."

"Good-night, Tex."

CHAPTER FOURTEEN

Houston placed a call to the real estate company that was listed on the sign next door to Mr. Germain's house. "I saw your for sale sign on a house I might be interested in. Could I make an appointment to see the place today?" She gave the address of the house she was interested in, and was given a 4 p.m. appointment. She decided she would dress up and wear the dark brown wig. Her usual makeup consisted of lipstick in a light shade of watermelon, but for today she would put on a darker red, some eye liner and color her cheeks.

Next night..........
"Sure glad you met with that real estate lady, Tex. I feel a whole lot better knowing the house is empty."

"Me too. I was able to unlock the back door when the real estate agent left me alone for a moment. She answered her phone and walked into the living room to talk. Hopefully she never discovered the door I unlocked. It would be so easy to get access to the house, but if she relocked the back door, we can still get in. I've got a few tricks left over from my old life.

"Willy, you drive around the block and park in the playground parking area that we saw yesterday when we were driving around. Then walk back to this house. If I've gotten in, I'll have the front room curtain slightly pulled back, walk around to the back door and come in. Got it?"

"Sure do partner. Hope no one can hear my heart pounding. Sounds like a jack hammer to me."

Houston got out of the car and Wilamina took off slowly driving down the street, heading for the park.

As Houston approached the back door she hesitated, cocked her head aiming her right ear towards Mr. Germain's backyard. She held her breath and listened intently. *That does sound like a power tool of some kind, maybe an electric saw.* She quickly tried the door handle and to her relief the door opened. Quickly she slipped inside, rushed to the front room and cautiously pushed the curtain ajar.

She didn't have to wait long. Her friend came through the back door and whispered, "I hear that same sound I heard last night. What you think that creep is up to?"

Houston moved the curtain back to its original position and pointed to the stairs, signaled they should start climbing. In a very low voice she said, "We need to be very quiet. Let's go and see what we can see. You've got the video camera, right?"

"Hey Tex, you're working with a pro. Course I brought it and my cell phone. Sasha showed us both how to work everything, thank God. I may be slow to learn something, but I never forget stuff. You know, I've never taken a picture in my life. I've never even owned a video camera or phone before. The only pictures I have of me were taken when they arrested me. Oh yeah, and again when our friends took pictures the day I was being released from prison oh, and again at that great party they gave for us."

They continued creeping up the stairs. They entered one of the back bedrooms and sneaked up to the window facing the suspect's backyard.

"My God, there's Mr. Germain holding and using the saw standing on a ladder." Houston grabbed the video camera from Wilamina and started to record the event. He was not wearing his back brace. He was using both hands and arms, climbing up and down the ladder. He stretched far out while balanced on one foot in order to use his hammer to nail on a board.

"We've got him!" shrieked Houston, muffling her voice with her hands.

At that very moment the cell phone started to play some fairly loud music and both women froze in place.

"What the hell is that?" asked Wilamina. As her head flinched back slightly.

"The f.......g cell phone." Houston grabbed the phone and rammed it down into her bra in an attempt to stifle the sound. She peaked out the window and saw Mr. Germain looking up at the same window. He quickly jumped down from the ladder and ran into his house.

"My God, Willy, I think he has heard us. What if he comes looking over here?" Houston grabbed her friend and said, "Let's go out the back door and hide behind the garage."

They raced down the stairs as Wilamina prayed out loud to Jesus. They went out the door and had just enough room to squeeze between the garage and the neighbor's fence. There were a few tall bushes and several trash cans to get around. They both squeezed in and squatted down just as Mr. Germain came running to the back door of the empty house. They could hear him opening the door apparently he went inside. Both frightened detectives were holding their breath. They couldn't see what he was doing or where he was. After what seemed like hours to them, they heard his footsteps, on the gravel driveway, coming toward them.

As he walked toward the garage he verbally threatened, "If you damn kids are lurking around here again, you're going to get more than you bargained for. I'm not calling the police this time 'cause I got a better plan. They'd probably just arrest you. My plan for you is far more painful."

Everything was deathly quiet for a second or two and then the two terrified investigators heard footsteps moving further away down the driveway. They waited breathlessly for what seemed like an eternity. Then slowly Houston inched her way through the bushes, walking sideways because of the tight fit. She was able to get close to the edge of the garage, peak out. She didn't see him. Wilamina was right behind holding onto Houston's pants pocket.

Wilamina whispered, "Wait up, I see a gate going into the other neighbor's yard. They backed up and Wilamina was able to gently open the gate. They carefully looked around, saw no dogs or people and crept into the yard. Fortunately, there were no more fences and they walked directly to the sidewalk.

"Let's walk slowly, like we have been simply taking a late night stroll," said Houston who was wide-eyed and sweat dripping down her face onto her sweater.

Wilamina simply nodded. Her voice having abandoned her.

As soon as they got back to their car they leaped in and collapsed on the seat. "My God, I've never been so frightened. Prison was a piece of cake compared to back there. Jesus, I've peed on myself. Oh, Tex, you've got a weeney for a partner."

"No problem Wilamina, my pants are wet too. We'll toughen up in time. We've got him. We've got the proof on this here video. His bacon is cooked. I'm calling Mr. Spade the second we get home. That is after I shower and I change my underwear."

They hugged briefly and Houston added, "We smell like a urine factory in this closed car."

Both started laughing which quickly increased to howling and continued all the way back to their home office.

Back at the office..........

As soon as Houston cleaned up and changed into dry clothes, she called Mr. Spade. "Hello Mr. Spade. Sorry to call so late, but Willy and I just got back home and we couldn't wait to tell you our fantastic news. We got Mr. Germain on video working an electric saw while standing on a ladder. He was working on the top floor at the back of his house. He wasn't wearing a back brace and all his body parts were moving just fine."

"Wow! You gals are 'sumptin else. Congratulations. I'll come by in the morning, say about 11 a.m. and look at the tape. Thanks for letting me know. See you soon."

"Bye Mr. Spade, later."

"Hey Willy, how about we split a beer to celebrate catching our first scum bag. Mr. Spade is coming by tomorrow morning to look at the video. He's really happy with what we filmed and thrilled the crook has blown his cover."

"I don't want to share a beer, I want the whole can to myself. It might help us relax us enough to be able to fall asleep some time soon. First I got to shower 'cause I stink. Then I'm getting on my pajamas and join you for a celebration. Hope I don't have nightmares about that man coming after us. I was really scared. That man is evil. We did good, didn't we partner?"

"Yes Willy, we did good."

CHAPTER FIFTEEN

Next morning.........

Mr. Spade arrived right on time. He was all smiles and carrying two bags tied with ribbons. Both women were standing at the front door, eagerly waiting for their new business friend.

"Welcome Jason," said Houston. She handed him the video camera and the three of them looked at the recorded evidence.

"Fantastic! This is the proof we've needed to stop that son of a b..... That crook sure met his match when you stepped in and took on his case. I'm proud of you two novices. You're amazing."

He handed a colorful gift bag tied with bright ribbon to each of them. "I've had these for a few days, just been waiting for the right moment to give them to you."

As he handed each of them their gifts bags, he timidly kissed them on their cheeks and quickly backed away.

Inside their respective bags they found a sweatshirt. Houston's was all white with black lettering. It read, "Detective Salt." Wilamina's was an all black sweatshirt with the words in white. It read, "Detective Pepper."

"This here is one of my proudest days," said Wilamina, tearing up. She grabbed Mr. Spade so quickly he hadn't time to object. She hugged him in her usual bear-like fashion, until he cried uncle. Houston showed her appreciation by taking hold of his hands, looking him straight in the eye and said "A big Texas thanks."

"Now ladies, you need to make out your itemized statement. I'll take the tape and have two copies made; one for you and one for me. I'll send the original to the insurance company's lawyer along with our statements all together in the same package. I bet we'll hear back quickly. The company has just saved a bucket-load of money and 'Mr. Scam' is hopefully out of business for good."

"I haven't had time to get that statement ready," said Wilamina.

"That's no problem. If you have time now I'll just go down the street and get the copies of the video made. That should give you enough time. Okay?"

"Yes sir, Mr. Spade. They'll be ready."

Wilamina got right to work while Houston put their sweatshirts away in the downstairs closet. The front door to their office opened up with a bang and in walked a tall, hefty man around thirty years old.

"Hello," announced Houston. "Can we help you?"

"I sure hope so. I sort of have a problem. Actually I've made a mess of things. What sort of things do you need me to tell you?"

"My name is Houston and over there typing is my partner, Wilamina. What do you go by?"

The stranger said, "Before I give you my name I want to know if you can look for a missing person? I have a friend who has been missing for almost two weeks."

"Yes. That is part of our work," answered Houston.

"Will whatever I tell you be confidential?"

"Yes, unless you're talking about committing a crime or hurting yourself or anyone else."

He still didn't offer his name, he just began to speak rapidly, barely taking time to breathe. "It's like this, this friend has been more than just a friend. I'm married and have a kid. My marriage sucks. My wife is bossy as hell. She has made my life miserable from day one. She's a control freak. If I try to divorce her she will make damn sure I have no relationship with my ten year old son, Richard. She bullies him too. He is a great kid and we do lots of stuff together. My wife is the meanest person I've ever known. I wanted to leave her years back, except I couldn't leave Richard and she'd never let me have him. The courts are always on the side of the mother even if she is hateful and harmful." He continued without taking a noticeable breath. "I know I sound like I'm making excuses and maybe I am. I desperately want a divorce. I'm not the cheating kind of guy. My friend, Charlene is really my girlfriend. We've been seeing each other for two years. My wife doesn't know anything about her. The problem is that Charlene has been missing for the past two weeks. She would never go away and not let me know that she was okay. I need you to find her. I gotta know she's all right. I really love her."

At this point he choked up and finally took a few deep breaths. "My name is Chance Young and my girlfriend's name is Charlene Kellog. My son is Richard and my hateful wife's name is Melody, but I call her Mel. She was definitely misnamed by her parents. Can you people help me?"

Just then Mr. Spade came through the office door. "Looks like I will need to come back later. How about giving me a call when your invoice is ready Wilamina and I'll either come back or you can mail it to me."

"Will do, Mr. Spade. I'll give you a call later and thanks."

He winked at her and left the office.

Houston looked over at Wilamina and said to Chance, the possible client, "I think I should tell you that Wilamina and I have been in this business for a very short time. You might do better with some agency that has more experience. We'd do our best, but there are other agencies with more experience. Have you gone to the police?"

"No I don't want to involve them yet. I don't want to hurt my son and he doesn't know about Charlene and me. Could you just do some snooping around? I'll give you all the information I have on Charlene and maybe we'll get lucky right away. Would you at least try for a short time to locate her?"

Houston again looked at her partner. Wilamina nodded, grabbed a note pad and pen and moved her chair next to Houston. They spent the next part of an hour obtaining basic information about Charlene, where to look and people to ask questions. The investigators agreed to get back in one week with what they had found or sooner if they located Charlene.

Mr. Young said, "This is my cell number. You can reach me anytime, even at night. I'm not staying at home right now. I can't be around that nasty woman worried the way I am. Please don't call my house unless it's an emergency. If you absolutely have to, you could say you're a co-worker. Give a fake name, say Mary. That's a pretty common name and since I don't know any Mary, I'll know it is you calling. That's if Mel gives me the message."

"If we need to see you, can you get away from your job?"

"Yes. Actually any time if it's necessary."

"Wilamina and I need some time to come up with a plan of action. We'll begin today making calls to the numbers you've given us. Do you have a key to Charlene's apartment?"

"I do. I've been to her place every day hoping to find some clues or ideas as to where she has gone or what has happened to her."

"Would you be able to meet us at her apartment tomorrow at noon?" asked Houston.

"I'll be there at noon. See you there and thanks. Do I pay you now?"

Wilamina responded, "No. I'll keep a daily record of everything we do, hours, mileage and whatever else we do. We charge fifty dollars an hour for the two of us. We will do our very best to keep the charges down."

"I'd appreciate that. I have some savings that Mel doesn't know anything about. See you tomorrow."

After Mr. Young left the office the two stared at each other with a mixture of excitement and anxiety. Houston was frowning while Wilamina was rapidly rubbing her hands together.

"Are we in over our heads here? Where to begin. We need to talk to Sasha real quick like. Maybe we should talk with Mr. Lagunta as well," expressed Houston.

"Do you think Mr. Young's wife knows anything about the girlfriend?" questioned Wilamina.

Houston responded, "I'd be surprised if she didn't. Two years is a long time not to at least get suspicious. He said she was very controlling and I bet she has had her eagle eye on him for a long time. Someone that hateful could get mighty clever and even dangerous."

Houston placed a call to Sasha who answered after the first ring. "Good morning Detective Sasha. This is your fan club of two calling for your advice."

"Good morning back at ya. What can I do for you guys?"

Houston summarized the visit by Mr. Young and asked for suggestions.

"Is her car missing?

"Mr. Young said yes it was. He gave us the plate numbers, year and make of her car." She added the details given to her by Chance and waited for the detective's response.

"My hands are pretty much tied, if he won't file a missing person report. The department has some serious guidelines we have to follow regarding missing people. See if you can't get him to change his mind tomorrow when you meet up with him at her apartment. I'll check out what I can and get back to you."

"Thanks Sasha. Wish us luck." Houston turned to her partner and said, "Okay Willy, time to put some kind of plan in action."

They agreed that tomorrow they would thoroughly search Charlene's apartment and hopefully find something that would help them. The plan for today was to go to Charlene's place of employment to and ask questions and then talk to her neighbors. Later on they would call their attorney and listen to what he might suggest.

CHAPTER SIXTEEN

The first call Houston made was to Charlene's best friend, Lynn Reynolds. Mr. Young said Lynn would know the most about Charlene's friends and other activities that Charlene was involved in. Both ladies became close friends because they lived in the same apt. building.

"Hello, Lynn here."

"You don't know me Lynn, my name is Houston Hayfied and I'm a private investigator. I wonder if you would be willing to answer a few questions about your friend, Charlene?"

"What's happened to her. I've been worried sick. Do you know where she is?"

"I don't know if anything has happened to her. My partner and me, we've been asked to try to locate her. We were given your name and thought maybe you could help. Could we meet?"

"I'm off today and tomorrow. Tomorrow morning would be best for me," responded Lynn.

"That would be great. What time and where?" asked Houston.

"I run around the park most mornings for my workout. There's a fountain in the center of the park. How about we meet there at 9 a.m.?"

"We'll be there and thanks for your willingness to help us. By the way, when was the last time you saw your friend?" asked Houston.

"Not sure of the date, but it was on Saturday, two weeks ago. We both have Saturdays off so we power walk\run around the park almost every Saturday. She simply didn't show up and that's so unlike her."

"Thanks again Lynn. See you tomorrow at 9 a.m."

Next Houston put in a call to Dr. Clarkson's office. He and Charlene shared the same waiting room and apparently worked together in group situations. There was no answer so she left her name, number and asked him to return her call.

In the meantime, Wilamina used her cell phone to call Mr. Woods, the manager of the apartment building where Charlene and Lynn rented separate apartments.

Mr. Woods answered the phone. His voice was shaky and he sounded quite elderly. Wilamina identified herself and asked if she and her friend could meet up with him tomorrow at 11:30 a.m. at the apartment building. "When was the last time you remember seeing Miss Kellog?"

"I'm not real sure, but it has been over a week. She sure is a nice young woman, so polite and thoughtful. Is everything okay with her?"

"As far as we know she's okay. See you tomorrow and thanks Mr. Woods."

Houston spoke up, "I have another thought, Willy. If Charlene is in private practice she probably has quite a few clients. I don't know much about the work she does. The closest we both have come to needing or using a therapist was the group we joined at Lancer's. If she sees lots of folks there is no way we can talk to all of them. The TV shows always talk about confidentiality stuff. Guess that's another question for Mr. Lagunta.

"I'm beginning to think we need a lot of people on our team. Looking for a missing person is definitely over our heads."

"I have an idea." said Wilamina. "Why not call Mr. Spade and see if he can help us with suggestions. We can also check with the Hunts. They both seem to know about a lot about investigating different kinds of problems."

"Great idea. Make the call Willy, first to Spade and later to the Hunts. Maybe Spade would like to have dinner with us here. You could whip together one of your great southern meals. It would be more private to talk to him here. A restaurant is too public."

Wilamina dialed Mr. Spade and he said YES with enthusiasm. "I'll be there about 6 p.m. tomorrow evening. Hopefully, I can help you gals. You sure did a great job for me."

"We sure have a full schedule tomorrow. It's almost like real business people," commented Wilamina. "We see Lynn at 9:00 a.m., Mr. Woods at 11:30 a.m. and Mr. Spade at 6:00 p.m. Maybe Dr. Clarkson will call back and we could squeeze in another person. If we don't hear from him today we should try again on Monday."

Saturday..............

Houston and Wilamina were waiting in the park next to the fountain a few minutes before they were to meet Charlene's friend, Lynn. A few walkers and runners passed by the two women.

"This is a real pretty place. We could walk around here most days to get in better shape. How about it, Willy?"

"Okay Tex, I'll walk, but don't you go and try to trick me into runnin. I'm not into huffin' and sweatin'. I like my figure just fine and there's nothing wrong with yours either."

"Willy, I'm just thinking about our safety. We may have to deal with others like Mr. Germain or worse." Houston stopped talking and squinted her eyes looking at an approaching figure. "Maybe that's Lynn coming our way."

A young, well-fit woman dressed in running shorts, T-shirt and tennis shoes, jogged up to the partners.

"Hi. I'm Lynn and I guess you must be the two investigators. I love your Salt and Pepper sweat shirts."

"Thanks. They were a gift from a satisfied customer. I'm Houston and this here is Wilamina."

Lynn asked, "Who has asked you to look for Charlene?"

"We can't share that, but we can tell you this person is very concerned about Charlene's whereabouts. Please tell me again about the last time you saw her and anything else you think might be important."

"Like I told you on the phone, it was two weeks ago. We did our usual jog around the park. She didn't seem like anything was bothering her, except she was quieter than normal. Charlene is a good person, a great friend, caring and thoughtful. I didn't see her all that week so I figured she was super busy. When she didn't show up last Saturday for our workout I got concerned because she always let me know if her plans changed. Saturday mornings were special to both of us. We could catch up on the events of the week."

"Do you know if she has a boyfriend?" asked Wilamina.

A long silence and Lynn began to walk in place. "Why do you ask that? She's single, good looking, and young, now who wouldn't be interested in her? In fact, I know several guys who tried to date her but she wouldn't ever say yes to any of them. I'm not comfortable talking to you anymore unless I know who is paying you. Is it a man or a woman?

Houston told her it was a man.

"She is my dear friend and I don't want to cause her any trouble."

Houston looked over at her partner and wrinkled her nose. Whenever she wrinkled her nose it meant that she had conflicts.

The partners had been together long enough now to learn how to read some certain gestures. Wilamina winked back at Houston which was her go-ahead sign.

Houston responded, "Chance Young gave us your name and asked us to contact you. I feel it's okay to say he is the one who's paying us to look for Charlene. He is very concerned and he doesn't want to go to the police yet."

"I'll cooperate anyway I can as long as his wife is not involved. That woman is pure evil. Chance has told Charlene and me terrible stories about her."

"We have not met or spoken to the wife," added Houston.

"Charlene is not a person who would ever want to break up anyone's marriage, but Chance's wife is a nasty piece of work. I've gotten to know Chance and he's a great guy. He loves Charlene and his son deeply and passionately."

Wilamina asked, "Has Charlene disappeared before and not told you or Chance where she was going?"

"No, never. She's much too responsible and thoughtful."

"Has she ever talked to you about any client that has concerned her? Maybe she told you she had safety issues concerning a client. Any sort of threats you can remember?"

"None. Anyone who knew her, loved her. She never talked about her clients. She's too ethical and too trusting for her own good."

Houston informed Lynn about the prearranged meeting with Chance at Charlene's apartment at 11:30 this morning and asked if she would like to go along with them."

"Absolutely! I live on the third floor and Charlene lives on the second floor. We can walk back to the building together after I've jogged around the park. I need to keep up my exercise routine. You can both join me and ask anything you want. We can walk around if you aren't into jogging."

"You ain't gonna start runnin' are you? I don't do runnin." said Wilamina emphatically.

"No ma'am. I prefer walking to running myself." responded Lynn with a grin.

They started walking around the park trail and eventually Wilamina said, "I'll just go on over to the apartment, you two keep going."

Lynn laughed out loud, "Getting tired Wilamina? I forgot you two might not be into this kind of exercise. Let's all go to the apartment."

They walked across the park and when they reached the apartment building, Lynn invited them into her place for coffee and to wait til 11:30 when Chance was scheduled to arrive. Lynn proudly showed them around her apartment. After coffee and chatting it was time for the meeting.

The three ambled downstairs and met Mr. Woods and Mr. Young standing and conversing in front of Charlene's apartment, number 202.

"Thanks for coming," said Chance who hugged Lynn and shook hands with the others. "Let's pray we find something that helps us find her. She would never disappear without letting Lynn or myself know her plans."

Mr. Woods said, "I wish you all good luck. I don't think I need to go inside her apartment so I'll just go back to my office. If I hear anything I'll let one of you know."

Wilamina handed Mr. Woods one of their new business cards. "Just in case you remember something. Actually I want to show off our new cards. Maybe you know of others who might need two fine private detectives," she winked at him as he walked away.

They started in the living room. Lynn commented, "Charlene was such a wonderful housekeeper. She always kept her place looking spotless, pretty and cheerful."

They found one dirty coffee cup in the kitchen sink. The bathroom told a different story. The towel was lying on the floor along with her running shorts and T-shirt.

Lynn looked hard at the clothes on the floor and said, "Those are her exercise shorts and the T-shirt she wore on Saturday. She usually wore the same outfit for our run. You can see it's got the 'Save a Pet, Adopt - Don't Buy!' logo on it. Looks like she left in a hurry. She must have taken a shower after we ran together and then maybe she got a phone call and raced out of the house."

The four continued checking every corner and drawer until Wilamina spotted a piece of paper that had apparently fallen on the floor. It was next to the desk.

"Don't pick it up, Willy. There could be finger prints. Using a pencil, Chance straightened the paper so he could read what was written on it. He read it out loud, "Road 45 go 2 miles--gas."

"Chance does this note make any sense to you?" asked Houston.

"Yes it does. There is a small picturesque lake off of Hiway 45. Charlene and I have gone there several times together. We could swim and picnic and be alone."

"Would she go there without you?" questioned Houston.

"I doubt it. We sort of thought of it as our special place. It was very private and peaceful. We'd even talked about building a get-away cabin there one day. The last time we visited that place was about a month ago. We've been working on my plans to divorce Melody and how to go about sharing Richard."

"Did Charlene ever talk to either of you about any clients that concerned her? Ever say she was afraid of anyone?" Houston looked at both.

"Not to me," responded Chance and Lynn agreed with him. Lynn added, "She did speak about feeling compassion towards most of her clients. She told me that some of them were seriously challenged by their difficult childhoods. She also said that not too long ago, Dr. Clarkson seemed to be getting overly friendly. She didn't give me any details except she added that some people can really take you by surprise. Said also she was considering looking for other office space."

Chance's gaze bounced from place to place. He cleared his throat and said, "Charlene never said anything about Clarkson to me. Maybe I need to pay him a visit."

"Chance, I left a message for Dr. Clarkson to call our office. We'll keep after him. If he hasn't returned our message by the time we get back to the office, Willy and I will go to his office and hopefully get to talk to him."

Houston signaled Wilamina to meet her outside the apartment. "We'll be right back in, keep looking around you two."

"Willy, I'm getting a bad feeling here. The police need to be notified. We've got to convince Chance."

"I agree. Somethin' doesn't feel right. From what everybody said, Charlene is too considerate to just disappear and not tell her friends anything."

They returned to the apartment and the four continued to look for anything that might lead them in Charlene's direction. There was a bookcase in her bedroom and Lynn had been looking through the books, albums and knick knacks that were stored there. She pulled out a book titled When Mental Illness Turns Violent. She opened to find a tablet that had some words written on it. "This is Charlene's handwriting and she has written *the life-long effects of cruelty in childhood* and listed these words, vengeance, obsession, murder."

"It's not surprising she has these sorts of books. She's a counselor and a licensed social worker and deals with all kinds of emotional problems with her clients. I know she and Dr. Clarkson run a group together for people with bipolar disorders and depression. She runs grief groups separate from Clarkson. She loves her work and is always reading and learning more."

"Chance, Wilamina and I are very concerned about Charlene and we both agree that you truly need to let the police know what is going on. Charlene may need help. Willy and I will do all we can, but the police are the professionals. What do you say?"

"Please listen to them, Chance. I'm beginning to get frightened and we need to do everything possible to find her. I'll go with you to the police station if you like," begged Lynn with crocodile tears running down her cheeks.

"You're right. Would all of you be willing to go with me to the station?"

"Absolutely!" the three announced in unison.

Houston placed a call to Sasha to give her a heads up about Mr. Young coming in to talk about a missing friend.

Sasha said she'd be waiting and for them and to simply tell the officer at the desk to let her know when they arrived.

"We're good to go," said Houston. "This is the right thing to do for your special friend, Chance."

CHAPTER SEVENTEEN

The four stopped at the Table Talk Cafe for coffee, pastries and basically to stall for time. They all agreed they needed something to calm themselves but the real unspoken reason was to put off facing the frightening possibility that something bad may have happened to Charlene. After they sat down and ordered, no one said anything. Silence hung heavily over their table. Lynn's lower lip was quivering, Chance was stone-faced and Houston was fiddling with a strand of her hair. Wilamina broke the silence by talking nonstop until the waitress took their order.

Houston spoke up, "I know we are dreading this, but Sasha is waiting for us. She's a great gal and will do whatever she can to make this as easy as possible. This is the right action to take for Charlene's sake."

Reluctantly, they finished their break at the cafe and drove to the police station. As soon as they entered the station the officer on duty said, "You must be here to see Detective Voss. Go right down the hall and open the second door on your left. She's expecting you."

They looked like a parade of mourners with their heads down and feet dragging as they slowly followed the directions given by the officer.

"Come in," greeted Sasha. "Good to see you, Tex and Willy." Houston introduced Chance and Lynn and they shook hands all around. Tears slipped from Lynn's tear ducts and she clumsily tried to wipe them away, but they were simply falling too fast to keep up with. She quit trying to stop herself from crying. She covered her face with her hands and sobbed quietly. No one said a word. They all waited for her to get herself under control. Chance was swallowing repeatedly and Wilamina blew her nose into the tissue that Sasha handed to her.

"I'm so embarrassed," said Lynn with a flushed face. "We don't even know if Charlene is in any trouble or not. Sorry. I'm okay now, for a while."

Chance patted Lynn on the back to comfort her while he did his utmost to keep himself under control.

Sasha opened a notebook and grabbed her pen. She asked Chance to tell her about his friend, Charlene Kellog. "When did you last see her?"

Chance spoke in a rapid fire manner and told her all about his relationship, marriage, son and so forth. It was like a flood gate had opened up.

Sasha could barely write fast enough even though she was using her own type of shorthand to keep up with him. When he finally took a breath, she asked a few direct questions and then asked Lynn similar ones.

Houston and Wilamina filled in with what they had learned from Mr. Woods as well as their attempt to reach Dr. Clarkson.

Chance then asked, "Will my wife have to know about this? If she hears about Charlene, she going to take out her anger and bitterness on my son. How can I protect him from her venomous tongue. She usually doesn't leave marks on his body, but she can wound him emotionally. She's mean, vindictive and secretive. People who don't do her bidding get punished in sneaky ways. She's caused lots of hurt for many folks."

Just then, there was a knock on the door. A tall, dark haired, olive skin man walked in. His very presence grabbed everyone's attention.

Sasha stood up and introduced Detective Lorenzo to everyone in the room. He shook hands all around and sat down in the chair next to Sasha.

"Sorry I'm late. Detective Voss and I are partners and we both like to hear all the details personally, if at all possible." Glancing at his partner he asked her, "Maybe you could summarize what's been said so far, 'cause I can see you've already written down a great deal."

Before Sasha could answer, Houston said, "Maybe I could sum up the reason we are all here. Would that be okay with you, Sasha and Chance?"

Both nodded and Houston proceeded to give a summary of the events so far. After she finished she added, "Wilamina and I are just beginning our private investigative business and we felt the police needed to be notified of Charlene's disappearance. We are doing our best to learn the 'ground rules' of when to bring in the police and when not to. Mr. Young came to our office and asked if we looked for missing people. That was the beginning of our getting involved. Mr. Young and Lynn convinced us that Charlene would not take off without letting at least one of them know where she was going. Willy and I became concerned about their friend and with Lynn's help convinced Chance to come to the police.

"Chance is married and has a ten year old son, Richard. He told us his wife, Melody constantly belittles and criticizes both of them. This has apparently been her habit or strategy for many years. He is afraid to divorce her because she will probably get custody of their son. Chance believes she doesn't want or love their son, but would keep him away just to punish him. He and

Charlene have been having an affair for about two years. He said he doesn't believe his wife knows anything about it. He has finally made up his mind to take steps to end the marriage and get a lawyer to help him gain custody of his son.

"He moved out of their home for a short period, but his son was so upset by his father's absence that he moved back in with Melody a few days ago. He is afraid something bad has happened to Charlene. He came to us because he didn't want the police involved. Melody would find out about his affair if the police were called. He is terrified she will be even nastier and uglier to Richard. He said she is a bully and enjoys intimidating others. Now you know what we know."

Detective Lorenzo focused his attention on Houston and with a twinkle in his eyes said, "Thank you for your detailed summary. I must say your sweatshirts are definitely an original way to advertise. I'm going to take a wild guess, you must be Salt?"

"Yep, and I'm Pepper," affirmed Wilamina enthusiastically. "My friends call me Willy."

A flush crept across Houston's cheeks. She stated, "Mr. Spade, a private investigator out of Seattle made them for us. It was his way of thanking us for helping him solve one of his cases. Do you know Mr. Jason Spade?"

"Yes, I've heard some good reports about his work. I also know two P.I.s out of Seattle. I have great respect for the Rickels. They are both efficient, clever and often think way outside of the box. They have a fine reputation, as does Mr. Spade. If anyone of them is mentoring the two of you, you're lucky. They all have assisted with our department before."

"What is mentoring?" asked Wilamina.

Sasha answered her, "They're all like Sharon, great teachers."

"Oh yeah, they mentor good. Sharon was the best teacher," responded Wilamina.

After several forms were completed and signed by Mr. Young and Miss Reynolds, the two detectives and both investigators mapped out a plan of action. Houston and Wilamina were to follow up with calls and a visit to Dr. Clarkson.

Chance handed over the note that had been discovered in Charlene's apartment to the detectives. Houston asked if it would be okay for her and Willy, Chance and Lynn to follow the directions given on the note and have a look around. "Chance knows exactly where the directions lead to since that was one of his out-of-the-way places he often met with Charlene."

Detective Lorenzo thought it was a good idea, "Let us know if you find anything meaningful or even questionable."

Houston looked mostly at Sasha. She seemed to be avoiding eye contact with the other detective. On the other hand, he had no trouble glancing frequently in her direction. This seemed to make Houston most uncomfortable. She repeatedly crossed and uncrossed her long, shapely legs.

Chance cleared his throat numerous times and muffled sobs were beginning to be heard in the room. He managed to say, "I'd appreciate any help you can give me. Charlene is the most wonderful person ever and she would never let me or Lynn worry like this. Please help us find her."

His shoulders moved up and down. He placed his hands over his face and soon his shoulders shook more noticeably.

"Sasha and Detective Lorenzo, thanks for your kindness and help," said Wilamina.

As soon as Chance and Lynn walked out of the door with Houston and Wilamina walking behind them, Detective Lorenzo asked the two investigators to remain behind for a few more minutes. He told Chance and Lynn, "Go on out into the front lobby. Your friends will be out shortly. I just need a few minutes with them."

Houston thought to herself, *Oh boy, here it comes. We've gone past some invisible police lines and now he's gonna to read us the riot act.*

"Please sit back down ladies. I've been clued in by Detective Voss about your prior relationship at Lancer's. Sasha seems to have a great deal of respect for the both of you. Sasha and I are both homicide detectives and we don't usually become involved with missing people, but since Sasha is asking..... well it's hard to say no to her. She's been my partner for less than a year, and she's already proven herself to be a great detective. My point is that we are making an exception for you. Please don't take advantage of your friendship with her."

"No sir. We'd never do that. We are really grateful for your help. Sasha's the best and we don't ever want to cause her any trouble." Wilamina looked toward her one time prison mate, "We sure don't want to make anything bad for you Sasha."

"I know, Willy. I'm okay and we're going to do what we can to find your client's friend."

Wilamina continued, "Detective Lorenzo, do you know that, Sasha was the most believable "H" in all of the prison. She could be a movie star."

The detective responded, " Yes. Willy, by the way is it okay if I call you by your nickname?"

"Sure, makes me feel like we're friends," answered Wilamina.

"Sasha has shared some of her prison days with me, but I'd like to hear more from the ones who saw her in action."

In her newly found business voice, Houston asked, "How do you plan to help us find Charlene? Also do we have to get your permission to check out our leads or what? We are working with Mr. Spade and he knows the ropes and will help us to not step on anyone's toes or get out of line. The same goes for the Rickels." She looked directly at Detective Lorenzo. He didn't look away and met her gaze with his piercing eyes. Neither seemed to want to look away from each other. Her look was challenging and he met the challenge with a playful smile.

Detective Lorenzo answered, "Go ahead with your plans to interview Dr. Clarkson and others that might shed some light on Miss Kellog's whereabouts. Just keep us in the loop. Try to stay out of harm's way. I will give you this piece of advice. You will be most successful if you stick to getting information, not giving out information. The less you say the more you can learn."

Houston added, "So does that work for you as well? Willy and I remain silent and you do all the talking?"

This time Detective Lorenzo showed off a full face smile and the laugh wrinkles around his eyes appeared. "Ms. Hayfield, we are on the same side here. So I think it would be prudent if we work in an 50-50 fashion. I listen and share and you listen and share. Everyone benefits and cases get solved."

Sasha spoke up, "So now we are working together, Tex. Please keep us up to date. You, Willy plus Chance and Lynn are going to follow up and look at the location Ms. Kellog had written down. Call us when you get back to your office and let one of us know what you found out, if anything.

The three women hugged and Wilamina and Houston shook hands with Lorenzo.

"When Lorenzo shook Houston's hands he asked her, "Do I call you Ms. Hayfied or Houston or Tex?"

In a voice cold enough to freeze the words instantly, she said, "I may not have your jail-free background or your education and title, but I doubt you have my hard-earned gut instincts. Call me what you will, Detective Lorenzo."

"Fair enough, Ms. Private Investigator Hayfield," he said as he thought to himself......*She's drawn a line in the sand. We'll see who crosses it first.*

CHAPTER EIGHTEEN

After leaving the police station, the four of them climbed into Chance's roomy Suburban and took off to the address that Charlene had written down.

Houston used the time traveling to ask questions of Chance and Lynn.

"Chance, tell me more about your wife and what's going on right now with the two of you."

"I moved back into our house after only a few days, for Richard's sake. Even though I was gone such a short time, he's been so upset that I left. He was breaking my heart. I could protect his feelings a little when I was there, even though she would say hurtful things to him when I was present. At least I could tell him I loved him and make up some excuse for her mean words.

"The odd thing is that Melody has been acting very differently the last few weeks. To tell the truth, she scares me more now. I don't know why is she behaving so strangely now, like nice? She's like a Jekyll and Hyde. She's mostly nice to everyone else if she wants something from them. But if they cross her, she can fire off nasty, cruel words faster than an assault weapon. She can hold a grudge forever."

"What exactly is she doing that is so different now?" asked Houston and Wilamina, almost in unison.

"She has a fairly decent dinner ready when I get home. Not like her usual thrown together mess. She usually would practically throw the food on the table and say 'EAT' and no complaining.' She hasn't screamed at Richard lately, at least not when I'm there. She talks decently to me and asked how my day went. She has been doing our laundry and not saying to either of us, 'You dirtied it, you clean it.' She fixes her hair in the morning. She hasn't done that for years.

"Richard and I are both waiting to hear the barrage of accusations and mean spirited words just before the rattlesnake bite. She's been spitting out poisonous crap for at least the last seven to eight years and some even before that. Thinking back, she changed about a year after Richard was born and every year since and she's gotten worse."

Wilamina asked, "When exactly did she become this nice Melody?"

"Can't say exactly. Maybe for the past few weeks. I've been so worried and torn up about Charlene I really wasn't paying close attention to Melody. I thought she started changing 'cause I shocked her by briefly moving into a hotel. I really don't have any idea why she is acting this way now."

"Chance, if she has been such a controlling person why do you believe she never knew anything about you and Charlene?" inquired Houston.

"We were very careful. We never met in public places. I could call her at her office and she would call me at mine, using only our cell phones. We never said anything incriminating on the phone. We didn't become....." a long pause and he cleared his throat. ".....become romantically involved for the first year. And we've spent much of the last year trying to figure out how I could divorce Melody and still be a big part of Richard's life. Charlene is as worried about Richard as I am.

"Lynn was the only one who knew about our situation. I never told my folks or even any of my friends. The same for Charlene. She only confided in Lynn. Charlene's folks are both deceased and she has no siblings. She never would talk much about her past. I felt she must have had a tough childhood. She did tell me she lived with an older aunt for a few years after her parents died. I didn't want to make her uncomfortable so I never pressed her for more history. I figured in time she'd share more with me. I believed it was important for her to confide in me on her terms and her timeline.

"Going back to your question why has my wife changed her behavior recently, I repeat I don't believe Melody ever once thought I would dare to leave her because of my love for Richard. She probably figured I'd stay until Richard was old enough to leave home. Then she'd think of some other way to make my life miserable. How in the hell did I ever find her attractive and sleep with her? I'll never forgive myself for that mistake."

Lynn patted Chance on the back and said, "You were young, stupid and led by male hormones."

Chance continued, "She told me she was on birth control pills and I was stupid, like you said, Lynn. When she told me she was pregnant, she became hysterical and threatened to kill herself. She said her parents were horrible people and would never help her, except to pack her one bag and throw her out of the house. She claimed she had no friends and I can believe that. I was raised to take responsibility for whatever I got myself into so I had no choice but to get married. She refused to get an abortion. No sense looking back. I'm going to make it right somehow for Richard and for Charlene. Not sure how, but I'm going to whatever I have to.

"We're almost to the turn off where Charlene and I come to picnic and be alone."

He parked the car and told them they would have to walk some distance to the lake. For the next ten minutes they walked on an seldom used dirt trail, strewn with light undergrowth. The lake was coming into view when Chance stopped abruptly and grabbed something off the trail.

Houston screamed out, "Stop." Don't touch anything. We don't want to mess us any evidence."

Too late, Chance was already holding something up in the air. He began hyperventilating and yelling out, "This is her bracelet. My God this is hers." He frantically raced ahead, calling her name and looking in every direction and behind every bush or tree. The others followed his lead.

Lynn was next to yell out, "Look over there under that tree. Oh no!" She didn't finish whatever she was going to say before she began to sob hysterically.

Chance raced over to see where Lynn was pointing to. He fell to his knees and grabbed for something, but Houston got to him in time to stop him from picking the article up.

Lynn could barely catch her breath. She was looking at a pair of pants that Chance had come upon. "I know those. She wears them a lot. This can't be happening."

"Willy, call Sasha or the other detective and tell them where we are and what we have found so far," ordered Houston in a shrill voice.

Wilamina took off like a track runner for the car to get her cell phone. Lynn yelled after her, "I've got my phone right here." She was already dialing 911 and told the operator to pass on the location and our names to the two homicide detectives, Voss and Lorenzo.

In the meantime Chance was racing around rapidly from one tree to another calling out loudly for Charlene. He had a harried, wild appearance and his vision was focused on the torn article at the same time. He was running blindly into bushes and trees.

"Lynn would you please help Chance go back to the car and wait for the police? Willy and I will continue to look around." Houston used the prison correction officer's tone to get the two to do her bidding. Much to her surprise and gratefulness they both started back down the path in robot style. Lynn was holding one of Chance's hands and leading him back down the path.

"Willy, let's continue down the path to the lake. You take the left side and I'll take the right side. They hadn't gone very far when Houston spotted a baseball size rock that had some kind of stain on it. She took off her cap and placed it next to the stone. "This will make it easy for the police to see it." They continued slowly searching and finally heard a siren.

Detective Lorenzo, Sasha and two other officers came into view.

Sasha addressed the women, "We left Chance and Lynn with an officer. Chance reluctantly handed us a bracelet and quickly broke down. He appeared to be in a trance-like state. He was shivering and pale as a ghost. Officer Moore is one of the finest policewomen when it comes to handling individuals in a state of shock."

Houston showed them the pants they just found exactly where they laid and the stained rock. Sasha placed both objects in evidence bags.

The six walked slowly toward the lake zigzagging through the brush and undergrowth following close to the path right up to the edge of the lake.

Detective Lorenzo stated, "Looks like we're going to need a bigger search team and the use of the dogs." He instructed Sasha to make the call and added they would stay until the search team arrived. The two officers with them were told to separate and walk in opposite directions along the edge of the lake.

Houston asked, "What do you want us to do?"

"We can use all available eyes so let's each walk off the path, spread ten feet apart and walk into the woods approximately fifty feet and turn back around. We walk the grid until the search team gets here. They should be here within the hour, or if we're lucky, in less time," answered Detective Lorenzo.

One of the officers near Detective Lorenzo leaned in toward him and said, "There is a place nearby considered by the young folks a good place to park away from prying eyes. There also a cliff area over-looking the lake. It's call Lover's Leap. You want me to go and check it out, Lorenzo?"

"Good idea. Take your partner and call back with whatever you find or don't find. We'll keep looking here until we get replaced by the team."

Houston asked Sasha, as they started to separate and walk into the woods, "This doesn't look so good for Charlene, does it?"

Sasha responded, "No, it's not looking great, but I've learned to never try to second guess evidence. The stain on the rock will be examined and if it is human blood then they will try to match it to Charlene's."

They walked about the fifty feet into the woods and were about to turn around when Sasha said, "Over here. This area looks like it's been disturbed." She'd been joined by the other three. Lorenzo said, "Let's mark this spot off with your tape, Sasha. We can block off this circle." Just then his cell rang.

"Go ahead. Officer Ronson." The detective listened for a minute, his expression never changed. Then he said to his partner and the two investigators, "We are going back to the car and go to another spot. You two officers please continue looking and when the other team arrives you can return to your other duties."

While the four were on their way to the other place down the road, Detective Lorenzo informed the others a car was spotted partially submerged in the lake.

Wilamina was teary eyed instantly and Houston asked, "Does the car fit the description of Charlene's car?"

"Apparently it is her car. The same make and color plus the license plate matches what Chance had given you."

Once they arrived at the scene and looked over the high ground and down at the lake they could see the rear of the car was just barely out of the water and the license plate could easily be seen. Officer Ronson and his partner had found the path leading down the hill. One of the officers had waded into the water and was looking inside the submerged car. He yelled up to his partner, "Can't see anyone inside. We will need the dive team here."

CHAPTER NINETEEN

Dive team arrived.........

The team was met by Detective Lorenzo and Detective Voss. The others were told to stay back and in their cars. Houston and Wilamina sat with Chance and Lynn in one of the police cars. The silence was deafening. Chance's features were distorted by his anxiety and anticipatory grief. Lynn wasn't in much better shape. Wilamina was praying with her lips moving soundlessly. Houston stared straight ahead not looking at anything in particular. Time stood still.

Houston finally broke the silence and asked Chance and Lynn, "Can you think of anyone, anyone at all, who might want to hurt Charlene? Maybe someone said something in passing to you, about her? And at the time you didn't think anything of it, but later you thought, that was strange. Can you remember any kind of odd remarks?"

Lynn wiped her eyes and answered, "No one comes to mind. Guys would notice Charlene all the time. She is really beautiful inside and out. Most of them were simply flirting and whistling."

Chance looked at Lynn and said, "She is truly beautiful and her soul is perfect. Lynn told you that Dr. Carlson seemed to confuse her. She thought that sometimes he said things that were inappropriate. I wasn't aware of this. She never mentioned ever being uncomfortable around him to me."

Houston continued her questions, "Did your wife ever threaten you with harm if you were to divorce her?"

"I never threatened her with divorce. I did tell her many times that I couldn't keep on living with someone filled with so much hate and begged her to go to counseling. I offered to go with her to no avail. Sometime ago, while I was at my wits end with her bullying Richard and demeaning me, I lost my temper and yelled at her that I wished she would simply disappear or suffer a sudden death. The next day she told me she was going to see someone about our problems. I don't know if she really did and if she did I don't know who she saw. Her behavior was slightly improved for maybe a month and then WHAMO, back to 'bitchville'. Melody did tell me that if I tried to divorce her she would make me sorry."

"Did she ever tell you what she would do to make you sorry?"

"No she didn't, Miss Willy. I know she had it real tough as a kid. Both parents were mean drunks. She's told me some horror stories about things they said or did to her, such as leave her alone for hours and sometimes even days when she was around age six or seven. The problem was that she would tell me these stories of abuse over and over. She was like a broken record, never getting past all the pain and hurts. She's a miserable and damaged person who seems to need to hurt others, including her own son and me. Sort of like payback for all the cruelties she experienced in childhood. It's like we were being punished for what her folks did to her. She is so filled up with rage and bitterness.

"Sometimes I felt such pity and sadness for her. She couldn't let herself enjoy anything. Payback is what she lives for. Makes no sense to me and never will.

"I'm going to save Richard and me somehow. I'll find a lawyer who can help us. I'll do whatever I have to stop us from living Melody's hell. Charlene will help Richard heal from Melody's cruelty. I can't help my wife, guess I never could."

Sasha returned and leaned into their car. "Chance we have not found Charlene, but we have found her car."

Chance turned even paler than before and said, "Where is it. I've got to see it. Take me there now." He yelled while struggling to open the car door.

"Okay Chance, but there is a problem, the car is mostly submerged in the lake. We have a dive team coming, should be here within the hour."

Chance scrambled frantically out of the car and started running in circles.

"All of you come with me. The car is a short walk around that hill and to the lake," said Sasha.

They all headed to the hill trying to keep up with Chance. He was almost race walking with Lynn close behind him.

Houston said to Wilamina and Sasha, "This doesn't feel too hopeful."

When Chance arrived at the spot. He could see the lake and the trunk of Charlene's car. It was still visible and the license plate could be identified. He started running, dove into the water next to the partially submerged car.

Detective Lorenzo yelled out, "Damn it Chance, don't touch anything! Let the dive team do their job. Get the hell away from the car you idiot." The detective waded into the lake and with difficulty grabbed onto Chance's feet and dragged him back to shore.

"Listen to me. You could be screwing up evidence if there has actually been a crime. I know you're upset, man, but get a hold of yourself. Here comes the divers now. Let them do their work. Sit here, don't move and you can see what's going on from here. If you don't, I'll have you placed in a squad car. Comprende?"

"Yes," said Chance, shivering and sobbing. Sasha handed a blanket she had in her squad car to Lynn who sat down next to

Chance and covered him ever so gently with it. He put his head down in her lap and covered his head with his hands, moaning quietly and shivering.

The divers were quickly suited up and into the water. They found no one in the trunk or within the car. Two divers started diving deeper in the area. The search lasted several hours and eventually reported that no body or any personal effects were found.

Houston commented, "This waiting is God awful. Now what comes next?" she asked Sasha who had just returned from combing the area with other officers. "The team will continue searching the woods until something is found. None of you can do anything right now. Would be best if you went on back home. You and Willy can follow up with Dr. Clarkson.

"Chance, you and Lynn can stay and help with the search or go back and help Houston and Wilamina with other ideas you might have. You need to get into some dry clothes. Maybe call your boss and let him know you need some time off. Lynn, what do you need to do about your job?"

"I can ask for a few days off because of a family emergency. Chance you might want to do the same thing. Richard must be terribly worried he hasn't seen you today."

"You're right. I've got myself under control now. Sorry about jumping into the lake. I'll take it as a good sign that no body was found. Charlene may still be okay. She's got to be okay. I'll go back and change clothes, call my boss and reassure Richard that everything is okay."

The four climbed back into Chance's car and took off for Whitefall. Once on the way Wilamina asked, "Won't your wife wonder what's going on?"

"I'm going to tell her a friend of mine has gone missing and I'm volunteering to look for her. I can add the police are asking for volunteers to be in the search. I've made up my mind to see a lawyer quickly as I can and find out about my options. I won't live in such a toxic house and there's got to be a way to get Richard away from her.

"Lynn, you must know some people to whom Melody has been ugly. She has been a patient in the hospital and you were one of her nurses. Do you have any ideas?"

"As a matter of fact, I do know someone who might be happy to describe Melody's behavior in the hospital." She addressed Chance, "Also Charlene told me that you were the one who had to attend teacher's conferences because the principal asked you to?"

"Yes, that's right," responded Chance. "I've been the one who usually attended the conferences, but one time I was sick and Melody had to go. She practically had one teacher in tears and was in a shouting match with Mr. Rosen, the principal. He called me and asked that in the future would I please attend the teacher conference alone or accompany my wife.

"The pharmacist that has dealt with Melody knows firsthand what a world class bitch she can be. Maybe he would be a character witness for me also."

Wilamina joined in, "Sounds like you will have quite a number of witnesses showing what kind of person your wife is. Too bad I don't meet up with her in some public place. I could piss her off and let her nasty nature come out. Of course, my partner would have the video running. What'a you think of my idea, Tex? I can be mighty irritating when I set my mind to it."

"Yes Willy you can be quite an irritant at times, but a lovable one. Not a bad idea though," responded Houston with an ear to ear grin.

Wilamina continued on with her fantasy getting more into it with each word. "Maybe I could accidentally bump into her, knock her down on her mean ass and offer my hand to her, but I trip and land my great ass on top of her. She'd be speechless and breathless and then Tex, you'd start recording whatever comes out of her mouth. Hell they might even have to throw her in jail for all her threats to me, an innocent, beautiful and dark skinned lady. Could maybe get my picture in the paper and our business would grow like crazy."

"Hold it down partner. You're definitely leaving Earth behind. Your imagination is going wild. Just to set the record straight, your ass ain't that great."

Chance spoke up, "You guys have begun to convince me that it's possible to get custody of Richard. I'm going back to the area where Charlene's car was found and help with the search. That's after I go home and check on Richard. I can't just sit around and do nothing."

Chance dropped Lynn off at her apartment and then continued on driving the semi-novice investigators to their office/apartment.

"Let's keep each other informed of anything that turns up. We'll try to hook up with Dr. Carlson and make a few other calls. Will you have your cell phone on?" asked Houston.

"Yeah. I'll call if there is any news. Thanks for helping me to keep it together. I can't let myself think that something bad has happened to Charlene."

Wilamina added, "Good luck, Chance. I'll be praying for you and Charlene."

"Thanks Willy."

CHAPTER TWENTY

Houston dialed Dr. Carlson's office. The secretary answered and asked the caller's name then connected Houston to the doctor. "What can I do for you Ms. Hayfied?" asked Dr. Carlson.

She told him she was working with the Whitefall Police Department to try to locate Charlene Kellog. "It seems Miss Kellog has been missing for two weeks and I'm asking if you have any knowledge of her whereabouts?"

"I've been wondering the same thing. What the dickens is going on with her? She hasn't shown up at the office for the past two weeks. We do groups together. She's never missed one group or even been late before. I've called her apartment several times, left messages and spoke with her landlord on two occasions. I thought maybe she had become ill or perhaps a family member had an emergency and she simply left to help out. Actually I don't know if she has any family in the area. She never spoke of a family. She is a very private sort of person. Her office phone has been very busy. I don't answer it so there will probably be quite a number of messages on it. A few of her clients showed up here confused and upset by her not being available. One man got pretty angry she hadn't called and cancelled his appointment. I have his name and number if you or the police want it."

Houston responded, "I think the police would be interested in that information. Someone from the department will give you a call. They may have some other questions for you."

"What sort of questions are you speaking of?"

"I'm not sure, Dr. Carlson. A Detective Voss or Detective Lorenzo may get in touch with you today or tomorrow. Are you going to be available at your office or at your home? Before we hang up I would like to ask you a question. How long have you known Charlene Kellog and when was the last time you saw her?"

"Let's see. We've shared this waiting room for more than one year. I met her earlier because she had referred several clients to me and we both became interested in working some groups together. We quickly saw the advantage and success of joining groups. All together I'd say I've know her a little longer than one year. I last saw her during one of our combined support groups. That was on a Wednesday or Friday, two weeks ago. I'm not sure which day, I can look it up if needed. It certainly wasn't like her to not show up. She never missed a group since we combined our clients. I'd hate to think anything terrible has happened to her. Such a lovely person. Tell the detectives they can call me anytime today or tomorrow."

"Thank you Dr. Carlson, I will pass that information on. Good-bye for now."

As soon as Houston ended her call to Dr. Carlson, she dialed the detectives number. The officer on desk duty put the call through to the Homicide Division.

"Hello Ms. Hayfield, Detective Lorenzo here. Detective Voss is out of the office at the moment. Can I be of assistance?"

"I just now hung up the phone after talking with Dr. Carlson. He said he doesn't have any idea where Miss Kellog is. He added the last time he saw her was two weeks ago and he's been worried. He said she has never missed a group with him since they started working together. He did mention she has received many calls which have gone to her answering machine and one of her male clients was quite upset she hadn't gotten in touch with him.

"I told him that either you or Detective Voss will get in touch with him today or tomorrow. He said he would be available any time." She gave him the Dr.'s number and proceeded to ask if there was any news about Miss Kellog.

"No news yet. The Search and Rescue team is working on the site and Mr. Young is searching the woods with one of my men. I have a personal question for you, do you have any gut feelings about Chance Young?"

"Yes I do. You're not one of those, those men who make fun of women's intuition, are you?"

"Absolutely not Ms. Hayfield. In fact, I'm a believer in the gut feelings of women and take their instincts seriously."

"Okay then, I think Chance is innocent of harming Charlene. He seems to be completely torn up about the possibility she may be in danger or worse. You sure you're not asking me 'cause of my jailbird time?"

"I'm so sure that I'd like to ask you and your partner to have lunch with me, so that I can get your ideas and suggestions about Charlene."

"You don't have to take us to lunch to find out what we're thinking. We both have big mouths and have no trouble telling anyone what our opinions are on most anything."

"I'd still like to take you both to lunch, say on this coming Sunday?"

"I'll check with Willy. She goes to church on Sunday and isn't free until after 1 p.m."

"Please check with her and let me know. If that time doesn't work maybe you could suggest another time, okay? Thanks for the information concerning Dr. Clarkson, and Sasha or myself will follow up today or tomorrow."

They said their good-byes; Houston told him she'd get back to him about lunch in the next day or so. As soon as she put the phone down, she wiped her forehead and noticed her hand was shaking. *What the hell's the matter with me. He asking us because he knows the value of greasing all the wheels not just a few. He's no more interested in me than I am in him. He's too important in his own eyes, too arrogant, too good-looking for his own good. Enough you idiot, it's only a business lunch.*

Wilamina had been watching her partner squirm around in her seat while she was talking on the phone. "That call sure made you antsy, Tex. Who were you talking to?"

"What'a you mean antsy, I was just trying to get comfortable in this damn chair. Gonna find me a pillow for my skinny behind, unlike your well-endowed one. I called the precinct to tell someone about Dr. Carlson and Detective Lorenzo picked up the call. He invited you and me to lunch this coming Sunday at 1 p.m. Said he wanted to get to know more about us and our gut instincts. He wanted to know if I thought Chance was guilty or innocent, and wanted to hear from you as well. No big deal. Do you want to go Sunday with him? Are you finished at church by that time, If not, he said we could pick another day or time."

"Sunday is fine if you could make it for 1:30 that would be better for me."

"I'll call him back tomorrow with that time. Don't be rolling your eyes at me. He's just another guy with all the baggage. Don't be fixing me up with him, in your half-black evil mind."

"Now Tex, don't go and get yourself all worked up over nothin'. We've both been locked up a long time and only natural we be thinking about you know what. I miss the lovin' and I'd bet you do too. So don't go and get too huffy with me. We is, no we are two healthy, young, good-looking, hot-blooded women and we weren't raised to be nuns.

"Am I starting to sound more book learned. I'm really trying to use the right words and not sound so ignorant."

"Willy, you sound just fine, as always. You are a smart and very wise person. You're the one doing the books and most of the computer stuff around here. There's nothing wrong with how you talk."

CHAPTER TWENTY-ONE

Wilamina was up early and getting herself ready to go downstairs to their office. She yelled at Houston, who was still in bed and told her to get her pale, skinny ass up. "I'm gonna go down now 'cause I have a lot of catching up to do. We've been running around a lot these last days. I'll make us something good to eat later."

As soon as she sat down at her desk she listened to the phone messages. Wasn't long after when a sleepy eyed roommate ambled in and sat down at her desk.

"Hey Tex, we got a message form Hunt Rickle's wife, Jessie. She asked if we three could get together for lunch one day soon. Said she'd be glad to meet us in Whitefall. She has several friends who live in the area who she'd like to visit. Wants to meet on Saturday in two weeks. What'a you think?

"Sounds like a plan, Willy. Hunt said his wife was a sharp cookie and could be a big help to us. Call her back at make the date. We can use all the help we can get."

Wilamina did just that and reported that Jessie sounded like a great gal. "Tex, I'm really gettin' a bad feeling about Charlene. I'm feeling bad for Chance and Richard if somethin' terrible has happened. Do you think she could be alive?"

"Doesn't look too good with every passing day, roomie. Let's take a drive and bring along Charlene's picture. We can drive the route to the lake and stop at any businesses we pass on the way. I remember a mom and pop store, an antique store and one gas station with a tire shop connected. At least we'll be doing something."

"Yeah. Good idea. Lordy, Lordy I'm starting to get that bad ache in my bones, like something bad gonna happen or already has. Who would hurt such a sweet girl? What about that client who got mad at Charlene 'cause she hadn't called him and cancelled his appointment? Maybe he was setting up an alibi. Guess I've been reading too many detective stories."

"The detectives have his name and I think they'll talk with him. I get the feeling we're not supposed to try to interview suspects, only talk with possible witnesses, like gas station attendants and store clerks. At least that is the impression I've gotten from Sasha and Mr. Rickels." Houston continued, "I think it would be okay if we asked Charlene's landlord more questions. Maybe he's remembered something new."

Wilamina was staring into space, trance like, when suddenly she jumped up from her chair and exclaimed, "I have an idea and it's gonna sound goofy. We need a photo of Melody. Could we just ask Chance for one or follow her around in the grocery store and snap a picture with our cell?"

"Are you thinking she might've had somethin' to do with our missing girl? Remember Chance told us she doesn't know anything about his affair with Charlene?" reminded Houston.

"I know. I said it was a goofy idea," reiterated Wilamina.

"Willy, I don't think it's goofy at all. I've been thinking about her for some time now. She's a control freak, mean, bitter and probably filled to the brim with rage. Remember she tricked Chance into getting her pregnant. He told us she had horrible parents who abused her in every way. She treats Chance like shit, but won't give him a divorce. I can imagine how angry and vengeful she might get if she knew he was messing around and wanted to leave her for some pretty, sweet, young woman. What would that sort of damaged, crappy person do?"

"Mercy, Tex. I think she could easily get rid of Charlene or whoever threatened her or even pissed her off a little. There are lots of women who have killed their boyfriends, husbands or the other woman and Melody has sounded pretty crazy and spiteful.

"How about we call Chance at his job and see if he would give us a picture of Melody. What could we say if he asked why we wanted it?"

Houston threw her arms up into the air and said, "Let's just tell him we need to know what she looks like in case we run into her somewhere and observe her hostile behavior, making a scene and being ugly to others. We would catch it on our cell and that would help in court to show the judge what a terrible mother she was. Hell, I'll just call him up now while I've got myself all worked up."

Wilamina handed her office mate Chance's number. Houston dialed. "Could I speak with Chance Young, Houston Hayfield calling."

"Hello Tex, is there any news? Houston could hear the fear in his shrill voice.

"No, Chance. We haven't heard any kind of news, yet. I'm calling to ask you something that might sound weird, but do you have a photo of Melody with you?"

"Yes, I have an old one taken about two years ago. I have it in my desk in case she ever showed up at my job. Why, what do you want it for?"

"Wilamina and me just thought we should know what she looks like in case we run into her. Maybe we would catch her on camera being mean to someone. Seems that would be helpful for you in court. It would be one more witness against her keeping

Richard. It seems logical if there are many witnesses who will talk about your wife's outbursts, it would show the judge how unfit and unpredictable she is. I know it's a long shot, but can we come to your office in the next half an hour and pick up the photo?"

"Yeah, sure Tex. Whatever you need. See you soon."

"Okay Willy, we gotta get movin'. We can pick up the photo on our way to talk to some folks."

They quickly got themselves dressed, organized and out the door. They drove off with a list of names and addresses. First stop was at Chance's office. They picked up the photo and then they were on to the next place. They pulled into a mom and pop grocery store and spoke with the owners. They showed them the pictures with no recognition noted. Third stop in the next block was a small dress shop. Again no help. Next door was an antique shop called Abigail's Shop. They were cordially greeted by the owner, Miss Abigail herself. She was wearing a lovely old broach. Hanging underneath the broach was a tag printed with her name, Miss Abigail.

Houston introduced her partner and herself and asked if she could show her two pictures.

Miss Abigail stuttered, "Are you the police? You aren't wearing uniforms." She looked at the first picture and asked, "Is the lady in this photo in trouble?"

"No ma'am," said Wilamina in a reassuring voice. "We are private detectives and we are trying to locate Ms. Kellog. Have you seen her?"

Miss Abigail adjusted her glasses and looked long and hard at both pictures. No ma'am, I've not seen this young one, but I have seen this here older one. She was here a while back, say several months back. She was quite rude, oh sorry, hope she's not a relative or a friend."

"No problem Miss Abigail. We've never met the woman ourselves. What did she do?"

"Well......I don't like to speak poorly of anyone, but that woman was a person I won't forget. She saw a vase she was interested in. She looked at the seventy five dollar price I had put on the tag and she immediately began to raise her voice and called me a thief. She said my prices were outrageous and my inventory was mostly junk. Then would you believe that after calling me a thief and my merchandise junk, she said, I'll give you twenty five dollars and not a penny more.

"Much to my shame I told her I wouldn't sell the vase or anything else to her, ever. I am a lady, a spinster lady and pride myself always for being polite to all. I rudely showed her the door. As she walked by me, she had a devilish smirk on her most unattractive face."

Houston and Wilamina thanked the owner and left her a business card with instructions to call them if she remembered anything else about either of the women in the photographs.

Back in the car they talked about Melody and the nasty impression she left with that sweet Miss Abigail.

"Next stop is the gas station. There it is. It's almost next door to Miss Abigail's place. Let's hope we get some worthwhile info. Let's fill up the tank while we're here," suggestion Wilamina.

Houston got out and picked up the gas nozzle and placed it into the car's receptacle. An older man appeared dressed in overalls with a logo of the gas station on his shirt. His name was Jose.

"Can I help you miss?" asked Jose showing a friendly smile.

"Yes you can. While my car is filling up could you look at these two pictures and tell me if you recognize either one?"

"Sure thing lady." He wiped his hands on his pants and took hold of the photos. "I believe I've seen this young woman before. She's come in several times in the last six months or so. Sure hope a pretty thing like this isn't in any kind of trouble. She was here about two or three weeks ago, My memory ain't so good no more so I can't say exactly when she was here."

"Do you keep receipts for a period of time?"

"Yes ma'am. Are you checking up on my record keeping? I'm a good tax paying citizen. Why are you asking? Who do you work for?" He was looking at the truck with Wilamina inside.

"Here is my card. My partner, Wilamina, in the truck, and me are both private detectives. We are the owners of Salt and Pepper Detective Agency in downtown Whitefall. Sorry, I should have introduced us earlier. We are trying to locate the young woman in this is photo. She disappeared two weeks ago. Her name is Charlene Kellog. She is a social worker and has an office also in Whitefall."

He studied the picture briefly and said, "Yes, she has come in several times. Like I said before, I seem to remember she was here just a few weeks ago. I think she said she was on her way to Lake Bountiful."

"Do you remember if she was with anyone or seemed upset or anything?" asked Houston.

"I don't remember anybody being in the car with her. Now that I think about it, she seemed to be in a hurry, but maybe not."

"Now please look at this photo and tell me if you recognize her."

It didn't take but a second for Jose to blurt out, "Oh, si. I recognize her. She was unfriendly, and very demanding. I was finishing up with another customer when she pulled in and honked her horn and yelled at me. She said that she was in a hurry. I saw her face good, 'cause I walked up to her window and told her I'd be with her soon as I could. She mumbled something under her breath and I swear I heard her say 'damn wetbacks'. I couldn't be sure so I kept my mouth shut, but I took my time getting back to her car. She paid by cash. I remember that because she almost threw the money at me through her window. I haven't seen her since and I better not see her again."

Jose paused a moment then added, "Now you got me thinking about it. She came in here same day that the nice lady was here. She came in before the nice one did."

Houston thanked Jose and handed him their business card with the same instructions she'd given to the others. She climbed into the truck and winked at Willy. "We got something from Jose my friend. He told me that Melody was in his station same morning, actually before Charlene showed up. I wanted to jump and shout out, gotcha bitch and kiss Jose, but being the reserved person that I am, I controlled myself. Unlike someone else I know."

Wilamina who was driving, pulled the truck over to the side of the road. "My Lord, Tex, do you really think we have some good evidence. Is it possible Melody did her in?"

Wilamina drove back onto the road and headed toward Whitefall. "Guess we might as well go back to the office. There aren't any more businesses between here and the turnoff for the lake. Plus I'm starving. Wanna stop at the Hot Tamale?"

"Sounds good, Willy." Houston called the police department and was told the detectives were out on a call. She left a message for one of them to call back as soon as they could. "We can stop at the Hot Tamale. They can reach us there as well as at the office. We have found two more character witnesses for Chance. Seems both Miss Abigail and Jose have no love for that woman, Melody. She reminds me of some of the nasty inmates at Lancers. Did you ever run into Birdy?"

"I don't want to ever think about that horrible woman, Tex. She was the devil's handiwork. I stayed as far away from her as I could. I'm ashamed to say, but I was glad when she got done in. I don't know if they ever found out who did it, but I would'a given that person a gold medal."

Houston continued, "Melody reminds me of Birdy and I've never even met her. Chance said she's been acting out of character. She's being nice to Richard and him ever since Charlene's gone missing. Why the hell would she change? Maybe she's known all along about Chance and his girlfriend. Now she knows some girl is missing and Chance is all upset and helping to look for the her. Maybe she did or didn't know who he was seeing, but now if she didn't know her identity she must suspect it's the missing girl, Charlene."

"We really don't know Melody, maybe we should meet up with her somehow?" Wilamina said thoughtfully. "I don't like judging others, especially if I don't even know them."

"I'm with you, Willy. I just can't figure how to do it without being too obvious. Let's ask Sasha about it. How about we stop at the police station after lunch and see if she has returned yet."

"Okay and then we can tell her about Jose and Miss Abigail."

CHAPTER TWENTY-TWO

Raul greeted the new investigators, "Glad to see the town's two most attractive private investigators again. Makes me feel safe to know you two are in the area," he playfully nudged Wilamina. He led them to a booth and asked for their drink order.

"Haven't seen you two for a few weeks. How's the detective work going? asked Raul.

"Praise the Lord," sang out Wilamina. "Our business is growing with each sunrise. We are learning more every week about what this investigating is all about."

Houston smiled at Raul and handed back the menus. "You feed us whatever you think is the best today. We love having you decide for us, Raul. It's great to try your new dishes and so far everyone has been a winner."

A cell phone rang and Houston rummaged through her large purse and finally found it and silenced it. In a whisper she answered, "Hi Sasha. Thanks for the call back. We have some news we think might be very interesting for the case. Willy and I just ordered lunch at Raul's Hot Tamale." There was a pause and Houston answered back, "Sure you can join us. Willy and I don't order. We let Raul feed us whatever the special of the day is. Okay, I'll tell Raul to add another plate. Oh, he's coming too? Okay that's gonna be four specials. See you soon."

A short time later, the homicide detectives arrived and sat down in the booth with the investigators. Raul quickly brought out four steaming plates of the day's special. In his enthusiasm, Raul announced, "You must let me know how much you like this dish. If you don't like it then lie. Only kidding, sort of. Hopefully you will find it delicious."

Their table remained quiet except for the sounds of chewing and satisfying moans. The plates were empty and the owner was praised for the fantastic meal. Houston began sharing what Jose had told her about Mrs. Young. "She had been at the gas station the same day as Charlene and she had been there about a half hour before Charlene. This was the last day Charlene had been seen by anyone. Jose has the receipts to show the date, the time and names. He did say Melody Young paid cash."

Detective Lorenzo offered a thumbs-up, "That sounds like very useful information. We also have something interesting to share. The stone that was found had blood stains on it. The stains have been definitely identified as belonging to Ms. Kellog. The real surprise is that there was a fingerprint, or more like a smudge, discovered on the same rock. So far we have no match. Because of your excellent detective work, we will have cause to bring Mrs. Young in for questioning and then we will obtain her prints. Her response to being questioned and the request to fingerprint her will be most interesting, I'm sure."

"Excuse me," offered Detective Lorenzo, "I have to take this call." He listened to the caller, as his face turned like stone, almost grim. "Voss and I have to leave." He laid out enough money for all four meals plus a generous tip, stood up and moved quickly to the door. He made eye contact with his partner. Sasha quickly moved in right behind him. Houston and Wilamina with their mouths hanging open, watched them as they sped off with the sirens blaring.

"They have a tough job. I hope it has nothing to do with Charlene." said Houston thoughtfully.

CHAPTER TWENTY-THREE

"Was the food so bad that they had to run out of here?" asked Raul with a toothy grin.

"Your food was delicious, the best ever. I'd like to take some cooking classes from you. They had a police call and had to go somewhere fast!" exclaimed Wilamina. "You think we should go back to the office, Tex?"

"Yes. If that call was about Charlene, they will let us know soon enough." Houston's cell sounded off. She listened for a moment and looked up at her partner and slowly shook her head, and answered, "We'll be right there." Looking at Wilamina she added, "Sasha said they've got a body. Asked if we wanted to come to the station. You heard my answer. Let's go Willy."

At the station..............

Detective Lorenzo came down the hall walking quickly, with Detective Voss practically running behind him trying to keep up. They both looked like they were responding to a fire drill.

Detective Voss grabbed hold of Houston's arm and announced. "Come with us. You can follow us or ride with us. A body of a female has been discovered in Lake Bountiful."

"Oh no!" exclaimed Wilamina. "This is gonna break Chance's heart, if it's her."

The four of them piled into the patrol car and off they drove with the sirens on.

"Who found the body?" asked Houston.

"It seemed a fisherman did," answered Detective Lorenzo. They rode the rest of the way in silence, each one lost in their own thoughts.

Didn't take very long to get there with the siren blaring. There were several other patrol cars plus the coroner's vehicle already at the site.

Houston and Wilamina nearly tumbled out of the car with a verbal warning from Detective Lorenzo to not touch anything and to stay behind him and Detective Voss.

The body was lying partly in the water and partly on the sand. A distraught appearing man was sitting a short distance away on a rock holding his head. There was a fishing pole and metal box next to him.

Officer Bennet informed the detectives, "That man over there is Mr. Ricon. He is the one who discovered the body. We've already taken his statement. He's waiting to see if you have any other questions."

"No, I'm sure you got all the information we needed. If we have more questions for him, then we'll get in touch. Thanks, Bennet."

Detective Lorenzo and his partner walked over to the body and uncovered the face, both nodded. Lorenzo looked up at Houston and nodded, "It's looks like her picture. Her driver's license was in her pocket, which seems odd. She is wearing the ring that was shown in one of her photographs. The Medical Examiner will match the dental records. Apparently she's been in the water for quite some time and water does disfiguring things to a person. She has a very small tattoo of a flower on her ankle."

The Medical Examiner spoke with the two detectives and told them that the wound on the back of the head was probably the cause of death, but he would have to do the autopsy before he could officially state the actual cause.

Wilamina was crying as softly as was possible for her, "Oh, Jesus, poor Chance. He loved her so and had fine plans for her and Richard. Why would somebody do this?"

Houston put an arm around her friend and wiped her eyes with the other hand. "Whoever did this better be caught soon a put away forever or put down, like a rabid dog."

Sasha walked over to where her friends were standing. "How would the two of you feel about going with me to inform Mr. Young about the death of his friend? You both apparently have a good relationship with him. It might be easier for him if you were both there."

Houston looked at her partner, Wilamina nodded. "Yes, we want to be with him when he gets this terrible news. Charlene's best girlfriend also needs to be told. If you want, we can tell her after we see Chance. She might be able to help Chance through this some way. I'm not very good with this kind of thing, but Willy here is a real understanding kind of person. We'll both stand by him as best we can." Her voice began to crack and she turned her face away, looked at the woods and said, "Shit happens to the wrong folks."

Detective Lorenzo thoughtfully said, "I'll drive us back to the police station; you can pick up your truck and follow Voss to Mr. Young's workplace. He's going to need some understanding friends around him."

They all drove in silence for most of the trip back to town. "By the way, how is the Salt and Pepper Agency doing? Have you been getting any new clients?" asked Detective Lorenzo.

Wilamina perked up and responded, "We've been doing just fine. Our business is really pickin' up, and our clients have sure been generous. Tex worries more than me." She climbed into the back seat of Lorenzo's car and added, "Is this your own car? I see there are cop lights on top."

"We are assigned cars that the department loans out to us to use for work related business."

After settling down Wilamina said, "Do you mind if I start singing? Singing gives me courage and calms me down. I feel so bad for Chance. Charlene's life was cut too short. Never gonna like it when a good one is taken too soon. I know she's okay now, but not so sure about Chance and his son." She started to hum quietly.

Houston related in a much subdued voice, "I need to tell you some things that Willy and me learned this morning, from the antique store owner and Jose, the gas station owner. Sasha, is there some way to check up on Chance's wife? Jose told us that for the past few weeks she has been a lot nicer then she's been for the past nine years. Why would she change from nasty to nice right around the time of Charlene's murder. Am I way out in left field? It seems suspicious, such a drastic change."

Detective Voss remarked, "Can't say much right now, but I can tell you we're checking several leads and Mrs. Young is on our list to interview. We've questioned one of Charlene's clients, the one who was apparently upset when Charlene hadn't informed him of the cancellation. When he was interviewed he was visibly upset to hear that Charlene was missing. It seemed he couldn't remember where he was Friday after his missed appointment and his weekend was a blur, according to him. He remains on our follow-up list.

"Today we have four or more coming in to be interviewed by Detective Lorenzo and myself. Oh, here we are. This is where

Mr. Young works." He pulled into a parking space turned off the engine and everyone sat motionless until Sasha whispered, "Time to do it, my friends." The three walked slowly towards the entrance, heads down, each with their own thoughts.

Detective Lorenzo remained in the driver's seat. "I'll wait here. I think the three of you will do a better job of giving Chance this life changing news."

The three identified themselves to the secretary and she walked briskly down the hall to fetch Chance.

Chance came out his office door like he'd been shot out of a cannon.

"You have news?" He yelled in a high pitched voice. He stopped suddenly staring at the three visitors, "My God, no. It can't be. She's too good of a person. This can't be happening. God couldn't let this be, not to Charlene."

He staggered toward them and Wilamina grabbed his arm and led him to the nearest chair. "Where is she? What happened to her and where did you find her? She can't be dead." Leaping out of the chair he started pacing, at the same time he was hugging himself. Wilamina kept pace with him as did the detective. Houston stood back and watched. Her eyes told a story that she was sharing in Chance's shock and pain.

"She's at the Medical Examiner's office, Chance," said Wilamina in her gentle, soft voice. She is dead. I'm so sorry." Her voice cracking.

"I have to see her. I have to see for myself. You may have the wrong person. That happens sometimes. I've read horror stories about a wrong person being identified. Please help me." His pleading eyes staring into Wilamina's tearful face.

Detective Voss responded, "We can take you there right now, if you want. I must tell you Charlene doesn't look much like herself. She has been under water for a long time. You sure you want to see her?"

He barely whispered, "I've got to be sure, this is so unreal. I feel like I'm going to explode. You could have made a mistake, that happens. Does Lynn know?"

"No." answered Houston. "Would you like me to call her now and have her meet us there, if she can get away from the hospital."

"No sense calling her until we know for sure if it's really Charlene."

Houston nodded, "A call to Lynn can wait." She said it more to herself than to the others.

Wilamina and Sasha walked on opposite sides of Chance to the car. After the five were settled and seat belts belted, Detective Lorenzo drove off. He remained silent and kept his eyes straight ahead. He thought to himself, *It's times like this I really think about checking out other careers.*

CHAPTER TWENTY-FOUR

They soon arrived at the coroner's building and the five seemed to move in slow motion as if they were in a funeral procession. Both detectives led Chance into the viewing area and stayed by his side. Wilamina and Houston were close behind them.

The attendant slowly removed the sheet covering Charlene's face and let Chance take a look. His legs gave way and he slipped to the floor, sobbing quietly. He was helped to a chair and every so often he would clear his throat and attempt to speak, but would start sobbing again.

"Does she have a small tattoo on her ankle?" asked Chance.

Detective Lorenzo asked the attendant to remove the sheet over the ankles. That was done and the detective said to Chance, "Yes, Chance, there is a tattoo of a small flower on her left ankle. I'm so sorry."

"Then she's really gone forever." Chance emitted a long, continuous animal sounding moan from deep within. Houston could no longer maintain control and also began to sob in earnest.

After some time passed, Chance asked, "How did she die? Who did this? Why would anyone want to hurt such a loving, kind person?"

Detective Voss responded, "The Medical Examiner said it looked like a blow to her head caused her death. It was probably instantaneous. A written report will be available in a few days."

Just then, Lynn, was escorted into the area. She was pale faced and red eyed. "Oh Chance, my heart is breaking for you and Richard. I'm so terribly sorry. It's unbelievable that anyone could harm such a beautiful person. She's the best friend I ever had."

Lynn knelt down in front of Chance and hugged his knees. They cried together a while longer. Chance agreed to let Lynn drive him home. Houston and Wilamina would retrieve his car from his work place and drive it to his home.

After some time passed and Chance seemed more able to talk he exclaimed, "It's time for me to level with Melody. Richard will still be in school so I can tell her everything. I'm going to tell her I'm getting a divorce and we are going to share custody of our son. If she argues with me, I'll threaten her with court and tell her I have many witnesses who will testify to her meanness and what a rotten mother and wife she's been."

Detective Voss was pacing up and down the hall and eventually she stated, "Chance, I want to suggest you hold off a day or two, maybe more, to give yourself a little time to get over the shock. I say this because we don't know who murdered your love, but we do have some suspects. I hate to spring this on you at this most terrible time for you, but I'm concerned about your wife's reaction to your plan. We haven't ruled out anyone yet and that includes your wife. My main concern is for your safety."

"Are you crazy? Mel doesn't even know about Charlene. What the hell are you talking about? She's mean and vindictive. She's not a killer. For God's sake, she knows nothing about my infidelity."

"Chance hold up a minute," advised Houston. "You believe she knew nothing for the past two years. You described your wife as controlling, vindictive, bitter and an abuser of you and your son. You told Willy and me that Melody had changed into a nicer person for the past several weeks. Think about it, she changed after Charlene disappeared.

"Willy and me we spoke to the owner of an antique store and to a gas station owner who both said the same thing. They said they don't ever want to do business with your wife again because of her nasty mouth and hostile attitude. Those two businesses are located on the way to Lake Bountiful.

"I'm not accusing your wife of anything, but maybe you and Richard could stay with Willy and me for a few days. Give yourself some time to think more clearly. We have plenty of room for the two of you."

"That sounds like a good idea to me," affirmed Wilamina. "Maybe you could tell her you are going to take Richard and go camping and fishing. Say you need time to get over your friend's murder. That will give the detectives time to start interviewing her."

Detective Voss jumped into the conversation, "You and Richard could be in danger. If your wife has behaved as badly as you've stated, she may actually need help, mental help. If you threaten divorce or sharing custody, and tell her about people who have witnessed her anger and meanness, you may send her over the edge. If she is the one who harmed Charlene, she could turn her rage and lack of control on you and her own child. Just a thought for you to consider."

"You know, as crazy as this is all sounding, I'm beginning to wonder myself why she has suddenly 'gone sweet' after the disappearance. She's been terrible for the past eight or nine years and why now would she start acting differently? I can't believe what I'm thinking. Is Mel actually capable of murder? I can't risk Richard's safety. My God, if she killed Charlene, she could do the same to me and then Richard would be alone with her. I can't take a chance.

"Houston and Wilamina, guess it would be the easiest thing to do if you guys take me home. Then when I tell Mel about me taking Richard fishing, she might not get too nasty in front of two investigators. I don't have to tell her that I was the one who hired you. I'm such a coward. Charlene might be alive if I hadn't been so cowardly. My God, I could've saved her. I'm never going to forgive myself. What have I done?"

Sasha got into Chance's face and grabbed his shoulders and said, "This is not the time for guilt or a pity party. You are not responsible for her death, but you are responsible for your son's safety as well as your own. Go home now with Tex and Willy and do what you need to do. I'll stop by tomorrow to see how you and Richard are getting along. Bye for now. I'm so very sorry for your loss."

CHAPTER TWENTY-FIVE

Melody and Chance's Home..........

"What are you doing home so early and who the hell are you dragging in?" Melody glared at the two visitors and they glared back at her. "You look terrible Chance, you're eyes are red and puffy. What's going on here?"

"This is Ms. Hayfield and Ms. Robinson. Maybe you remember I told you about my friend who has been missing for a few weeks. Well, she's been found dead. She was murdered." He choked up, took several deep breaths and continued. "She was found this morning by a lake. These ladies were hired to look for her. They've been kind enough to drive me home and will drive me back to my car later."

"Who hired these two? Don't tell me you paid to have them look for this woman who you say you barely knew?"

"No, Mrs. Young," spoke up Houston. "Someone hired us. We can't give you the name. Because of confidentiality issues. You understand of course. We simply crossed paths with your husband where he works when his office got the news of her death. He became very upset and the police woman in charge asked us to drive him home and give him time to compose himself. It's a known fact that people who are distraught are more apt to be in a car accident. We are glad to be of service."

"Mel, I'm going to need a few days off and seems like a good time to take Richard camping and fishing. I won't be much good at the office for awhile. Several others at the office are taking some time off for themselves as well, not just me. It'd be good for me and the boy, some bonding time."

"Bonding, you're bonded enough. I don't understand why this is becoming such a big deal for you. She was only a co-worker, not like a relative or close friend."

"You're right, but I've never known anyone before who was murdered and she was a very likeable sort. I'm going to pack and gather my fishing and camping gear and then let these kind ladies take me back to my car. It will soon be time for school to end and I can pick up Richard and we'll go for a short, fun trip. You won't have us to bother you. So you can have some free time."

Melody's mouth opened but nothing was coming out. She frowned and gave a slight head shake, like she was trying to clear her thoughts. She said, "This seems very strange. You suddenly going fishing. Maybe I should go with you."

"No no, Mel, this is a guy trip," stuttered Chance.

She challenged, "You've never taken a guy trip before, sure seems odd."

Chance felt himself starting to cave in. He looked over pleadingly at Wilamina and Houston, They both winked back at him. He looked back at Melody. With her mouth pinched up and mean eyes staring hard at him. He put his shoulders back and his chest out and said in a strong voice, "I should have been taking guy trips long before now, and I plan to do many more of them in the future. No women allowed." He turned and walked into Richard's bedroom. He stopped a moment, turned back to the living room and announced, "I'll be ready in less than fifteen minutes ladies. You three have a friendly chat while I pack."

Ear-splitting silence followed until Houston said, "This here vase looks like an antique. I love the old stuff, reminds me of my grandmother. Do you collect antiques, Mrs. Young? I've been looking for a good and inexpensive antique shop. Where do you go to shop for the older stuff?"

"That was my aunt's vase. She got it from an old relative of her husband. There's a store not too far away, but I wouldn't recommend it. The old biddy wants too much for her junk. The good stores are located in and around Seattle. Too far for me to travel just for an antique."

Soon Chance returned with gear and suitcases in hand.

"Sure looks like a lot'a stuff for just a few days," said Melody rolling her eyes at him.

"It does, doesn't it. Never know about the weather or other unforeseen events. I want to be prepared and not caught off-guard. Bye now, Mel."

Melody remained standing in the doorway watching them drive off. She clenched her jaw and ground her teeth. She crossed her arms tightly over her chest and muttered under her breath, "You'll never get away, not in my life time. I just need a plan. I can take care of this, just need a plan."

CHAPTER TWENTY-SIX

Chance and Richard were soon settled into the women's apartment, above their office. They were glad they had an extra bedroom and could offer a safe place for them. Wilalmina cooked up a feast for dinner with Richard's assistance. The young boy talked nonstop about everything he could think of. It was as if he finally had a female listening to him, not the other way around. He said to Wilamina, "This is the first time I've ever talked so much to a grown lady. My mom usually does all the taking, and I'm always afraid I'll say the wrong thing and she'll get mad. I like you Ms. Robinson."

"I like you too, Richard. I'd like it better if you would call me Willy. That is what my friends call me and I definitely want you to think of me as your friend."

"Okay, Willy. That's a funny name for a lady, but I like it."

After all four finished eating and shared in the clean up duties, Chance asked if he and Richard could be excused. "I have some things to talk over with my son and this is as good a time as any. This talk is long overdue."

Houston immediately spoke up, "You two stay right here at the table, Willy and I have work to do in the office downstairs. We have some serious catch up paper work. We should be busy for quite a while. Come on Willy, let's get hopping."

"Sure thing, partner," stuttered Wilamina rubbing the back of her neck. "Take your time Chance, we've got tons to do downstairs."

As soon as the women closed the door, Chance asked Richard to come and sit by him at the table. "I have some things I need to share with you. Things I should have talked about a long time ago."

Richard slowly sat down and began to cry softly, quickly wiping tears from his cheeks.

"Why are you crying, Richard?"

"Cause you're going to leave me. I won't be able to stand it." He began to sob in earnest and his dad grabbed him in his arms and cried with him. After some time, they both became calmer and the crying stopped. Chance began saying how much he loved his son and would never leave him. Then he proceeded to tell him most everything, age appropriate, from the time of Richard's birth to the death of Charlene. Time seemed to stand still while Chance talked. He became tearful every so often. He eventually got out most of the story. Richard had a few questions, which his dad answered honestly.

"For a time, Richard, you and I are going to live in an apartment. You will continue going to school and I will continue to go to my job. Your mother apparently has some serious mental problems and she is going to get some help. I don't know what the future holds for us, but I promise you it will be far better than the past has been. I'm so sorry I've let you down, but no more. I love you so much and I'm going to do what's right for both of us from now on."

Chance opened the apartment door and called down to the two who were waiting on pins and needles. He told them the talk was over and they could be back up to their own place anytime they were ready.

Houston and Wilamina had no clue what was said for the past few hours, but they were delighted to see Chance and Richard standing together hugging each other tightly. They were red-eyed and wet faced, but smiling.

"Praise the Lord," said Wilamina. "We can all sleep peacefully tonight."

Several days later..............

Detective Voss brought Houston and Wilamina up to date. "We have been busily interviewing all possible leads from many sources. Three possible suspects have been eliminated. They all had airtight alibis which checked out. Dr. Clarkson and Mrs. Chance Young continue under suspicion. Dr. Clarkson willingly took a lie detector test and gave a blood sample. Mrs. Young refused the lie detector test, stating she had heart problems. Her doctor did verify she does have an enlarged heart and high blood pressure. He stated the lie detector test would not, in itself, be dangerous for her health, but Mrs. Young's anxiety level could put her at risk. She was ordered to give a blood sample, which she did under duress. We're expecting the lab report at any time. We also obtained a search warrant and had her car gone over with a fine tooth comb. Should have the results back today or tomorrow."

Houston responded, "What a bunch of bunk. Young's wife has no heart. How could she possibly have problems with something she doesn't even have? I won't be surprised if her blood was found on Charlene's clothes, not after so many people have said how mean, hateful and unpredictable she can be."

Wilamina added, "She is a piece of work, a damaged piece. I was surprised how easily Chance had moved Richard and himself into our place. I bet he's somewhat relieved but still sleeps with one eye open. He's got Melody backed up against the wall. I know he is being as careful as possible, and watching his back. She doesn't know that he and Richard are staying at our place. Chance has found an apartment and plans to move into it in about a week. He talked with Richard's school principal and explained what's going on. He said he would be the only one to pick up his son. Richard knows not to go with his mother if she shows up at school. If she does, he is to go directly to the principal's office who will call the police."

"Hold on a minute you two, a report was just handed to me, " said Detective Voss. "Looks like we've got a match. I'll have to call you back later. Bye"

"Did you hear that, Tex. The blood work of Melody matched. What'a you think will happen next?"

"Don't know. We'll just have to wait till Sasha calls us back. Sure hope this is enough for the police to arrest her. Oh, I just had a sad thought about Richard. It's gotta be mighty rough to know your mother may be a murderer. Let's get busy doing something Willy. I need to get my mind on something else until we hear for sure she's been arrested for murder. Think how bad Chance is gonna feel knowing his wife was driven to murder. He could even feel guilty about getting the love of his life murdered. That's some heavy burden."

"I'm gonna double up on my prayers for him and his son," offered Wilamina, making the sign of the cross . "Some folks cause so much misery for others."

Melody is arrested..........

Detective Lorenzo and Detective Voss rode together to Melody Young's home. They were followed closely by two squad cars with four policeman.

Melody answered the door, "What the hell do you guys want now?" she belted out with her face all red and moist. "Chance has turned you all against me. He's always telling lies about me at work, even lies to Richard. What's that fornicator been saying to you?"

"You are under arrest for the murder of Charlene Kellog," announced Detective Lorenzo. He continued to read her the Miranda Rights. Detective Voss, with efficiency, placed the handcuffs on Melody's wrists.

Melody, with venom spewing from her eyes, spit at Detective Voss, whose lightening responses avoided the sputum. "If you try that again, you will be wearing a protective mask," barked Detective Lorenzo. He directed the two officers to take Mrs. Young into custody. "We'll meet you back at the precinct, officers. Thanks for your help." The two detectives could hear profanities and threats being screamed out at the arresting officers. "That little bitch had to die. She was destroying my home. She bewitched him. He was so weak. All you men are worse than worthless, you're evil. You destroy everything you touch. You're all rabid pigs, Satan's army," continued to screech Melody.

"Sounds like a confession to me. And in front of six officers of the law no less," remarked Detective Voss, smiling like a Cheshire cat.

"I have an idea Sasha, why don't you call your friends Houston and Wilamina and tell them about Mrs. Young's arrest? Ask them if they would like to join us for dinner tonight or tomorrow night, as a sort of celebration."

"I like that idea. The girls will be so thrilled for Chance Young and his son. The problem of Melody has hopefully been solved. Give me a minute and I'll try to get them on the phone right now." She dialed her ex-jail buddies and spoke with Houston. As soon as she finished talking with her friend she gave her partner the okay sign. "We're on for tonight, Lorenzo. They will meet us at the Hot Tamale at 7 p.m. You wouldn't be having an ulterior motive for this date now would you?"

"I don't know what you are suggesting, Sasha. I just think they deserve to do a little celebrating since they were a part of finding justice for an innocent young woman, Miss Kellog, and for saving Mr. Young and his son from any further abuse."

"Whatever you say, partner. Let's get back to the precinct. We've got a mound of paper work to wade through. I feel kind of sorry for Mrs. Young. She is obviously not a professional killer. She left her prints all over the crime scene like on the rock she used to bash in Charlene's head and all over her car. She put the bloody body in her own car and dumped her in the water. She's really a mental mess. Hard to figure that a good person like Charlene is gone. The only thing left behind is so much pain. Enough of this for now. Let's get this paper work over 'cause I'd like to have time to go home and change clothes before our dinner celebration."

CHAPTER TWENTY-SEVEN

Detective Lorenzo waited until the three women were seated before he sat down. "Hard to be a gentleman to three ladies at once," said the detective.

"What are you talking about?" asked Wilamina.

He responded, "I usually pull the chair out for a lady to sit down and then I seat myself."

"Heck, if a man pulled out my chair, I'd think he was wantin' me to fall on my ass," blasted Wilamina.

Sasha laughed out loud. "Willy, you need to learn how to be treated with respect. Remember what Sharon's group's work was all about?"

"Yeah, I remember," expressed Houston. "You get the treatment you expect. So we should expect flowers, candy and a pulled out chair."

"Maybe we should take a class, to learn us about being ladies," replied Wilamina.

"Forget it Willy, we can learn as we go along. Sasha can clue us in."

They all placed their dinner orders with the waitress. Raul brought over two bottles of wine to their table. "I understand this gathering has to do with a celebration of sorts. So glad you've graced my restaurant for a happy event."

Most of the conversation centered around questions as to what could happen to Melody Young. The detectives shared their personal experiences with trials and sentencing of convicted murderers and the length of time it can take to bring about justice for survivors and victims of violent crimes. The subject of follow up care for Chance, Richard and Lynn was discussed. Houston brought up the Grief Clinic and the good work that can be done in support groups.

After the meal ended, Detective Lorenzo looked directly at Houston with his dark, penetrating eyes and said, "I'm still planning on lunch this Sunday with you and Wilamina. Is that right?"

Before Houston had a chance to respond, Wilamina said, "Yes sir, you have a date with us two ladies."

"Great. We meet here at 1:30 as planned. Now I can tell you a little more about Mrs. Young. She was sent to Lakepoint Hospital for a complete psychiatric workup, evaluation and recommendations. During the transporting of her to the precinct and while the officer attempted to interview her, she became more confused and combative. She had to be restrained and was taken by ambulance to the hospital. She was admitted to the psychiatric ward. She can be held for seventy-two hours, longer if need be, and then depending on the doctor, she could be admitted for a much longer assessment time. The good news for Chance and his son is that she won't be going home for a very long time. She appears to be a very sick woman. She's certainly not able to go to court and respond sanely to a charge of murder. At least not at this time."

Detective Lorenzo asked if anyone knew when and where there would be a funeral for Miss Kellog.

Wilamina responded, "Yes there is going to be one, but Chance doesn't know just when. He's gonna call us or Lynn will, and let us know when and where. Do you want me to let you know when we find out?"

"Please do, Willy. I believe Sasha and I would like to be there."

"Absolutely," replied Sasha.

Dinner was finished. They enjoyed a decadent dessert and both bottles of wine were emptied! Detective Lorenzo thanked Houston and Wilamina and told them they had the makings of two fine investigators. He thanked them for being so professional and innovative.

Sasha added, "See you guys later. Thanks for all you did to help Chance and our department. You're the best."

CHAPTER TWENTY-EIGHT

Funeral for Charlene Kellog at Lake Bountiful.....

A small group of mourners were standing together at the place that Chance had picked for a memorial service for Charlene. The love of Chance's life had been cremated and he brought her ashes to the spot that had been so special for the two of them. The place their relationship had grown into a beautiful love affair. The same place where that relationship was so brutally ended by hate, jealously and mental illness.

Miss Kellog had no living relatives that Chance or Lynn knew about. Chance shared with Houston and Wilamina that he knew so little about Charlene's past. He added that he had the feeling she must have had a very difficult childhood because she never wanted to talk about it.

This somber group consisted of Richard, Lynn, Houston, Wilamina, and Detectives Lorenzo and Voss, Charlene's office mate, Dr. Clarkson and his wife, Charlene's landlord Mr. Wood, and surprisingly the principal of Richard's school showed up. Five other women and two men joined the group as well. They introduced themselves as clients of Miss Kellog. They all agreed she had been such a caring therapist and would be sorely missed.

Chance thanked everyone for their presence and for their kind support. "Charlene believed in second chances for all. She was non-judgmental. She didn't have a mean bone in her body.

Kindness was the only way she knew how to treat everyone no matter how they treated her. My only regret is that my son didn't have the chance to get to know her. I have to believe she is near and will always be." He covered his face with his hands and Richard placed his hands on his dad's back.

Lynn spoke briefly about her best friend and what she learned about kindness and forgiveness from her.

Chance then took the urn with the ashes and emptied it into the lake.

Wilamina raised her face upward and began to softly sing Amazing Grace. One by one, she was joined, by the other mourners. Tears mingled with the singing.

Before anyone could start to walk back to their cars, everyone was invited to a picnic meal. The plan was hatched by Houston, Wilamina and Sasha. They headed back to their truck to gather the food prepared by the loving hands of Wilamina: fried chicken, mashed potatoes, fried okra and all the trimmings. They had paper plates, plastic silverware and blankets to place on the ground. The weather was warm and the blue sky was thankfully cloudless.

Chance made a toast. All raised their paper cups filled with apple juice toward the sky. "Your time was too short Charlene, but you've left a long stream of kindness. Your loving nature touched many hearts and because of you, we're better people. Thank you."

CHAPTER TWENTY-NINE

"I've got it all settled, Tex. We'll visit our friends at Lancer's Prison this coming Saturday," said Wilamina. "We're gonna get to see Sammy, Sharon, Mela and Warden James. Dr. Gibran is on vacation so we can't see her this time."

"Good job, Willy. It'll be great to see them all face to face again. Talking on the phone isn't as satisfying as seeing someone in person. I hate to think about Sharon having to stay there for a long time. She's too good of a person to be behind bars. She killed her sister to save others and out of mercy for her sister."

"That's true, Tex, but she's making the best of it. The good Lord is watchin' over her. I believe she'll be gettin' out sooner then what the judge ordered."

The phone rang and Wilamina, the designated secretary and treasurer answered. "Salt and Pepper Detective Agency. Oh, hello Miss Abigail, course I remember you. I'm Wilamina. What can I do for you?"

She listened for quite a spell and then responded, "We can see you today, this afternoon around 2 p.m. Would that be okay for you?" After a short pause, Wilamina said, "Great. See you later."

Houston was watching her friend talk on the phone and when the call ended she asked, "Well, what gives with that sweet old lady?"

"She said someone is stealing her flowers right out of her garden. I think she was crying, I could hear her sniffling on the other end. She's coming in today. Sure hope we can help her, cause she's so darn sweet and innocent. She just makes you want to put your arms around her and protect her from the world."

"Remember Willy, she did stand up to Chance's wife. She may look like a frail old lady, but underneath she may be a tiger."

Later the same day...............

There was an almost undetected knock on the agency's door. Houston moved quickly to open their door, "Come in, Miss Abigail. No need to knock. Please come in and take a seat. Willy and I are both anxious to hear your problem. Hopefully we can help you."

"Thank you ladies. It's so kind of you to see me so quickly. I'm embarrassed to bother you with such a small problem, but I'm becoming quite unnerved by the disappearance of my beautiful flowers. The thief must come at night."

Houston asked, "How long has the flower stealing gone on?"

"I think it has been going on for a month or so and always on a Thursday at night, because Friday mornings are when I discover the loss. It started so slowly I hardly noticed, but this last Friday my favorite roses were cut and taken. I tried to stay up late and watch my garden, but I fall asleep so easily now. Guess I'm getting prepared for the coming, long, eternal sleep.

"Can you help me? I don't mind sharing my flowers, but this last time was simply too much."

Houston responded, "Yes, we can and we will help. Do you still have many flowers left in your garden for the thief to steal?"

"Oh yes, there are plenty left."

Houston looked over at her partner and said, "How about we come over this Thursday evening and plan on spending the night in your living room. What time do you usually go to bed?"

"Always by 9 p.m., no later than 9:30."

"Okay. We will need to sneak into your back door at 9 p.m. Our car will have to be parked somewhere out of sight, probably down the road from you. I suggest you don't tell anyone about this plan. If you have a light on the back porch, be sure to turn it off and close the drapes in the living room and lower the lights. Do you understand our plan, Miss Abigail?"

"Yes I do. This is actually beginning to sound like quite an adventure. It's like a Miss Marple story. Rather exciting. Don't you both agree?"

The investigators nodded and smiled. Miss Abigail was shown to the door and thanked for choosing them to help her. When they were alone, they began laughing in earnest. "I don't know who Miss Marple is, but I think this is the most excitement that Miss Abigail has had in a long time," chuckled Houston.

CHAPTER THIRTY

Thursday night at Miss Abigail's.....

Thursday evening arrived with Houston and Wilamina standing on the back porch of Miss Abilgail's home, at the agreed upon time.

"Hello, ladies," whispered Miss Abigail wearing a flowery robe with matching slippers. "You're right on time, like I expected. I must say I've been quite jittery all day long about this evening. I do hope you won't be putting yourselves in any danger over some silly flowers. I can't bear to think you were harmed trying to save something so unimportant."

"Don't you worry yourself none, Miss Abigail. We know how to protect ourselves," stated Wilamina with a twinkle in her eyes.

Wilamina took the first watch. They would trade places every three hours. Wilamina was to wake her partner up at midnight to take her turn watching the front yard garden. They drank some tea and ate a few cookies that their client had put on the coffee table for them. Houston then made herself comfortable on the couch. Wilamina situated herself in a hard back chair next to the draped, large living room window. She was positioned to the side of the window, but had a complete view. The living room was completely dark, in fact, there wasn't a light on anywhere in the house. There was a half moon beginning to show itself, which would shed some minimal light on the garden.

A little before midnight, Wilamina woke Houston. "Your turn partner and I'm glad to take my turn on the couch. I was gettin' mighty sleepy the last hour. I was afraid to drink much, 'cause I'd have to hit the bathroom. Someone was sure to show up the minute I left the rock hard chair. Reminded me of when I was little. I was suppose to watch the chicken coup at night sometimes, and as soon as I nodded off that damn fox would grab a hen. I got a lickin' a time or two for fallin' asleep. Tex, you better go pee now, while you got the chance. This whispering don't come easy for me."

"Good idea, Willy. I'll make a quick trip to the bathroom and then you can lie down on this comfy couch. I just hope you don't snore loud like you usually do. I may have to cover your face with the pillow." She grinned and moved quietly to the bathroom.

"Oh sure, you're gonna suffocate your own partner and then live the good life with all our money."

"Hey, Willy. The only thing you'd be leaving me with is the bills. I'd just have to commit some crime so as I could live the good life back in Lancer's."

Wilamina made herself comfortable and was asleep within minutes, snoring quietly.

Houston did a few exercises in the chair to help herself wake up and to stay alert. When 3 a.m. rolled around she felt wide awake and decided to let her friend remain asleep. By 4:30, Houston's eyelids were beginning to droop, suddenly she noticed slight movement out in the front yard.

She was aware there was a person but couldn't make out if it was a man or woman. Whoever they were, they were definitely messing with the flowers and holding a bucket.

"Willy, wake up! We got ourselves an intruder." Houston poked her partner and placed a hand over Willy's mouth, in case she made too much noise.

"What's happening? It's my time already?"

Houston pointed to the window and whispered, "Our thief is out there. You go quietly out the back door. I'll count to ten and then race out the front door. You run to the front and we can both grab the person at the same time."

When Houston heard the back door close, she started counting. When she reached ten, she turned on her flashlight and ran out the front door heading at the figure holding a pair of shears. She yelled, "Don't move sucker, you're surrounded. At that very moment Wilamina came flying around the house and leaped at the intruder, knocking him down and landing on top of him. Houston, quick as a bunny, was aiming the flashlight at the two tangled bodies on the ground. She let out, "Oh my God, Jose, what the hell are you doing stealin' flowers from your neighbor? You can get up Willy before you crush him."

Jose was attempting to catch his breath, barely able to squeak out, "Lo siento, lo siento, I'm so sorry. I'm not a bad person. Just taking a few flowers I didn't think would be missed."

By now, Miss Abigail was downstairs, standing inside the front door with her mouth hanging wide open. "No, I can't believe it. It's Jose! " she gasped.

With much effort and groaning, Jose and Wilamina managed to stand up. They were wiping off flowers and dirt from their clothing and faces. Miss Abigail requested everyone to come inside. "Jose, you must have an explanation for what you've been doing."

They all followed her into the kitchen. The lights were turned on and Miss Abigail put the tea pot on to boil.

Wilamina gently took a few squashed flowers and leaves out of Jose's hair. "Hope I didn't hurt you, Jose."

"No problem, Miss Wilamina. But, they could use you on my favorite football team. Their defense guys are not so good. Where did you get your training?"

"From livin' in a tough neighborhood and Lancer's prison."

Jose looked at her with a curious expression on his face. "Sounds like an interesting story. Hope you tell me about it someday, that is if I'm not going to jail tonight."

As soon as tea was poured and everyone had a chance to calm down, Jose explained why he was taking flowers from his sweet neighbor's garden. His elderly mother is living in the local nursing care facility. She is very old, feeble and becoming weaker with every passing week. One of her most favorite things in life was her garden, especially her roses. Jose visits her every Friday and brings her a small bouquet of Abigail's flowers. "I don't have time to run to the flower shop, it's way at the end of town and doesn't open until 9 a.m. I need to be working my station by 6 a.m. to 7 p.m. or later every night. I didn't think you'd miss a few flowers, I took only five or six very early Friday morning. The flowers last pretty good until Friday evening when I can visit mother. I'm sorry to cause you to be frightened. I should have asked, but I was embarrassed. Please forgive me. I'll clean up the mess, in your beautiful garden. Do you want to call the police?'

"Heavens no!" exclaimed Miss Abigail. "I'm just sorry you didn't ask me. From now on you can come by every Friday afternoon, and I'll have a nice bouquet ready for your mother or you can come by just before you plan to visit her and we can make up a bouquet together. It would be my pleasure to share my beautiful flowers with someone who loves flowers, like I do. Especially someone who appreciated roses like me."

Tears were streaming down both Jose's face and Wilamina's face.

"Kindness always makes me cry. I'm so glad everything has turned out okay. I really like this detective work, Tex. We get to make some fine new friends."

"Yes Willy, I've discovered there are many good people around. It's just the few bad ones that smell up the place. Well, I'm beat. Time we got ourselves home and get some shut eye."

Miss Abigail said, "I'll get in touch with you tomorrow afternoon. After you have some time to sleep. You can send me a bill and I'll gladly take care of it. I'd be happy to give your business a great recommendation. You are two fine investigators. Goodnight dear ladies."

Jose added, "You ladies come to me if you have any trouble with your truck. I'll be talking with you soon. Can you give me your business card again? I need the phone number."

"You bet, I love passing our card around. See you both some other time. Good-bye."

CHAPTER THIRTY-ONE

Visit to Lancer's Prison..........

Houston and Wilamina arrived at their old place of residence, a half an hour before visiting time was to start.

"I'm feeling all funny inside," remarked Wilamina. "Like a bunch of crawly bugs are dancin' in my stomach. I can still hear that old judge say those terrible words, **guilty**! I thought my heart would stop and my skin would fall off. I cried and cried 'til I threw up. I couldn't stop crying what seemed like hours. Royal was there in the court room. He was bawling and cursing the judge and the lawyers. Worst day of my life. I was ashamed and scared.

"And I also remember that very same day they put me inside this very prison. They gave me those awful clothes to wear, after makin' me strip in front of all those nasty looking strangers. I was too ashamed to ask Jesus for help. I was hopin' He wasn't watching."

"I can remember that shit too, Willy. I'll never forget the mean eyes of the judge who looked like he was almost thrilled when he sent me away for twenty years. I was so pissed at him and at the idiots on the jury. I hated everybody. I was too mad to be scared. I couldn't believe my own mother lied in court, but then she was so messed up. Her brain was soaked in alcohol and didn't work so good. I couldn't really blame her. Her life had been hell.

I'm not sorry one bit that I killed that son of a bitch. Just wish my mom wasn't so screwed up with booze and dope.

"Gives me a strange feeling to be sitting here on the outside, waiting to walk in voluntarily. I'm not sure what would'a happened to me if Sharon hadn't started her programs and if Mr. Lagunta hadn't shown up. Thanks to Rachael, one of the other therapists from the Grief Clinic who knew Mr. Lagunta.

"It's time, Willy. Let's go in and visit our friends. The correctional officer is waving us in. This time we are the visitors and we'll be walking back out in an hour or so. Freedom is such a great word."

Warden James and Mela Washington, the night nurse, greeted the two ex-inmates with hugs and beaming faces. The warden directed them to her office. "We're going to use my space for this glorious visit. Lunch is being prepared by several of your buddies, and they have special permission to bring out the food shortly. Sharon and Sammy are already waiting for you inside."

As soon as they arrived at the warden's door, Wilamina began to sniffle. A correctional officer opened the door and Sharon and Sammy jumped up out of their chairs and ran to greet their ex-cell mates. Wilamina managed to hug everyone with her usual bear hug stretch at the same time. "Thank you, Jesus for this glorious moment of reunion," she sang out.

Houston took a moment to look over her old friends and thoughtfully said, "You both look great. Sammy you've lost some weight, looking good. Sharon I don't know how to thank you for what you did for Willy and me. You taught us how to look at our lives in a different way, a more respectful way.

"So great to see everybody again. We owe our new and joyful lives to all of you. Sammy, soon you'll be out and living life like it was meant to be lived."

There were tears, laughter and tender embraces until it was time for lunch. A knock on the door interrupted the warm scene. The warden opened the door and admitted a correctional officer followed by Luella and Berri carrying the food trays. The whoops and hollers began all over again when Wilamina and Houston saw two more of their ex-cell mates. Everyone was talking at once, sounding like a huge convention.

Houston and Wilamina let Sammy know that she could live with them until she made other arrangements after she was released. Sharon shared how the programs were progressing with the unfailing help from the warden and how a few other prisons for women were considering adding the self-respect type workshops as well. Sharon's program was to be the blueprint for success. Everyone was thrilled and interested in how the Salt and Pepper Agency was doing. A brief synopsis of the ex-inmates cases was talked about and each one of the current inmates had their time to tell what was going on in their lives. The warden and Mela were both teary eyed at the joyful exchange of news and encouragement, one to the other.

"Our time is drawing to an end, my dear ladies," said the warden, sadly.

Everyone gave hugs and wished each other health, joy and hope for a beautiful life, where ever life finds them.

Once back in their truck and on the road to home, they both remained silent all the way back to Whitefall, with their own personal thoughts.

CHAPTER THIRTY-TWO

"Tex, would you like to come to my church today?"

"No thanks, Willy. I get enough religion during the week, with your Jesus talk and gospel singing. I'm not complaining, my friend, I just don't want to overdo it. I might become one of those crazy Bible thumpers and find myself standing on some street corner yelling at sinners."

Wilamina laughed hard and loud, "And I'd be standing in front of you yelling, save me sister, save me. I'll come home right after church lets out to pick you up. We'll get to the restaurant right on time. I bet Detective Lorenzo will definitely be on time. You do remember our date with him, don't you?"

"Yes, Willy, I remember. I wish we didn't agree to meet with him. That Lorenzo is a guy who likes to get his own way. Bet he comes from people who have money and are used to gettin' what they want. He's too smooth to suit me. I like'm more rough around the edges. You know, a guy that wouldn't fall over in a faint if I hit him with my fist or kissed him so hard that his eyeballs nearly fall out. I can't be the kind of gal who can't say what she wants or what she thinks."

"Now don't fret, my friend. Mr. Detective only wants to get to know us better. No harm in that. I like him 'cause he's not afraid of being himself. He's a strong thinkin' man with a good looking ass. See you soon after 1 p. m. Tex, I wouldn't go and hit

147

the detective in the jaw, he'd hit ya back and harder. Now honey, you might try the kissing part. Bet he'd surprise you."

Detective Lorenzo was waiting outside the restaurant door when Wilamina drove up and parked.

Houston spotted him and mumbled, "He's waitin' to do some gentleman thing. I know what he's up to and he's not gonna trick me. I knew a pimp one time, smooth as glass, until I let him know, with my fist, that I wasn't gonna be one of his girls. That's when he showed his true colors. For a skinny little guy he could sure fight. Surprised the hell out of me. I still never worked for him or anyone else."

"Tex, you be nice. The detective ain't no pimp. He's one of the good guys. We just got to get some practice with being treated respectfully. "Hi Detective Lorenzo," hollered out Wilamina through her open window.

"Hello ladies, you're right on time." He reached to open Houston's door, but she was too quick and nearly jumped into his chest. "Whoa, sorry, guess I was too slow for you." Then he walked to the driver's side and asked Wilamina if he could open her door.

"Yes sir, detective. I like this lady-like stuff. Tex, hasn't warmed up to it yet. Give her time."

Once inside the restaurant Houston, once again, quickly sat down, but Wilamina waited for the detective to pull out her chair. They smiled at each other and Wilamina sat down as gracefully as she could manage. "I have to admit," she said, "I had to take a peak to make sure the chair was gonna be there before I plopped myself down."

The detective laughed out loud and Houston looked as if she'd been chewing on lemons.

"First off, I'd like to ask you both to call me by my first name, Sark. We're not working now. This is a friendly get together so that we might get to know each other a little better."

"You can call me Willy, Sark. I guess you mean when were not on a case we can be more friendly-like?"

"You got it, Willy." He looked at Houston and waited for her to say something.

"You can call me Tex or Houston or whatever you want. Makes no real difference to me."

"I happen to like the name Houston, so that's what I'll stick with unless we're on a case and then I'll address you as Miss Hayfield. Okay, Houston?"

"Okay, Detective Sark."

They ordered from the menu. While waiting for their food, the detective asked them both of their impression of investigative work.

"I love it so far, except for the death of Charlene and the pain and sorrow it has caused for Chance, his son and Lynn," answered Wilamina. "We get to help others and get paid for doin' it. Doesn't seem right to make money from someone's sorrow, but I don't mind having a bank account with somethin' in it. I like having money to pay for things. I've had to do some things I didn't want to when I was younger. I'm not one bit sorry about stealing things, like food, but I always felt ashamed and afraid."

"Willy, you were trying to survive," confirmed Houston. "No one should fault you for that. I've done my share of taking what didn't belong to me. Most was necessary, but not all. At least we never sold ourselves. Down deep I knew that was a road that led nowhere, except to hell."

"Tex, I never told ya that I was tempted, long time ago. Had a boyfriend who almost convinced me I needed to prove I loved him. He said that if I really loved him I'd go on street duty. I was fourteen years old. Guess I didn't love him enough. He got himself shot dead and I never dropped a tear."

"How about you Detective Sark, you ever do some stealing or anything else illegal?" asked Houston, crossing her arms and visually offering a challenge.

Before he could answer, the waitress was placing their food in front of them. He waited until the server had moved away and looked directly at Houston. "I was never a choir boy or the well-liked high school athlete. I lived in a very nice home, in a well-to-do neighborhood. I was an average student, nothing special. But, what went on behind the closed door in my home was not what anyone expected.

"My dad was a mean alcoholic. He beat my mother, my older brother and me. The only time the house was peaceful was when he was at work or at the bar. We all dreaded hearing the garage door open. He'd stagger in, yell profanities through the door and the three of us tried to disappear. My brother Tico tried to stop him from hitting mom, but dad turned on him. He broke Tico's arm and nose. Mom did nothing, but cry.

"When Tico was sixteen he ran away from home. I was thirteen, terrified to be alone with just mom and me. My mom was more afraid of what her parents and the neighbors would think of her, if they found out her husband was a beast. She didn't even pretend to care about what was happening to her own sons. She was so superficial and beautiful, but empty inside.

"To shorten the story, Tico wound up in Juvenile Hall and dad bailed him out, brought him home and immediately started in drinking and screaming at Tico again. Dad went crazy and started pounding on him with frightening force. My brother tried to get away, tried to fight back, but dad was much bigger and stronger. Mom did try to help Tico, but dad hit her so hard she was knocked out. I think I was screaming the whole time and something told me that this time, someone was going to die, if I didn't do something. I got dad's gun from the bedroom and walked into the kitchen and shot my father, dead, one shot to his head. Mom died a few days later from her head injury. I was eventually sent to live with my Aunt Rosita. Years later, Tico was murdered in prison.

"At some point in my teenage years, I made up my mind to be one of the good guys. My aunt was a kind, wise lady. She helped me set my life in the right direction. If it hadn't been for her, I'd be dead by now." The detective stared down at his shoes and remained quiet. Houston and Wilamina appeared frozen on the spot. Their mouths were hanging open and both remained silent.

"Sorry ladies, I didn't mean to go on and on. Guess you heard far more than you needed or wanted to. I haven't told many this story. Not sure why I picked you two, maybe because I thought you'd better understand then some others."

"I don't know what to say, Sark. I had you pegged as a spoiled, rich kid. I was so wrong. You're the sort of person Sharon was trying to teach us to become. To respect ourselves, to make right choices, to become our own heroes. She taught us to raise above our childhood abuses and use the abusive experiences as ladders so that we would climb out of the hell-hole we came from. That's exactly what you did."

"Don't get me wrong, Houston. I'm no saint. I still have to fight hard to keep myself under control when I'm confronted with abusers, especially those that are hurting kids or pets.

"Tico didn't have a chance. He was so mistreated most of his young life by a father and a mother who should never have had kids. Sometimes he even took the beatings that dad meant for me. He just wasn't big enough or strong enough to fight off a drunken bully."

A cell phone buzzed and Wilamina answered it, "Hello, oh yes I can do that. I've just finished lunch and I can be there in fifteen minutes." She put the phone away and addressed Houston, "That was a church friend. She needs my help. Would you mind much if I took the truck? Sark could take you home, maybe?"

Houston had a look of disbelief and asked, "Willy, what sort of emergency does this friend have?"

"I'll tell you later as soon as I get home. Thanks for lunch, Sark, and for sharing some of your life story with us. I'll see you both later." She quickly moved through the restaurant, got into the truck and drove off.

"Your partner is certainly a caring individual. Would you like dessert and a coffee refill?"

Houston was still focused on the door through which her partner had so abruptly departed. "That's so strange, her leaving that way. Didn't know she had made such close friends at her church. More coffee and a dessert would be great."

Lorenzo ordered dessert then continued, "I've shared a great deal this afternoon, far more than I ever intended, but I'm feeling good about it. Do you want to tell me your impression of investigative work so far or anything else about yourself?"

Houston hesitated for a moment and with her eyes casted downward said, "Willy shows her emotions far easier than I do. I'm a very private person. I can never remember being comfortable talking about myself, especially my feelings. Talking always got me in trouble, as a kid. Talking about feelings, got me laughed at or hit. God forbid if I had an opinion.

"My mother was a train wreck from drugs, booze and her mean-spirited parents. My life as a kid was something like yours, strange as that sounds. I was a scared little girl, scared of everybody. Not sure how that changed, but I did learn quickly enough that I'd better fight back. First with my mouth and if that didn't work, with my fists if I was ever gonna make it to become a teenager.

"Mom brought lots of dirt bags home. They stayed a night, a week, maybe even a few months. They were all bad news. My brother, Lee, got out of the house long before. He was ten years older than me. So with him gone, I had to take care of myself and my pitiful mother. I guess our backgrounds are sounding sort of alike. I also killed someone, defending my mom. You just made better choices than I did. At least now I have a decent future ahead of me."

"So does this mean we can someday be friends? Friends who sometimes go to dinner together?" asked Detective Lorenzo.

"Sure, friends go to dinner together. Willy and I go out to dinner a lot. But I think you are talking about a date? I haven't been on a date in such a long time. I'm not sure I've ever been on a prearranged date. Sark, I need more time to get to know you, and to get more comfortable in my new skin."

"Dating is one way to get to know someone. How about this? When you feel like it, you ask me to go on a date with you. I hope you won't make me wait too long. Houston, I'm not one of the bad guys. Sasha knows me pretty well, ask her opinion of me," suggested the detective as he grinned and winked at her.

"That might work, but don't be holding your breath. I'm not promising anything," replied Houston.

The detective didn't speak for a moment, he appeared to be looking into space. "Houston, I just had a strange thought. You and me, we've killed somebody in defense of another. Not sure what to make of it. Want me to take you home now?"

"I'd appreciate it, Sark."

CHAPTER THIRTY-THREE

"Willy, we've talked about writin' to Sharon. I'm gonna try it. I've never written this kind of a letter before. Hope I don't sound too stupid or silly. I just feel so good about my life right now and I want her to know that she made this all possible. I hate thinkin' of her sitting by herself, surrounded by those cold walls, maybe in danger. Here goes,"

Hi Sharon, You've been on my mind lots of times. I want you to know how much you've done for me. I don't know how things would have been for me if you had not come to Lancer's Prison and started your program and group work. I know you didn't come voluntarily, but I understand why you did what you did to your sister. You are the kindest person I know, except for Willy. She's also got a soft heart.

They would've kept me locked up another fifteen years or so. My life never changing. Trying to survive watching my back every moment. Expecting nothin' good. Feeling bad like always about my sick, addicted mother. My brother kept trying to help her and not getting very far with all his efforts. His own life being wasted.

If you didn't help me I could've become like some of the other inmates. Some will give up hope and become like rabid dogs. Maybe I would have become like that too. I know I'd survive, but what kind of person would I end up like? Makes me sick all over to think about it.

Guess I'm rambling on. I want you to know that the program you wrote and the group run by Brooksie and Lucinda saved me. You changed me. I found my insides weren't so dirty and damaged. I learned about my good and decent parts. I'm not a bad person. Maybe bad acting at times, but not really bad through to the inside of me. I believed that shit, family and others told me when I was only a kid. I was gettin' messed up by messed up grownups. They were cowards. They lied to me, lied to themselves, hurt me and tried messing with my mind and body.

Your program let me see I could choose to be whatever sort of person I wanted to be: honest, useful, a real friend and pay my own way. Maybe I'd find a guy who loved me and showed it, maybe I'd even get married. I don't know about kids, my own, I mean. I'd be afraid that I'd mess them up. I don't know how to be a mom. I never really had one.

Sorry I'm going on and on. This is the first letter I've ever written. Not sure about the spelling, but you can get the idea. You don't belong in a prison, but maybe it's a good thing you're there 'cause you're changing lives.

Willy and I talk about you a lot. We hope Mr. Lagunta can bring justice for you like he did for us.

> *My thanks is all I have to give you, but know I'll always have your back.*
> *Your friend*
> *Tex ...... Houston Hayfield (case you forgot my real name).*

Wilamina sat in her chair behind her desk. She watched her friend write feverishly. Writing and erasing, then more writing and more erasing. Houston's tongue was slightly visible peaking out between her lips. After a great deal of animated effort on Houston's part, she announced she was finished and asked her partner to read over her letter.

"Sure will, partner. I don't think I've ever seen you so involved in anything as much as you worked on that piece of paper. Hand it over. I'll be glad to read it." A minute later, she handed the letter back and said, "You did one fine job and will surely make Sharon happy and proud. I'm happy you see me as a kind person too. You, my friend are also a very kind soul. My turn to put my feelings down on paper."

> *Dear Sharon,*
> *My prayers got answered the first day I walked into the mess hall and sat at the first group meeting table. You are a blessing to many hurting souls. You gave me hope and a way to make my life a blessing for some other folks. I never heard the word respect when I was growing up. You brought Tex and me together. You didn't do it on purpose, but your teaching is what did it. Tex is my first real friend and I'm hers. You taught us, with Brooksie and Lucinda and now even their husbands, showed us how real friends treat each other. So many good folks have done so*

much. I can never thank everyone enough, but I say my prayers for all of you every night. Every night the good Lord gets to hear how great you and the others are.

When I used to sing my gospel songs, I sang with a deep pain inside. Now I sing with a joyful heart. I still get the blues once in awhile, but that's okay, cause now I'm helping others and that makes me cry happy.

Tex and I will be at the prison when they open the gates and you walk out, same goes for them pearly gates. If we go first, then we'll be standing tall welcoming you. If you go before us, I'm counting on you greeting us.

Thank you, sister. Willy or Wilamina

CHAPTER THIRTY-FOUR

"I got a call from Warden James today to let us know Sammy Long will be released in the next two weeks. Dr. Blackmore is planning to pick her up and drive her to the Sea Horse Restaurant for a surprise party. He's gonna have his secretary send us invitations. The warden said he is asking lots of folks. He wants us to come and bring a date or a friend. Sasha, Brooksie, Lucinda and the other social workers from the Grief Clinic plus husbands and boyfriends are also invited. The doc is going to have his wife and most of his staff there.

"What kind of useful gift can we come up with, Willy? Something she needs and that we can afford."

Wilamina answered, "Remember the gift certificates for clothes and household goods we got? They came in real handy. The warden also said that Dr. Blackmore is gonna let Sammy stay in one of his apartments 'cause it's only a block from his office. She won't be needin' a car to get to work then. That man is truly a saint."

Houston was staring off into space. Wilamina asked her, "What you looking at, Tex?"

"Nothing. Just got stuck on that word date. We can bring dates. We got no dates, Willy. No prospects at all. Maybe we could bring the Rickels to the party, but that would be stupid.

Sammy don't know them. Maybe Sasha will have an idea. Let's call her later and see what she says."

"Yeah. She's got lots of ideas," remarked Wilamina. "You know she's never talked about any guy in her life. What'a you supposed is gonna on with her? She's great looking, smart and lots of fun to be around. Hard to believe she's not being chased by guys. I don't think she likes women."

"No, I don't either. We don't know much about her past. We need to be better friends to her. Let's have her over for dinner. Maybe a drink or two will help to loosen her up and she'd share things about herself. Willy, give her a call and pick a time. Say, you don't mind me asking you to do most of the phone calls, do you? You're really good on the phone, like a pro."

"Thanks for saying that, Tex. I'll call her and bet she'll have some ideas about dates for Sammy's party."

Wilamina made contact with Sasha and she accepted the dinner offer for the next night.

The next night...............

"Thanks for the dinner invitation. Willy your cooking has become legendary. Maybe you could work in a fancy restaurant, or better yet, own your own and be the head chef."

Wilamina's smile lit up the room. "I love cookin' and feedin' people, all kinds of people, young and old. Makes me happy inside. But, no ma'am, I like this detective job, for now. I get to do some helping folks in trouble and get to cook and feed them at the same time. Fit's me just fine."

Houston offered their guest a drink. What's your pleasure, Sasha? We got wine, beer and pop."

Sasha chose a glass of wine, walked slowly around the small kitchen, and looked at the few photos attached to the refrigerator.

"Now this one is a classic, the two of you standing at the gate of Lancer's Prison."

"Yeah, that was the day Willy was released. She cries every time she looks at it. Hope you don't mind me askin', but Willy and me were wondering if you have time to date anyone. Seems like you're always working. Don't mean to be nosey, but we've both noticed how the guys at your precinct are always eyeing you up and down every time we make a visit there. You do know you're a real looker?"

Sasha looked down at the floor, a slight flush appeared on her cheeks. "I've had my share of dates in the past. They didn't go so well. I guess I didn't make very wise choices. I almost walked to the altar once, had the wedding dress ordered and one week before the grand event was to take place, the shit hit the fan. The man I thought I knew and admired, turned out to be a scam artist. He was a stock broker and was ripping off his clients, big time. My folks were two of his victims. He hurt them bad, along with others, including some of their friends. My confidence in picking a mate was shot all to hell. My folks have recovered financially and never once blamed me, but I blamed myself for being blind and stupid. Now I have a hard time trusting myself, when it comes to a personal and romantic relationship."

Wilamina and Houston listened intently and remained silent for a few minutes. Wilamina was the first to speak, "He was the stupid one. Honey, never blame yourself for someone else's sins. Whoever he was, gets the blame and the guilt and all of the consequences.

"Child, don't you remember the lessons Sharon gave us? Don't take on somebody else's shit. You were in love. You believed in your man and it turned out he was a damn liar and thief. You hold your head up, walk straight and try again."

Houston added, "Sorry you had such a painful lesson but you're no coward. Time to try again. If Willy and me with our past shit can keep trying then you sure as hell can too. You're history is more like the story of a saint. We are no saints, but we ain't givin' up a shot at happiness.

Two weeks later at Sammy's surprise party..........

Dr. Blackmore invited a number of mostly friends and a few strangers to the Sea Horse Restaurant. The restaurant faced the ocean and was located about two miles from the town of Whitefall.

Dr. Blackmore was Sammy's employer when she attacked her partner, Louny. The attack apparently left Louny a paraplegic. Sammy was sentenced to eight years in Lancer's Women's prison. Louny had some mental issues. She was diagnosed as bi-polar, but wouldn't take her medications regularly. She was extremely jealous of the time and love Sammy bestowed on her three dogs. So one day, when Sammy was at work, her messed up partner tortured and killed the dogs. When Sammy discovered the horrific crime, she nearly beat her partner to death. Louny received serious damage to her back when Sammy threw her against a desk. The surgeons said the paralysis could be permanent or not. Time would tell what her results would be.

The good Dr. Blackmore, a veterinarian, became Sammy's dedicated advocate. He visited her regularly at the prison. He always encouraged her to keep her hope up for a future. He promised her she would have a job as his assistant when she was released. He brought her books to help her learn more about her job as an assistant.

Mr. Lagunta took on Sammy's case pro bono. He had done this previously for Houston and Wilamina. He was successful in obtaining a reduced sentence for Sammy and today she is being released from prison.

Sammy sat quietly in the doctor's car for some time. Then said, "I'll never know how to show my appreciation for all you've done and especially for your belief in me. I've read all the books you brought me over and over. I'm going to work harder than anybody you've ever hired.

"So we are going to a restaurant to celebrate my release? Doc, you've done more for me than anyone else has, you and Mr. Lagunta. He took on the court system. I can't wait to start working in your office again. I've sure missed you and the animals. How soon do you think it will be okay for me to get a dog?"

"Give yourself a little time to adjust to your freedom, your job and your new life. Sammy, you owe me nothing. Do your best, forgive yourself and enjoy working as my special assistant. You studied hard while incarcerated and now we're all going to reap the benefits. The apartment you'll be living in has a fenced back yard, not big enough for a large dog, but maybe for a couple of small dogs. I just bet the right pet will soon find you. Mother Nature has a way of matching us up quite well."

Dr. Blackmore parked his car and he and Sammy walked into the restaurant. A few of the well-wishers almost knocked Sammy down, trying to all hug her at the same time. They shouted in unison, "Welcome to your new life, Sammy!" Hugs, tears and a thousand good wishes were bestowed on the now ex-inmate.

Sammy blubbered into the handkerchief her new boss handed her.

"I can't believe you're all here for me." She stopped for a minute and looked at the smiling faces, "I never thought this could happen to me. I don't have enough words to thank you all."

Wilamina, in her usual fashion, bear hugged her ex-prison mate. Houston shook Sammy's one available hand, nearly shaking her teeth loose.

Eventually, everyone greeted and congratulated Sammy on her release. She spotted Mr. Lagunta in the group of well-wishers. She roughly grabbed his hands and said, "You and the doctor are my two saviors. I'll be in the shadows for the rest of my life watching your backs. I'll be always be ready to protect you both from any harm."

"I appreciate that, Sammy. You are a good person and a good friend to both of us. Hopefully, neither of us will ever need protection," said Roco Lagunta with a big smile.

Dr. Blackmore introduced Sammy to Lacona Monroe. "Sammy, Lacona is the amazing manager of the local pet rescue shelter. She is devoted to animals of all kinds, much like you are."

"So nice to meet you, Sammy. The good doctor has told me so many wonderful things about you. Looking forward to getting to know you better and working miracles with you. Dr. Blackmore is one special person and he has a fine staff," said Lacona.

"Thanks, Lacona. I'm thrilled to meet another animal lover. The world needs more of us," responded Sammy.

Sammy made a point of thanking everyone and continued to wipe away the tears rolling down her cheeks.

Sasha was standing way in the background. She finally moved forward so as to be noticed by Sammy.

"Sasha! What the hell are you doing here?" screeched Sammy. "How'd you get out? You just disappeared from Lancer's. The warden said you got real sick and that's the last we heard."

Houston informed Sammy, "Sasha was an undercover cop. She was working for the police and all the time we thought she was a hooker. She's now a damn good homicide detective. Can you believe that? Our nasty ho turned out to be a cop."

Sammy's mouth fell open, "Sasha you were the best damn ho I've ever known. What an actress! I'm gonna hug you 'cause I've never hugged a cop before. Never wanted to. Well, that's not really true. There was Salina who worked in the court room. What a doll. Too bad I wasn't her type. Great to see that you're okay. That warden was a pretty good actress too."

"Sammy, I'm thrilled to see how hard you've worked to now be starting a good life, " said Sasha. "You deserve only the best of everything. We'll be getting together soon, you, Tex and Willy. We have much to share."

Brooksie and Lucinda were the social workers who facilitated the group that Sammy was assigned to in prison. They both introduced their husbands, Luke and Tony. Sasha introduced Detective Lorenzo. Detective Lorenzo introduced his friend, Monte Jacks, nicknamed, Stoney.

After the main meal was devoured, a large cake was set down in front of Sammy. It was decorated with a dog and cat figure and the words, WELCOME BACK SAMMY! WE'VE ALL MISSED YOU! signed, THE PETS.

The tears started flowing like a river from Sammy, Wilamina, Lucinda and Brooksie. The others simply wiped and blew their noses.

There were several envelopes next to the cake in a basket. She choked up immediately after opening the first one. She handed it to Dr. Blackmore. He asked if she wanted him to read it out loud.

She nodded and handed all of the envelopes to him. "You sure you don't want to do the honors, Sammy?" She again nodded her head.

There were many gift certificates for various places totaling over twenty-five hundred dollars. Dr. Blackmore's gift was a handwritten note saying she would be living rent free in a house he owned for as long as she needed.

Sammy looked frozen on the spot. She didn't appear to breathe or bat an eye lash. After a long, silent few seconds, she took Dr. Blackmore's face in her hands and said, "You will never be sorry. I'll be the best damn assistant, the best damn friend and the best damn person you've ever known." She kissed his forehead and gave him a Wilamina bear hug.

CHAPTER THIRTY-FIVE

Six months later..........

Monte Jacks, aka 'Stoney', had been working as a sub-contractor for Luke Jones, the landscaper and husband of Brooksie. Stoney was quite taken with Wilamina when they both attended Sammy's prison release party. Being a shy man, he hesitated for months wanting to approach her. Wilamina was also interested in him, but since practicing 'lady behavior' wouldn't take the initiative.

With Brooksie's persistent urging, Luke agreed to host a party and put Stoney and Wilamina at the top of the guest list. They also invited Houston, Sark, Sasha, Lucinda, Tony, Dr. Blackmore, Sammy and Leona, along with three staff members of the veterinarian's office, Ruth, Melba and Jackson. Sammy and Leona had developed a romantic relationship almost since their first meeting six months earlier. They happily discovered that they were mutually attracted to each other. What began as a love of animals eventually evolved into a love for each other and the pets.

Houston found many excuses to place herself with Detective Lorenzo, but she was still struggling with trust issues.

"Tex, what do ladies wear to a picnic?"

"You're asking me? Willy, when are you gonna stop this lady-like crap? Be yourself, for God's sake. You're a warm, sexy, outgoing, attractive woman with a fine ass, so you say. Stoney is a down to earth kind of guy. I think he's shy and you've been scaring him off with your lady shit. Don't you like him?"

"Hell yes. My panties get wet every time I see him, but I want to be treated with respect like a lady, like Sark always does."

Tex responded, "He's respecting you to death. Do what comes natural at the picnic. Wear comfortable clothes and tennis shoes. I'm wearing my well-worn Levis, red blouse and I'm bringing a sweatshirt in case it turns cold. Detective Sark will probably be dressed in a suit, like always. He's a gentleman alright, maybe too much of one for me.

"Willy, have you ever been to a picnic? We'll be sitting on the ground. I'll take a blanket for us. Brooksie and Luke are bringing the food and drinks. We might even play baseball or football."

"No. I've never been to this kind of a party. I've eaten on the ground before 'cause there was a time we had no table or no chairs; but, I wouldn't say it was fun. I've never played those games. I've played other games, like hide and seek from the cops or see who could steal the most food from the neighborhood grocery store without getting caught."

"If we play football Willy, maybe you could tackle Stoney and give him one of your famous hugs. Bet he'd love that. He might even surprise you with his response."

"My God, we might just rip each other's clothes off and go at it, right there in the park."

"If you do, partner, please head into the woods and try to keep your 'Hallelujahs' and 'Amens' to a low roar."

CHAPTER THIRTY-SIX

The picnic.............

With help from Lucinda and Tony, Brooksie and Luke brought fold-up tables and chairs. They also took care of the food and beverages. They laid out a great spread of fried chicken, mashed potatoes, corn bread and several different kinds of salads.

As soon as everyone arrived, Brooksie yelled out, "Come and get it while it's hot." No one needed to be asked twice. Sammy and Leona brought a huge watermelon for dessert and a basket of homemade cookies.

Since Stoney brought a football, it was decided by a show of hands that a game of touch football was next after they all finished filling their faces and stomachs. Sammy and Leona organized two teams. Sammy's team was made up of Dr. Blackmore, his staff, Sasha and Stoney.

Lacona's team was made up of Houston, Wilamina, Brooksie, Luke, Tony, Sark and Hunt Rickels. A few had played the game before, but the majority were novices. A so-called "game" began and quickly turned into a comedy of errors. Raucous laughter, snorting and giggling filled the playing field. The better players tried to instruct their team mates, with little success. Most simply fumbled along. Tripped over each other or over their own feet. Half of the time they couldn't remember whose team they were supposed to be playing on. What the game lacked in professionalism, it made up for it in comedy.

By pure luck alone Wilamina managed to catch the ball. She ran like her feet were on fire whooping and yelling, "Get out of my way. I'm comin' through." Which she did, right into Stoney. She knocked him flat on his back and she landed squarely on top of him.

Tony, the make-believe referee belted out, "Touchdown!"

Stoney was making very little effort to get up, seemed to like the position of his opponent. Wilamina raised herself half-way up and then planted a big kiss right on Stoney's mouth.

Houston threw her arms up high and hollered out, "Score one for our team!"

Everyone cheered and Lacona's team was considered the winner. A fantastic day was enjoyed by all. Home-baked cookies and fresh watermelon finished up the celebration. Stoney and Wilamina were sitting on the ground sharing a large piece of watermelon. It was unanimously agreed upon that this picnic should become an annual event.

Sasha announced to the group just before everyone dispersed, "I have a small house, and a very nice backyard with a large covered patio and fire pit. I would love to host an outdoor party, say in two months."

Sasha's offer was heartily welcomed and all would meet again in two months. Most everyone then gathered their belongings and walked off in other directions.

Houston asked Sark to wait up. She took him aside and whispered, "I'm asking you to go out to dinner and dance with me. I understand the Hot Iron Dance Hall has good food and a great western band. We've done business lunches and many coffee meetings and you said you'd wait for me to ask you on a real date. I'm asking now. Hope I'm not too late."

The detective looked away and slowly turned his dark eyes to Houston. "It would be my honor to go on a real date with such an interesting and exciting woman. It's been a long wait for me. I hope you'll find it worth the wait. I know I will."

She looked deeply into his kind, mysterious eyes, touched his shoulder and quietly said, "Thanks for waiting and thanks for saying yes."

CHAPTER THRITY-SEVEN

"Sammy and me talked a lot at the picnic," said Houston. "She is so happy. She told me Lacona treats her real good every day. She said she never knew life could be so great. She's crazy in love. I'm so happy for her. I bet this is her first real loving relationship. Her other partner sounded unpredictable and cruel. She also said that they plan to buy a house and move in together in a few months. They've found an older house on two acres close to both of their jobs. Sammy said they both want to make a caring home for unwanted critters. You watch, it won't take long before they'll have all kinds of animals living in every corner of their place."

Wilamina nodded her head and responded, "It warms my heart to know Sammy is so happy. She's such a good soul. They make a great team. We make a great team too, sister. Without the romance part, of course.

"Lacona and I hit it off pretty good. She's a real nice lady. She kept repeatin' how wonderful Sammy is. I wouldn't mind being one of their pets. They sure love all their creatures. How about we get a kitten? A little kitten don't need a big yard. I could sure love a little, fluffy bundle of joy. Lacona said she gets mamas and kittens dumped at her shelter all the time. Maybe we could have two little fellows. They could keep each other company when were gone investigating somewhere."

"Willy, if you want a kitten or two, go get yourself two fluff balls. I sort of like dogs better. I like cats, I've just never had one of my own. What happens if you and Stoney hook up and we live separately? What about the kittens?"

"Why you say, Stoney and me, what about you and Sark?"

We're gettin' way ahead of ourselves, partner. We got a goin' business, it's growing, and we're learning more every day. No matter what, we'll be partners for many years until we're too old to chase down the scum bags."

"Okay Tex, I'm gonna call Lacona right now and tell her we want two kittens. Lordy, I'm already getting teary-eyed just thinking how happy two baby kittens are gonna be. The little tykes truly need us. Maybe we can get a black and a white one and call them Salt and Pepper."

She placed the call, "Hello, can I please talk to Lacona? Oh, Okay. Maybe she could call me back. It's about adopting two kittens." Wilamina gave her phone number to the secretary, hung up and told Houston that Lacona hadn't shown up for work yet.

Noon time rolled around and Lacona had not returned Wilamina's call so she called the shelter again. This time Ruth, the secretary, said she still hadn't shown up and she didn't answer her home phone or cell. She added, "This is not like her at all. She's always been responsible and on time. She's the most on-time person I've ever worked for."

"Maybe Sammy would know what's goin' on. Have you called her?"

"No I haven't. You're good friends with Sammy, would you mind calling her and then let me know what you find out?"

"I'll call right now and get back to you," said Wilamina. She placed a call to Dr. Blackmore's office. No one answered. Her call went to the messaging service. She told Houston and they agreed that the doctor must have had an emergency. "I'll try again later today. I can wait one more day for my little balls of fluff."

Earlier that same morning.............

Lacona had received a call from some unknown woman asking her to please go immediately to a designated spot. She gave her directions, and told Lacona that she would find a badly injured small dog tied to a tree. The caller stated she needed to remain anonymous, that she was fearful for her own safety.

Lacona quickly drove to the area where she had been told she would find the dog. She called Dr. Blackmore's office as soon as she got to the location and found the injured and bloodied dog. She was in the process of telling the secretary that she was located on Blue Sky Road. While she was still giving directions, a shot rang out. Lacona dropped the phone and fell face down on the ground. She didn't move again.

Ruth was still connected and kept repeating, "Lacona, Lacona, what just happened? I heard a sound. Answer me. Can you hear me? Lacona answer me!" she screamed. She set the receiver down and ran to the back office and told Dr. Blackmore and Jackson what she had just heard on the phone. She gave them the directions that she'd been given before Lacona quit talking. The two men charged out the backdoor, jumped in the van and drove like madmen to the area relayed by Ruth.

It took them almost twenty minutes to find the road and within a minute they spotted Lacona's car. They flew out of their car yelling out to Lacona and quickly spotted her lying face down next to bloodied dog tied to a tree. Dr. Blackmore immediately checked her pulse, "She's alive, but her pulse is weak and her breathing is shallow. Jackson, dial 911 for an ambulance and then call the police!" he yelled.

The doctor turned her over very carefully and found a great deal of blood on her shirt and on the ground. He applied pressure over the wound and talked reassuringly to his unconscious friend, "I'm going to press down hard on your chest, Lacona. You're going to be okay. Help is on the way.

"Jackson, bring me a blanket and some sterile dressings. Her pulse is slow but slightly stronger. You're doing just fine, Lacona. Hang on dear."

He yelled again at Jackson, to bring some other items from the van. As soon as his assistant returned with the items the doctor stated, "I'm going to start an I.V. You will have to keep pressure on her chest to stop the flow of blood."

They both worked quickly and efficiently. They gently talked to their patient with encouraging words. The siren announced the arrival of an ambulance. The two paramedics immediately went to work. They had her on the gurney, in the ambulance and on the road to the hospital in minutes. The siren blasting the need for speed.

Two police cars arrived and after speaking with the doctor they began to tape off the crime scene. They told the doctor to go on back to his office and they'd catch up with him later.

The small, miserable dog started to whimper. The doctor picked up the pitiful creature, carried it back to his van. He quickly looked at the injuries and wrapped the young dog in a blanket. He told Jackson to drive them quickly back to the office. The doc needed to attend to the little patient. He spoke to the badly wounded animal softly using words of comfort and assurance.

"I'll call Sammy as soon as we get back to the office if she hasn't returned from the house-call she's on. Hopefully, by that time the hospital staff has had time to assess Lacona's condition. Jackson drove back to the office in record time. They arrived before Sammy had returned from the house-call.

Sammy had been on a follow-up visit to a client's home. Her job included making home visits to do follow-up care of some of the more seriously ill or injured patients that the doctor had recently treated.

Dr. Blackmore waited nervously for her to return to the office. He wanted to tell her face to face about her partner and drive her to the hospital.

In the meantime he had Ruth call Houston and Wilamina and clue them in about the apparent attempt on Lacona's life and ask them to meet the doctor and Sammy at the hospital.

A few minutes later, Sammy came in through the back door, "Hi guys, our little surgery patient is doing great and even his parents are gonna recover. Just a little humor for the troops."

Dr. Blackmore took Sammy by the hand and led her into his tiny office to give her the terrible news. Sammy immediately began to hyperventilate and stammer, "No, no, impossible. You have the wrong person. Why would you say such a thing. Hell, doc, you're supposed to be my friend."

"I am your friend and that's why I'm shaking your shoulders and loudly telling you to get in the car, I'm taking you to the hospital so we can see how Lacona is doing. You've got to hold it together for her sake." He led a zombie-like Sammy out the back and helped her into his car. Jackson followed them out to the doc's car and the doctor instructed him to call Dr. Cone, a retired veterinarian. "He will take care of the dog we just brought in and cover for me 'til I can come back. I'll call as soon as I have some information about Lacona's condition."

CHAPTER THIRTY-EIGHT

Sammy's eyes were wide open, not even blinking. She was breathing heavily and sat speechless in the doc's car until he stopped abruptly at the emergency entrance. He moved quickly to get out and ran to the passenger side to pull, with some force, to get Sammy out of her seat and into the hospital. Sammy appeared almost catatonic.

Houston and Wilamina arrived a few minutes before Dr. Blackmore. As soon as they spotted his car, they ran over and hugged a rigid Sammy. They told her that her partner was in surgery.

Sammy was so shaken up she was practically incoherent. It took the three friends to maneuver her into a chair and then again with some force, help her to sit down. Houston told her what she knew about why Lacona was where she was found. She related what Ruth had told her. "The phone call from some unknown woman reporting an injured and tied up dog. Lacona talked with Ruth about the call and where she was and the next sound Ruth heard was possibly the gun shot. She couldn't get Lacona on the phone again. After hearing that, Dr. Blackmore grabbed Jackson and drove to the spot and found Lacona bleeding and unconscious. The ambulance arrived and brought Lacona here. Now you know what we all know."

Dr. Blackmore added, "I spoke with the doctor by phone just before Lacona was taken into surgery. She has lost quite a bit of blood, but he feels her vitals are holding their own."

"Is she going to make it, Doc? asked Sammy pleadingly with her eyes, lips and chin trembling. "You've got blood on your clothes Doc, my God! That's **her** blood."

The doctor attempted to distract her, "Sammy, I have heard great things about the surgeon who is working on her. I believe she is going to recover. It may take a while, but with all of our support, your's particularly, she should be okay."

The two homicide detectives walked quietly up to the group and Detective Voss asked, "Any news yet?" wiping at her swollen eyes and wet cheeks.

"Not yet, Sasha," responded Wilamina. "She's still in surgery."

Detective Lorenzo glanced at Sammy, then directed his remarks to Dr. Blackmore, Houston and Wilamina. "The area where Lacona was found has been marked off as a crime scene. Fortunately, it rained last night and there were multiple visible tracks. Some of the tracks were from Lacona's car and your van, Doc, others were from the ambulance and the two patrol cars, but there was one other set that led off into the woods. There were footprints from the car to a spot near the shooting. Prints going back to the car. The car turned around and drove back to the main road. We have a very good set of prints from the suspected auto and possibly the suspect's footprints as well."

Sammy, roughly took hold of the detective's collar and her eyes widened. She blasted out, "Are you saying that someone shot her on purpose? Impossible! She's loved by everyone she knows. She's the kindest person on earth. Who? If something' happens to her, I don't want to see another sunrise."

Detective Lorenzo gently removed her hand from his shirt and held on to it. "It's too soon to know anything for sure, but we must cover every base, just in case."

Everyone eventually sat down in the recovery waiting room. Wilamina took off for the cafeteria and brought back coffee and sweet rolls for all. Sammy held her coffee in one hand and the roll in the other, both untouched. She appeared frozen in place. Anxiety, fear, confusion, and slow brewing rage hung like a dark threatening cloud hovering over the small group. The doctor's shirt and pants were covered in dried blood, Lacona's blood. Detective Lorenzo had gone back to his parked car and grabbed one of his sweatshirts and handed it to the doc. Blackmore mouthed, thank you, and put it on. He was relieved to cover-up the bloody reminder.

It was about two hours later, which felt like more than two days, when the surgeon, Dr. Hoyt came into the room. From his expressionless face you couldn't tell if he was bringing good news or bad news. He walked directly toward Sammy, who was still seated holding the untouched coffee and roll.

"Your partner is alive and resting quietly for now. The bullet did some extensive damage. At the moment she is stable and will be kept heavily sedated for the next twenty-four to forty-eight hours. The next few days will tell us more. We removed her spleen, repaired a tear in her right lung and will need to do more later. She will remain with us for some time. She will require more surgery to the stomach area in the next week, provided her recovery goes as well as planned. She is a young, healthy woman and I see no reason for her not to recover completely in time and with some rehab. The next forty-eight hours will let us know how she's going to do. She will remain in intensive care for as long as necessary.

"You may go and see her for a few minutes now and again later tonight. She will be kept sedated until tomorrow, to keep her comfortable and aid the healing process. Any questions?"

"Is she going to live? You must understand, she's got to live." Sammy's voice breaks.

"I believe if all goes as planned, she will be just fine, thanks to the emergency care rendered by Dr. Blackmore and the ambulance staff. There is going to be a long road of slow recovery and more surgery. Now Lacona's body, mind and spirit need to do their part. It takes a team all doing their best to bring about a favorable outcome. Looks like she has a great team on her side right here.

"Sammy, you can follow Nurse Rafael to take a peek at your partner."

Sammy walked shuffling her feet. She stumbled slightly and the nurse took her by the hand for support. Sammy was navigating strictly on auto pilot.

Right after Sammy left the room, Detective Lorenzo and his partner asked Houston and Wilamina to step outside with them. "We have some news about Chance's wife, Melody."

Houston spoke quickly to Dr. Blackmore, "Tell Sammy, we'll be right back. We need to speak with the detectives for a minute. Thanks for saving Lacona and being the kind of man that you are."

Outside the emergency doors, Detective Lorenzo informed the two investigators, "Mrs. Young has made a half-hearted suicide attempt. Another evaluation is scheduled and she's being placed on suicide watch. The staff report her as cunning and often times irrational and violently acting out. She yells profanities at the staff. When she makes a call she screams, swears and cries at the person on the other end."

Houston asked, "How is the charge of murder gonna play out? Will she have a trial or what will happen next? Surely, she can't ever go free. She may be crazy, but crazy as a fox. She planned the murder and then carried it out."

Sasha added, "Our court system does have some serious flaws, but I believe that justice happens more often than not. I understand that Chance and his son have moved to an apartment. I believe he plans to sell the house. I also heard he has filed for divorce. That woman certainly has torn up their lives, but more tragically, has ended the life of a lovely young woman. Jealousy is a powerful motivator for crime. But, in my humble opinion, mental illness is the true culprit. Melody's childhood sounded like a constant nightmare which apparently left her emotionally damaged.

"Now it's a waiting game with trials, appeals, sentencing and more appeals. I can't see her getting out for a long time. Her confession will definitely improve the prosecutor's case.

"Now our focus is solely on the perpetrator who shot Lacona. Lorenzo and I are going to give it all we've got right now. We have time to devote to finding the suspect. Murders or attempted murders are not plentiful in Whitefall, thank goodness."

CHAPTER THIRTY-NINE

Chance Young showed up, unannounced at the Salt and Pepper Agency. He was standing at the door when Wilamina unlocked it.

"Chance! You scared me. I'm glad to see you," she said cheerfully.

"Sorry about not calling first, but I found myself in your neighborhood and decided to see if you were open. Can I come in for a minute?"

"Of course. Is everything okay with you and Richard?"

"Sort of, well that's not completely true. I'm struggling and I thought I could get your and Miss Hayfield's opinion on something."

"Come with me, young man. I was just about to make breakfast for Tex and myself. Now I'll just make more for all of us. How about some great Southern cooking?

"That's real nice of you. I hate to be a bother. I'm really not very hungry. Maybe I could just have a cup of coffee?"

"No bother at all. Come on up to our place. You'll get hungry as soon as you smell my great cooking."

After Chance had time to swallow most every morsel on his plate and finished off the last roll on the platter and gulped down his coffee, he started to say something, but got all choked up. He blew his nose and began, "I think both Richard and I are having some problems with our feelings. Mel has called and talked to or I should say, screamed at both of us. She's making Richard feel real sad and even guilty for her being in the hospital and locked up. I'm so angry at her, sometimes I scare myself. The worst part is she's messing with Richard and it's tearing him up. He's so confused. I don't know what to say to him. I'm so powerfully lost with Charlene's death that I just don't want to be around without her. I know that's selfish 'cause I have a great son, but ...." he started to sob in earnest and couldn't finish his sentence.

Houston and Wilamina let him cry it out. They both pulled up their chairs right next to him. Houston laid her hands on his knees and Wilamina put her arms around his shoulders. When he was able to compose himself, he asked if they thought the Grief Clinic could help Richard and him.

Both women said an enthusiastic 'Yes!' at the same time. Houston added, "Try it for one or two sessions and decide for yourself. They also offer support groups for kids your son's age."

"Why not change your phone number?" asked Houston.

"I didn't want Richard to think we were completely abandoning his mother. Part of me does feels guilty for marrying her in the first place, but the worst is what happened to Charlene, because of me."

Wilamina asked if he wanted her to call Brooksie and set up an appointment?

"Sure. Why not. I've got to do something."

She dialed the number, asked for Brooksie and, waited briefly until she picked up. Wilamina explained why she called then handed the phone to Chance, "She wants to talk to you."

"Hello Brooksie, sorry to bother you." He was silent for a moment, apparently listening, then said, "That would be great. Thank you. We'll be there."

He hung up, smiled at his investigator friends and stated, "Richard and I have an appointment tonight at the clinic. I already feel better 'cause I'm doing something. You guys are the best, and Wilamina, you are the best cook! Thanks a million for everything. I'll let you know how we're both doing later. Thanks again."

After Chance left, Houston commented, "That Brooksie and the clinic staff are somethin' else. Do you think we'll ever be that good at helping others?"

"Sure thing, Tex. They have been doing it longer, but we're gonna catch up. We just helped Chance to get on the right track. Now let's get to work. We've got to work with our detective friends to find the creepy coward who shot Lacona."

"I have another idea, Willy. Let's find out what we can do for Lacona's shelter. I've also been thinkin' it might be a good thing for Sammy to stay with us until Lacona gets better. I don't like the idea of her being alone every night, not eating, just brooding and stressing. I worry about what Sammy will do if she finds the shooter first. How about it, partner?"

"Absolutely! I love both ideas. I'll call Ruth and run your ideas by her. Or should we just go and ask Sammy?"

Houston answered, "Let's go right now. If we're standing in front of her, it will make it harder for her to say no to us. I bet she'd be more comfortable with us. She can let out her anger better around her ex-jail friends. The good doctor and his wife have done so much for her. She might be afraid of shocking them if she starts spitting out the venom she feels for the shooter. I bet she needs to let it out. I would."

They arrived at the vet's office just as Ruth was unlocking the front door.

She looked up at the two, "I'm hoping you're bringing good news, it's just too damn early for any bad news."

Houston answered, "We want to ask Sammy if she would move in with us while Lacona is in the hospital. We also want to ask about helping at Lacona's animal shelter while she's recovering."

"My goodness," responded Ruth. "I'm beginning to wonder if I should have been making friends with ex-cons instead of with church goers. You guys are amazingly thoughtful."

"Sammy has spent the last two nights at the doctor's house, but your offer might be a better choice. She and the doc will be here shortly. They are making a quick trip to see Lacona.

"I'll get the coffee going and then give the shelter a call. A Mrs. Jarvis agreed to help out for a time. The dear Dr. Cone, a retired veterinarian, is doing all he can to fill in also."

A half-hour later, the doctor and Sammy could be heard coming in through the back door. Ruth asked them to come to the front, Wilamina greeted them both with a hug. "How is Lacona doing today?" she asked.

Sammy smiled, showing off most of her teeth, "She's talking, hurting and glad to be alive. Today the detectives plan to interview her. She's improving with every passing hour, so guess that means I'm going to make it, too."

Sammy let her friends know how much she appreciated their offer to bunk with them. She glanced over at the doc and he winked back at her. "After I see Lacona at noon, I can go and pick up my things and be at your place right after I visit Lacona again at 5. I wanted to spend nights there at her side, but the nurses talked me out of it. My boss has done so much for me and he and his wife deserve a rest." She winked back at the doc.

Ruth informed Houston and Wilamina that Mrs. Jarvis would be happy for any assistance and asked them to be at the shelter today at noon.

"Sounds like a plan," said Wilamina. "Maybe we can take home a few fluffy kittens. That would be helping the clinic, don't you think, Tex?"

"I think you're ready to be a mama to some little fluff balls. We'll have to stop and get some supplies for them on the way home. Somethin' tells me that Sammy won't be our only new roommate."

CHAPTER FORTY

Sammy moved into Houston and Wilamina's apartment that afternoon. After putting her things away she joined her friends for one of Wilamina's special meals. Sammy talked nonstop and her ex-cell mates listened attentively. While their ears and eyes were focused on the talker, their hands were busy gently petting the eight week old kittens. One was mostly white and the other all black, of course, named Salt and Pepper.

For the time being Sammy was finally talked out. Houston began to share their plan to work part time for two days at Lacona's shelter by feeding, walking, cleaning and answering phone calls. "We will do whatever Mrs. Jarvis or Dr. Cone need us to do. They know we run our own business, so if we have to leave to do investigative work, that will take priority. Did you hear that Dr. Cone is willing to work five days a week, until Lacona can return? He is a fine man. You know, since we've left Lancer's, I've met more fantastic men than I have in the first thirty-so years of my life. I thought most all men were lying pieces of crap, except for my brother, Lee, of course."

Sammy spoke up, "I just remembered, I forgot to ask you both somethin'. You remember the wounded dog that Lacona was trying to help, just before she was shot?"

Houston and Wilamina both nodded.

"The little guy is improving and he would improve a lot faster if he was out of the hospital cage. I'm gonna adopt him. Lacona asked about him and I know she would like for us to keep him. Can I bring him here at night? He'll sleep next to me. He's sort of like our kid. It's okay if you say no and I'll for sure understand." She tried to keep her face blank, but just couldn't keep the pleading expression from her eyes.

Houston responded, "We thought you'd never get around to asking us. We borrowed some special dog food from Ruth and made a quick trip to the pet store. Your little fellow needed his own toys and stuff. We got a dog carrier so you can take the little tyke back and forth from work to home."

"You guys are the greatest! Best friends I've ever had. Actually, the only real friends, except for the doc, of course and now Cona. Now that's sumpin'. My first real buddies I met in a f...ing prison. That'd make a great movie."

CHAPTER FORTY-ONE

It had been more than a week since someone had tried to murder Lacona. Detectives Lorenzo and Voss had been working overtime. There had been a murder that same week by a drunken, enraged husband. He stabbed his wife to death. So the homicide department was buzzing with paperwork, follow-up leads, interviews and crime scene work.

Detective Voss was the one to interview Lacona after she was released from the intensive care unit to the surgical recovery unit. The detective talked first with the nurses about Lacona. She was told that the patient was doing amazingly well. A spectacular bouquet of flowers had just been delivered to her room. She was also informed that Lacona's partner was visiting her right now.

"Hello Sammy and Lacona. Hope you don't mind if I ask you a few questions?" asked the detective. "Wow! Those flowers are magnificent."

Sammy responded, "The surgeon did a fantastic job. I just spoke with him and he said she is on the mend. Lacona has so many friends. I'm not surprised if one or more of them sent the flowers. There was a card, but it wasn't signed. The card said 'love hurts'. Neither of us can figure out who sent the flowers. I bet someone will eventually fess up. I'm gonna throw a big party when Lacona is released and feeling more like herself. There are so many people to thank for taking such good care of her. The doc told us that depending on how she progresses, she might be able to go home in a week or so, then return for daily physical therapy. She'll be needing to see the physical therapist for quite some time.

"I need to get myself to work, so I'll let you two talk. Bye, Lacona, see you tonight." Sammy kissed Lacona's forehead and gently touched her cheek.

The detective held the door open for Sammy and then spoke to Lacona, "I've got a few questions. Do you feel like talking to me right now?"

"Sure I do. I'm getting stronger every day. Ask away."

Detective Voss asked if Lacona knew of anyone who would want to harm her, anyone mad enough to do what they did. Lacona told her that she barely remembered what the voice on the phone sounded like. The voice was of some female sounding person. She tricked her into going to the place where she would find the abused, tied-up dog.

Detective Voss suggested that the person may have been disguising their voice. After some gentle prodding by the detective, Lacona remembered a lady who brought in an injured dog to the shelter several weeks back. She wanted to give the dog up and gave some story how the dog had come to be hurt. Lacona said she believed the lady was lying or covering up for someone. "When I asked her how the injuries happened, the lady grabbed for the frightened and badly injured pup and screamed at me. She yelled, "I'm taking him home! I thought you people were here to help."

"I called for another worker to help me with this very distraught woman. I refused to let the woman leave with the dog. I told her I was going to call the police if she didn't leave the dog with us. Luckily, I had her name and phone number and one of my quick thinking workers ran outside and wrote down the woman's license plate number and make of car.

"After she stormed out of the door, leaving the shaking dog in my arms, I notified the police department of a possible animal abuse case. Next, I drove the little fellow to Dr. Blackmore's office. A day later, he notified me that the dog had apparently been beaten with something heavy, maybe a bat. He also said the young dog was holding his own. He set the broken leg, stitched up his head and the deep cut on his back side. He believed, in time, the patient would heal completely, at least from the physical wounds. Sammy is keeping an eye on him and looking for a possible home for him. She named him Precious.

"Something else just popped into my head. That ladie's name was Sheri Winters. She had bruises on her arms and one on her face. I was so concerned about the dog, I forgot to ask her about her own marks. She may have also been abused and was afraid of the abuser. Maybe afraid he would find out she took the dog to a shelter. I hope I've been some help. I still feel a little groggy."

Detective Voss responded, "Would you mind if I called your office and asked for the worker who wrote down the car license plate numbers and any other information pertaining to Sheri Winters?"

"Please do. The worker's name is Susan. I know she'll be glad to help. We did file a police report, so your department may already have the information on file."

"You're right. I'll place a call right after I get into my car. You've been a big help. Now please rest. I'll talk to you later, Lacona. Thanks again."

The detective called her office from her car, spoke with Lorenzo and asked him to get the report. By the time she arrived at her desk, the car owner's name and address were on her desk. As soon as she saw the name, she blurted out, "Maybe there's a connection." Lorenzo looked at the report, the car belonged to Sheri and Ralph Winters. "So this Winters woman tried to relinquish an abused dog to Lacona's shelter and two weeks later an attempt was made on her life. Another abused dog is the bait and the Winters' car is involved. We need a warrant to get the tire prints from their car. Seems like a huge jump from dog abuse to attempted murder. I'll start checking more background information on the Winters. If God is on our side, the tire prints will match her car to the crime scene prints."

"I have a thought Lorenzo, we've been focused on people that Lacona may know, but what about people Sammy may know. She is far more apt to have a few enemies. I know first-hand that she pissed off a few inmates and guards at Lancer's. She never had trouble mouthing off if someone got her worked-up enough. I can ask my ex-cell mates if they know the Winters or know of them. Maybe something useful will turn up."

Lorenzo agreed, "You're right, why don't you do some checking with the warden and that Sharon Primm inmate. I think you trusted the night nurse as well, Mela something. They might have a few ideas. In the meantime, I'm going to follow up with Sheri and Ralph Winters. Let's hope this is a break for us. Let's you and I both pay them a visit as soon as we have more background info on them. We sure as hell don't want to spook them. Their car could have been stolen. I can quickly check to see if they made a complaint. We need the tire print identification yesterday! We can get a warrant after we've spoken with them. That is, if your gut instinct starts to twitch."

Sasha added, "The assistant warden, Malina and her muscle bound, moron for a husband could even be involved. I know they are both incarcerated, but that wouldn't necessarily stop them from getting involved in some way. I believe that Malina has a "long arm reach" into the underworld. She was one self-serving bitch. I'm going to make some phone calls. Maybe I could run this by Tex and Willy?"

"I'm going to be seeing Tex this evening. I could mention this to her and report back to you tomorrow."

"It seems that you two are getting along quite well. I've never seen Tex so up-beat, smiling every time I see her. You must be doing something right."

"Sasha, I find her amazing. Her standoffish demeanor is one way she protects herself. I'd like to get my hands on her mother's throat and all the asses that abused the two of them. I can't imagine what horrors she experienced, but she is a treasure, an uncut diamond.

"What about your private life, Sasha? I get the impression that you also put up a shield. You just do it differently than Tex does."

"Problem is, Sark, I'm not so sure I'd recognize a good guy even if I fell over him. I need someone who really gets me.'" She mumbled as she walked away from her partner, "He'd have to be an open book, a cellophane man. Someone I could see through, a man without secrets."

CHAPTER FORTY-TWO

The investigative agency's phone was unusually busy. They received a call from a Mrs. Ball. She sounded elderly and slightly confused. She asked if a detective could come to her house because she believed her housekeeper was stealing from her. Wilamina listened to the older lady's concerns, got her phone number and made an appointment to make a house call. Secondly, a Mr. and Mrs. Jensen called to ask for an appointment to talk about their son.

A short time later, Wilamina received a call from a woman claiming to be Mrs. Ball's housekeeper. She said it was important that she meet with the investigators before they saw Mrs. Ball. Wilamina hesitantly agreed and set a time several hours before the time they were to meet her employer, Mrs. Ball.

Meeting with housekeeper..........

"My name is Alicia Rains. I've been Mrs. Ball's housekeeper for close to eight years. Thanks for meeting with me. I thought it might be helpful if we were to talk before you see my dear employer."

"Could you tell us about yourself and how you came to be Mrs. Ball's housekeeper?"

Alicia responded in a sad tone, "Did she call you and say I've been stealing from her? Her son John hired me. He told me he was worried about his mother's forgetfulness. He shared with me that he had pancreatic cancer and his prognosis wasn't good. He felt it important to plan for his mother's care, in the event that he passed she would be taken care of.

"We talked many times about what the best plan would be. Eventually, he asked me if I would become her legal guardian after his death. She only had one older sister who passed away recently. John was a kind and a loving son. I'm a widow. My husband passed away nine years ago. My only living relative is an elderly cousin who lives in New York. Mrs. Ball has been my family for the past seven going on eight years.

"John and I came to an agreement. I worked for his mother for two weeks to see if she was comfortable with me. We liked each other right off the bat. We became good friends. She is my family and I love her. She's been more like a mother to me and certainly kinder than my own mother. Anyway, the lawyer set up the guardianship paper work so that when John died, everything was in order.

"When he died, she took it real hard. She's more forgetful now and there are times she doesn't remember that John is gone. She talks about him coming to see her. She's always been a sweet, kind, lady, but she's slowly disappearing mentally. So far, I've been able to take good care of her. I live in her home. I cook, clean, drive her to doctor's appointments and assist her with basic needs. We regularly drive to the beach. I take chairs so we can sit and watch the ocean waves. She loves the ocean.

"It's breaking my heart to see her become afraid of me. And now it seems she believes I'm stealing from her. I don't know what to do to put her mind at ease. Her doctor told me that paranoia can be a characteristic of Alzheimers. He also said that it oftentimes lessens with time.

"If you need to see my guardianship papers, I can give you the lawyer's phone number and you can see them for yourselves."

Houston and Wilamina glanced at each other. Wilamina said, "I'm so sorry for the both of you. Must be terrible to care for someone, grow close and then have to watch them mentally slip away."

Houston added, "Maybe the three of us could talk with her attorney. He might have some ideas on how to help her. I've heard about support groups for all kinds of medical problems. Why don't you make an appointment for all of us? Most anytime will work for us."

"I'll do just that. I know she is expecting you this morning because she told me she had friends coming this morning. She needs to have you show up. I won't stay in the room while you talk. Hopefully I will have made an appointment with the lawyer before your visit is over."

"Thanks Alicia. See you at her house in an hour."

After Alicia left their office, Houston said, "Willy, would you mind going alone to talk with Mrs. Ball? I'll take on the meeting with Mr. & Mrs. Jensen. They are coming here without their son. I'm glad to have business, but our schedule is getting squeezed. We're also helping out with the shelter and working on Lacona's case. I'm not complaining, mind you, just want to do a good job."

"No problem, Tex. Before I go how about I call our ex-warden and see if she's heard any jailhouse gossip about "Malina, the Terrible." We know she's been incarcerated in another state, but maybe she's working on payback. She's someone who would hold on to a grudge forever. We need to do something."

Houston suggested, "How about we visit the warden and Sharon. We can get another visit in and find out if they've heard any scuttlebutt. Maybe someone has it in for Sammy, so to get back at her, they hurt the one she loves? That makes me think about the note on the flowers that Lacona received, it said, 'love hurts.' Seems like a strange thing to say to someone lying in a hospital bed."

"Yes, Tex, that does sound like a strange note to send a patient. But I like your idea about a visit. It's always a pleasure to see our good friends, face to face. I'll make the call."

Later that morning..............

Wilamina made the visit to Mrs. Ball, as agreed. Alicia opened the door and greeted her. "Please come in and have a seat in the living room. I'll go tell Mrs. Ball you're here."

Wilamina nodded and gave Alicia a wink of conspiracy.

"Hello, Mrs. Ball. My name is Wilamina Robinson. I'm the investigator you spoke to on the phone."

"You're a black lady!"

"Yes'm. I was born this color. Would you like to sit down and tell me what has been upsetting you."

"Oh yes, let's sit and talk. I've never had a black lady in my house before."

"Well then, ma'am, maybe it's time you did. I'm pleased to be the very first black visitor to your fine home."

They both sat down and Wilamina began, "You have a very nice living room, Mrs. Ball."

"Thank you, my dear. I've lived here most of my life with my husband. Can't remember when he died, but it must have been a long time ago. My son would remember the date."

"Would you like to tell me about your housekeeper and what you believe she has stolen?"

"Mrs. Rains has worked for me a long time." She stopped and looked around the room, staring at nothing in particular, then went on, "I don't know why she's taking my things like my special broach, a tea set and even my glasses. Why would she want my glasses?"

"Have you asked her about these missing items?"

"Why? She would just deny it. I'm an old woman and I can't be having her stealing from me. Just last week, I found her holding my check book. She told me she was simply paying my bills. My son pays the bills. She can't fool me. What are you going to do about this terrible business, Miss uh........."

"Miss Robinson, but you can call me Wilamina, if you want to.

"Wilamina, that's a pretty name. You don't look like a detective. Shouldn't you be wearing a uniform?"

"No ma'am. My partner and me, we are investigators, not policewomen. Sometimes we work with the police department on certain cases. I have a question for you. How about some time this week, I bring along a police person and the four of us talk with your housekeeper? Perhaps we can get this problem of missing articles straightened out."

"That sounds okay. The police will get to the bottom of this. What if Alicia won't tell the truth?"

"The police have their ways of getting to the truth. Can you tell me what your housekeeper does for you?"

"Yes. She cooks. She's a very good cook and she keeps the place looking nice."

"I understand she takes you to the beach and you sit and watch the waves. She must be a very thoughtful person."

"Oh yes, she is. I love the ocean. She does too. She helps me take a shower and washes my hair for me. I don't know what I'd do without her. I'm getting tired now, would you call Alicia for me. She's in the kitchen."

"Certainly. You rest yourself, I'll be right back."

Wilamina got up and walked to where she figured the kitchen would be. When she found it, Alicia was mixing dough on a floured board. "Alicia, she says she tired and asked me to fetch you. I'm going to come back in a few days, with a friend of mine, a police lady. I think Mrs. Balls' doctor and lawyer need to be made aware of her confusion. A police uniform may be of some help. I don't know for sure, but I'm all for calling in anyone that could put her mind at ease. I'm going to say good-bye to her and then call you and let you know when Detective Voss can meet me here."

When Wilamina walked back into the living room, Mrs. Ball looked startled. She stammered, "What do you want?"

"Mrs. Ball, I'm Wilamina, the investigator. We've been talking for a while."

"Oh yes, of course. Did you know my son is very ill? I think he said, it's cancer. I'm so worried about him. Where is Alicia?"

"I'm right her, dear. I've brought you some hot tea. After you drink this perhaps you'd like to lie down for a short nap?"

"Yes. That would be lovely."

"Bye for now Mrs. Ball," said Wilamina. "Don't you worry your sweet head anymore. We're gonna get this all figured out and make sure you're well taken care of."

Alicia walked Wilamina to the door and they agreed to talk soon about options for caring for Mrs. Ball. "Alicia, I'm glad she has you to watch over her, for now. Her world is very foggy right now. I'm gonna say some prayers for her."

CHAPTER FORTY-THREE

While all the time Wilamina was at Mrs. Ball home, Houston was in the office interviewing Mr. and Mrs. Jensen. They made the appointment in order to discuss their concerns about their seventeen year old son, Roy.

Mr. Jensen began by saying, Roy hasn't been acting himself for about three, maybe four months. Would you agree with that, Macy?"

"Yes Ken, that sounds right."

"He spends much of his time in his room. He used to share his thoughts and give us a run down on his day most every evening, but no more. His grades have dropped down to C's, even a D in gym. He's always loved going out for sports, but he seems to have lost interest. In the morning he used to wear his pajama bottoms to the breakfast table. Now he is fully dressed before he leaves his room. Even his appetite has changed. He's always been well-liked and has many friends, but he doesn't seem to want to have anything to do with them anymore."

At this point in the conversation, Mrs. Jensen began to cry softly. Her husband put his arm around her and gave her his handkerchief.

"My wife is afraid he is taking drugs. We asked him about drugs and he got angry and said 'no way,' and stormed off to his room and refused dinner. We met with one of his favorite teachers and he said he's tried to talk to Roy, but with no luck. The teacher told us the school is having a drug problem. Several kids have been expelled for bringing drugs to school. Last week, when Roy was at school, Macy and I went through his room with a fine tooth comb. We didn't find anything. We felt terrible about doing it, but were relieved to find nothing. What can we do to help him without losing his trust?"

"Does he know that you've come to see me?" asked Houston.

"No ma'am. We're afraid to go to the police for fear of getting him into more trouble. There's counseling service offered at his school, but we are trying to protect his privacy and I doubt he'd be willing to go anyway. Maybe you can do some investigating without Roy knowing. We hate to be so sneaky, but we're desperate. He's a great kid, popular with everyone who knows him. Girls chase him and the guys seek his companionship. We just want him happy and productive again."

Houston asked for Roy's school schedule and other questions about times, places and so forth. "I'm gonna talk with my partner today. We'll try to come up with some sort of plan. I'll need a way to get in touch with one of you without Roy's knowledge. I'll get some kind of report back to you at the end of this week. This is Monday so you can expect to hear from either one of us by Friday."

Mrs. Jensen opened her purse and retrieved her wallet and handed two recent photos of Roy to Houston. One was a full face shot and the other was him standing and dressed in his track uniform.

Mr. Jensen asked about fees and was told about the hourly rate and the extras. Houston told them not to worry about the expenses because she and her partner were very considerate of their client's pocketbooks. She explained about the itemized statement they would receive.

"I understand how tight money is for most people. I also know you are worried, but the teen years can be difficult for both the teen and the parents. Me and my partner we'll do our best to help you to figure out what's changing your son's behavior."

Later that day...............

Wilamina told her partner how the interview with Mrs. Ball and Alicia went. "The poor dear is so confused. I left her for a few minutes and when I returned, she didn't recognize me. I think it would be best to meet with the lawyer, her doctor and Sasha, in uniform. Alicia needs to be present as well. The five of us should be able to figure out what would be best for Mrs. Ball and for Alicia.

"If it's okay with you, I'm gonna set up an appointment for all of us somewhere. Maybe here at our office, someone else's office or even at Mrs. Ball's home."

"Sounds good to me, Willy. So you don't think there is any hanky-panky going on with the housekeeper?"

"Absolutely not. The dear old lady's mind is slippin'. It's so sad to see how others suffer when one's mind begins to disappear. Her housekeeper is very kind and is doing a great job of taking care of everything. She is losing her good friend and it's breaking her heart.

"How did your morning go with the Jensens?"

"Willy, we've got to put our heads together and come up with a way to check out their son, without him knowing. Sounds like he's been one great kid, but for the past several months he's a changed son."

"My thought is that we need to observe him before, during and after school. We're gonna have to figure out how to do that. There is a teacher at the school that might be able to help us. He's already tried talking with Roy, with no luck. I'd like to be parked at his school to watch him, when he gets out today. Can you do that with me?"

"Sure. I'll make appointments for Mrs. Ball's case and that will fit in between the times we need to be watching the Jensen's son.

CHAPTER FORTY-FOUR

School parking area...............

Houston found a good place to park at the edge of the parking area. They could see the front of the school building and the entire parking lot. She showed Wilamina the pictures of Roy Jensen. They both pulled out their binoculars and made ready to wait for the students to pile out of the main front doors.

Wilamina noticed four guys waiting across the street. "Tex, look at those fellows over there. They look too old to still be in high school. They smell like trouble and look more like gang members than students."

"You're right. They look out of place here. They're looking to score, the assholes. If they're not dealing in drugs, I'll eat my hat."

The school doors opened and a throng of loud teenagers poured out on to the sidewalk and into the parking lot.

"There he is. He's that one in the Levi's without all the holes. What's the matter with these kids today, dressing like poor folks, like the homeless have to, but don't want to?" expressed Wilamina.

"I think our boy is headed for his car and look there, those four jerks are moving towards him."

Roy was talking with two clean cut looking students, but when the two boys saw the four rough looking guys head towards them, they turned and walked the other way. Roy started to walk faster toward the parked cars, when one of the big, nasty looking guys jumped in front of him and grabbed Roy by his shoulders. Roy froze and the other three then placed themselves in a circle around him. Some of the students that were headed for their own rides, kept right on walking and seemed to give the strangers a wide berth.

"Okay Willy, you ready to put our fighting skills to the test? I say we walk right over to Roy and stand with him. Let's just see what those scum bags do. Keep the cell phone ready to punch in 911."

"I'm ready, willin' and shakin'. Let's go."

They moved quickly over to where Roy was surrounded and Houston shouted, "Hey Roy, what the hell you doin'? I thought we was to meet up with you?" She didn't give him time to respond. They just walked right up to him, pushed one of the unkempt bullys to the side. Wilamina followed her example and also pushed. Then they took hold of Roy's arms and led him back to the front of the school.

Roy didn't resist their pulling him along. His eyes were as big as grapefruits, and his expression was one of disbelief.

"Roy, we're taking you into the school. Just keep walking and we'll explain what's happening once we're inside." Roy remained speechless but did as he was told.

Once inside, Houston said in her toughest voice, "Now young man, let's go sit on that bench over there and you tell us what's going on with those thugs. My name is Houston Hayfied and this here is my partner, Wilamina Robinson. We are owners of an investigative agency and we been hired to find out what kind of trouble you've gotten yourself into."

Roy turned pale and kept staring at the two women. "I don't know what to say. Is this some kind of trick? Maybe you're both part of their group."

"Tell you what, Roy. I can understand you are confused and not too trusting right now. We three are going to march into the principal's office and get this all straighten out."

That is exactly what they did. They introduced themselves to the principal and explained why they were involved. Roy then tearfully related his story how he had been approached by those four guys about five months ago. "At first it was just one guy who said he'd been watching me and was impressed with my running track record. He went on to say that he noticed how popular I was and wondered if I'd be interested in making some easy money. I told him I didn't have any extra time and thanked him and walked off.

"The same guys came back about a month later. The biggest one of the bunch came back again with another guy and they walked me back to my car. They were friendly and polite and invited me and some of my friends to a party they were having with a live band. They gave me the address and suggested we all just come for a few hours and see if everyone has a good time. They said there would be no strings attached. The band was great and lots of fun could be had by all.

"I told some of my friends, both guys and girls, about the party and the live music and about ten or so agreed to go. We did go. The band was fair. There was tons of food and alcohol. Several of my buddies got wasted, so did a few of the girls. A couple left the party shortly after we got there. They said they were uncomfortable. I was too, but I didn't want to leave my friends who had stayed. It was my invitation that got them there. I sort of felt responsible.

"The party got wilder and wilder and finally I was able to convince most of my friends that it was time to leave. We all came in separate cars. Two guys were too drunk to drive so I made them leave their cars. We piled into the two cars left. Mary was sober so she drove three of the girls home and I drove the four guys back to Tom's house. His parents weren't home so they had time to sober up. Two of the girls and one guy stayed at the party.

"Those same thugs showed up at school a few weeks later and cornered me. They said the party was a huge success and they were throwing another one. They wanted me to bring more kids. I said no way. They took turns beating me in my stomach and my back. They never hit me in the face, guess they didn't want the bruises to show.

"I've been able to avoid them until today. Maybe they just left me alone for the time being. I was so ashamed for having asked my friends to go to that horrible party. Some of them really got in trouble. Sally, one of the girls who stayed at the party, got into some drugs. She's been having problems ever since.

"Those guys are peddling drugs and whatever crap they can sell. I don't know how to make up for what I did, inviting my friends to go to that horrible bash. This is going to break my mother's heart and my dad will be so disappointed in me." He wiped his cheeks and nose as his head dropped into his hands.

The principal, his secretary, Houston and Wilamina remained silent throughout Roy's story.

Mr. Marshall the principal, eventually responded, "I'm practically speechless, enraged and saddened, at the same time. I'm not angry at you Roy, but at myself for not noticing what was going on right under my big nose. I feel like I've done a very poor job of letting my students know they can come to me with their difficulties. I'm setting up a meeting with the teachers first thing tomorrow, followed by a program for the entire student body with their parents. Roy, can you identify the four criminals for the police?"

"Yes sir, but I'm afraid for my parents, if I do."

"Mr. Marshall, I have another suggestion," stated Houston. "Miss Robinson and me, we can identify those thugs. In fact, my partner was quick enough to get their pictures on her cell phone. We have friends at the police station and they can probably tell us the best way to handle those four punks and whoever else is involved."

"Great idea Miss Hayfied. Thank God Roy's parents brought you their concerns about their fine son. Will you notify the police today and let me know what the next step is?"

"My partner will call the department right now to see if someone could come now and get this all started."

Wilamina did just that and added that she also needed to let Roy's parents know what was going on and to tell them he would be home later. Tears started down Roy's cheeks again, "Boy, I sure screwed up. Hope someday they can be proud of me again."

CHAPTER FORTY-FIVE

Houston paced around and around the kitchen table.

"You workin' yourself up to saying somethin'?" questioned Wilamina.

"Willy, I'm not so good at talking' the feelin' talk. I can sure spout off when I'm pissed. I can butt myself right up into someone's face and tell'm how mad I am. Mom wasn't much for teaching the sweet ways of talking. I don't know if she was ever okay in the head. Maybe the drugs and booze messed up her brain or maybe she needed that stuff 'cause she wasn't born right. My point is, you're the first person I've spent any amount of time with who could talk from the heart. Maybe 'cause you had a black mother who sang to you. I can't seem to make nice with the words. I'm so different from you. I'd like to be more like you, easy for you to hug anyone and say soft words."

"Tex, you're an honest, street smart friend, the best kind of friend. Your face, your eyes, talk for your heart, sister. I know you love me 'cause you treat me good. You'd take on the world for people you care about. I trust you with my life, anytime, anywhere. You're the best kind of friend."

"Maybe I could go with you to church, one time. Not for all that Jesus talk, but for the singing. Your wailing really moves me, can't put that feeling into words. Somethin' just stirs inside of me. I don't feel natural using gushy words."

"How about you come with me this Sunday. I promise, you won't be thrown into a nearby river with the reverend screeching, 'Jesus saves.' You can sit in the way back and walk out anytime. I'm in the choir so I'll be up front, wailing."

"I'll think about it and let you know Sunday morning."

"How are you and the detective gettin' along?"

"I'm not sure. He tells me how wonderful I am. A lot! I just can't make myself say those kind of things to him. Last night he used that love word and I about peed on myself. First thing I wanted to do was to run away. Those words scared the hell out of me. I was afraid I was going to throw up.

"I've mentioned to you that long ago when I was a little girl, some of mom's boyfriends and her pimp would mess with me. The sick bastards would whisper in my ear they loved me and what they were doing to me was because they loved me. Can't seem to stop those voices when Sark and I are fooling around.

"I'm a mess. He deserves someone in better shape. Do you think I'm screwed up for life?"

"Tex, I've seen how Sark looks at you. He knows about your loving heart, your brain, and your beautiful body and soul. That includes all body parts. What we've got between our legs is a gift to be shared with someone special. Sex is to be enjoyed by both, a shared pleasure. Your man may want to hear the love word, and he deserves to. If you told him the story you just shared with me about being messed with as a little girl, he could surprise you with his response. Your detective is a patient and wise man. I don't believe he's going anywhere without you. He's waited a long time just to date you. I bet he's willing to wait a long time to hear the love talk. The past is over, now it's our turn and our time."

"Thanks Willy, I'll chew over what you've said. I'll go to your church this Sunday, but don't be thinkin' it's gonna become a habit. Speaking of men, how are you and Stoney gettin' along?"

"He's one fine man, in every way," she emphasized the "every way," and rolled her eyes. "He owns a couple of acres just a few miles outside of town. The land has a small view of the ocean. He's set on building a house and a barn like thing, to hold equipment and stuff. He's got the foundation laid out. He asked me if I like the plans, and if I think five bedrooms would be enough. Hope he's not hoping for a dozen kids. I'm okay with some, but not a mob. He's hard working, honest and kind. You should see his muscles. He's all man.

"I've been holding off, you know, doing the nasty, but I don't want to keep on waiting. This being a lady is killing me. We have a date for Friday night. He wants to take me someplace special. He stuttered and stammered when he said we should dress nice. I love his shy way of askin' or tellin' me things."

"Willy, you're doing okay. Be yourself. This romantic stuff comes easily for you. I don't believe sex is a problem for you or for me, it's all the words that lead up to it that I don't like. Guess I'm gonna have to try harder. Maybe you could say a prayer for me when you're doing all your praying for half the population."

"Tex, I've been saying special prayers for you since before we left Lancer's cement walls.

"The Jensen's called us earlier, but I forgot to tell you. They're all doing just fine. They are really a great family. Roy is gonna take some boxing lessons and even some kick boxing at the same time. His dad is taking the boxing with him. Warms the heart so see a lovin' family in action."

CHAPTER FORTY-SIX

Hospital visit..............

"Good morning Cona, you're starting to look more like yourself. Your color is better. How'ya feeling?

"Much better Sammy, I think I'm going to be released soon. I need to get back to the animals and my responsibilities. This laying around isn't my idea of a good life. How are you doing?"

"I'm great, now that you are doing better. I have two surprises for you. First one, you asked about the little dog that you went to help when you got shot. I felt he was meant to become our first pet together. I'm staying with Tex and Willy right now, temporarily. They have an extra bedroom and invited me to stay with them and they were happy to let Spirit stay with me at night. Spirit goes to work with me during the day. He loves everybody and even tries to cheer up the other patients. One of the 'dog patients' Spirit has really warmed up to, happens to be the abused dog that a very upset woman wanted to leave at the shelter then changed her mind and you wouldn't let her take the dog away. Well that little guy is also recovering nicely and Doc says he can leave the hospital soon. We named him Precious. So, if it's okay with you we got ourselves our first and second pets. Right now I can only take Spirit on my house calls. He's just like you Cona, he loves everybody and they love him back. I've been calling him Spirit but you can name him whatever you want. Precious needs more time to learn to trust humans again."

Lacona's sweet face was bathed in tears of joy. "Oh Sammy, those are perfect names for both. You always amaze me with your thoughtfulness and tender heart. Both dogs are the best gifts ever, next to you, of course."

Sammy sat on the edge of the bed, stroking her partner's face and drying her tears with her hand. "Cona, when I thought that you might not make it, I knew I wouldn't either. I've never felt such feelings for another person in my entire life. I've loved my dogs, but my feelings for you are different. When my dear pets were tortured and murdered I felt only rage, some sadness, but mostly rage and violent hate. When you were close to dying, I was only thinking about how to join you. I didn't think that way when my dogs died."

Lacona took hold of Sammy's hands and looked deeply into her soul and said, "We have found love, and I believe with all my heart, that love is eternal. So even If I were to go first, you would never be without my love. Invisible yes, but just the same, real.

"I'm so excited about our first pets together and I bet they'll only be the first of many. I can't wait to see Spirit and Precious."

"I'm going to talk to the real estate person about maybe making an offer on the place we've been looking at. The one with a few acres. Hopefully, before long we will be making monthly payments on our very own home.

"Cona, do you have any idea who might have done this to you?"

"Not a clue. Maybe it was someone suffering from a mental illness. I have no explanation, only questions."

CHAPTER FORTY-SEVEN

Detective Voss talked with Sammy and asked her if she knew of anyone who might have it in for her.

"Sure as hell. There's Louny, my ex. I'm probably on the top of her list of people she hates. She's for sure second on my list and Lacona's shooter is number one on my list. I hate that piece of crap, Louny. Wish I'd never met up with her. Why are you asking about her? You know she's paralyzed. She's in a fucking wheelchair, that I put her in. I don't know where she's living and I don't want to know. We've had no contact since my trial. She was there, looking pitiful in her wheelchair. I saw her lookin' at me with those sick, mean eyes, filled with cruelty. Whenever I looked around in the court room, there she was staring at me with those pinched up lips. All I saw were my three loving dogs, all bloodied, broken and dying. They were innocent and always gentle with her. How could she do it? I'll never get over it, how anybody can hurt the innocent and helpless is beyond me.

"Louny was seated in her wheelchair when she heard the judge sentence me to Lancer's. I watched her smile, her eyes laughing when they took me away to prison. She couldn't know about my early release, could she? I thought there were rules about confidentiality. The good Warden James and her staff wouldn't say anything, would they? That bitch, Malina, the assistant warden, and the over-sexed, drug selling doctor were sent to different prisons, not Lancer's. Are you thinking they could possibly be involved?

"You're not thinking that Lacona was targeted by Louny, are you? For Christ sake, she can't even walk."

"That may be true, but she could have hired someone to do the deed. Look Sammy, this is all about gathering information, separating facts from fiction. I'm going to do some checking around. For your information all victims have the right to know a release date. My department is going to follow through with every lead and every possibility, till we find the shooter."

Sammny offered to do some checking herself, which Sasha said was not such a good idea. "You could mess up our chances of finding the perpetrator by letting the wrong people know they were being investigated. Let us do our job. Do not try to find Louny or have any contact with her. Bad guys start running and hiding when cops or others start snooping around them. Promise me you'll not do anything to jeopardize the investigation. If you put your nose in, you may be putting Lacona and yourself in harm's way. I'm asking you to stay clear of the ongoing investigation. I'm asking you as your friend and as a cop."

"Not fair using our friendship, but I promise to stay in the background and let you guys do your job. If you promise to let me know what's happening and to keep Lacona safe."

"We've had your partner under observation since she was admitted to the hospital. Once she's released, that's another story. Lacona, you and your friends need to keep your eyes open and be on guard every moment, until we have bagged the predator. I will keep you informed of any progress or whatever is going on. Now if you think of anything else call me or Lorenzo. You can always leave a message and we'll return it quickly. We good?"

"Yeah. For a retired ho you make a pretty good cop. Thanks for caring and watching over my Cona. Bye Sas."

"Sammy, remember what you learned in Sharon's program at Lancer's? Do you remember when you were asked if you could have made a better choice when you nearly beat Louny to death? Do you remember what you said?"

"Yeah. I remember. I said, I should've walked away from that rotten piece of garbage and never looked back. In fact, I should've run away as fast as my big feet could take me."

"Sounds to me like that would have been the better choice. Bye, Sammy."

Back at the precinct...............

"Hi partner," said Detective Lorenzo. "You learn anything helpful from Sammy?"

"Lorenzo, I've got a gut feeling about her ex-partner, Louny Robbins. When Sammy and I were sharing a cell in Lancer's, she described her ex-partner as manipulative, aggressively hostile and diagnosed as bi-polar. She refused to take her medications regularly and when she didn't she became mean as a caged cat. She tortured Sammy's three beloved dogs, killing two and the third one had to be euthanized because of the severity of his injuries. A person capable of that could definitely pull off other violent crimes.

"Think about it, Louny partially paralyzed from a beating by Sammy, finds out that her partner has been released from prison early. Then discovers Sammy has a new love in her life. She could be twisted with hate for the one who put her in a wheelchair. Maybe enraged and hires someone to hurt Sammy back by killing the new girlfriend. What's your opinion on the possibility of the ex orchestrating this payback shooting?"

"Sounds possible, Sasha. We've got access to a great data bank, start feeding it your questions. I'll work on the Winter's background. Maybe there is a connection between Sammy,

Lacona and them. Mustn't forget to be careful not to raise their awareness of our possible interest. Wouldn't help if they knew they were on our radar. Do you think Sammy can be quiet about all this?"

Detective Voss answered, raising her eyebrows and shrugging her shoulders, "I made her promise, but she's close to the edge of wanting to get her hands on the shooter. Controlling her temper is not one of her strong suits. Her main concern is the safety of Lacona. Seems like Dr. Blackmore and her dogs were the only ones who treated her decently, until Lacona showed up.

"It's seems so strange to me that I feel so close to three women I met in prison. Life is so odd. Relationships are so complicated and remain a mystery to me. I hate admitting this again, but I thought I was a better person than the inmates, when my undercover work began in Lancer's. I've learned how wrong I was. I've had my share of the good life, plenty of everything. They had mostly pain of all sorts, abandonment, violence, betrayal, torture, poverty and neglect. Look at what terrific women they are now. They may be the best friends I've ever had. Who'd think it?"

"I think you're selling yourself mighty short. See you later, partner. Just for the record, I consider you a good friend and hope you feel the same way about me."

"Thanks Sark. I do. Considering you're a man and my track record isn't great with men. Later, friend."

CHAPTER FORTY-EIGHT

Lunch date with Jesse Rickels..........

"This get-together is way overdue, but I'm glad we finally made it," said Mrs. Jessie Rickels. She had a big smile and shook hands, with a firm grip, with Houston. She then moved her hands to shake Wilamina's, who ignored the outstretched hand and gave the famous Wilamina bear hug instead.

Jessie added, "Wilamina, Hunt told me about your great hugging. I'll be happy to tell him now that I too have been the fortunate recipient of your strong arms. I understand you've both spent some undeserved time in our local prison. What do you think of prison life? If you don't mind discussing it with me. I have some strong opinions regarding the negative results caused by the incarceration for the mentally ill, addicts, the severely abused and those falsely sentenced."

"I don't mind at all," replied Houston. "My first reaction to my first day of incarceration was pure terror, then anger followed by embarrassment. I became a number that day, no longer a human being. I thought I'd probably die inside those walls. Some of the guards were mean, even sadistic and the other inmates looked like a bunch of hungry wolves. Luckily, there was a good warden, but a rotten assistant. If it hadn't been for the warden, a few other inmates, Sharon Primm and a handful of decent employees, I'd never have made it out alive. I'd either be done in by another inmate or by one of the sicko employees.

"Did I give you too much information, Jessie?"

"Not at all, Houston. You've shown me the ugly world faced by many prisoners every day. Prisons are meant to keep the out of control humans away from the general population. In my humble opinion, I suspect that some good guys falsely imprisoned turn into bad guys. The mentally ill are not bad, they're sick. Sick people need to receive help, not punishment. Prisons do a good job of teaching the lost how to become more lost and the violent to become more violent. They can permanently squash all hope from the very ones who most need hope. Sorry I'm on my soap box. A bad habit of mine, which Hunt is always telling me to step down off it. He says, talking does little, it's action that counts."

"Your husband is a good man, Jessie," added Wilamina. "He was very kind to us from the first time we met him. I felt like Tex did, when they took me from the courtroom to jail in handcuffs. I was so ashamed of myself for having to be taken away restrained, in tears, in front of my brother. He was sobbing. Broke my heart. I couldn't even pray, 'cause I didn't want Jesus to see me like that. Sounds stupid now, but the first day inside Lancer's when my clothes were taken away and me standing naked and being washed down like some filthy animal, I thought I was gonna die. I just didn't know when or how, but for sure I was gonna die.

"Sharon's program changed everything and so did Mr. Lagunta. They both saved my fine ass. There are some who need to be locked up 'cause they're just mean and don't give a shit about anybody. They're the ones who've lost all hope. Those folks who caused misery for others on purpose and repeatedly belong locked up for the safety of everyone.

"The folks with head sickness, they don't do mischief on purpose. Like you said, Jessie, they need help not punishment. Punishment never works but rehabilitation might."

Houston asked Jessie, "How'd you get so interested in prisons, the individuals incarcerated and private investigating?"

"I'll give you the short version because it would take a week to give you all the details. My sister was murdered ten years ago. She was an addict. She took most any drug she could swallow, snort or inject. Her addiction began with the legitimate need for pain relief. Her crap of a husband beat her frequently. The last time it happened when he was drunk and enraged. He broke her back. Hence, the pain pills which then became a downhill battle against any and all drugs, legal or illegal. Come to find out, after her death, the abusing husband furnished her the illegal dope. He was a dealer and her supplier.

"To go on, she went missing, her body was found three weeks after she'd been murdered, beaten and unrecognizable. The dentist was able to identify her only by her dental records.

"The police did all they could, considering their shortness of manpower, money and motivation. Murdered drug addicts are not high on the list for most law enforcement agencies, as far as solving who done it. Court justice leaves a lot to be desired. A year after her death, there was still no real evidence or suspects. Her case was put on the back burners.

"That's when I decided if the murderer was going to be caught I'd better get to work. I always suspected her husband, but he supposedly had an airtight alibi. So I quit my day job. I was an accountant working for a large firm. Hunt thought I'd gone crazy, but he supported and understood what I felt I had to do. He became my investigative partner. He was an electrician and a part time computer salesman. Eventually, he quit both jobs and together we started the agency. We've never looked back.

"It took us almost a year of long hours and almost no days off, but we found my sister's killer. He's sitting in a cell right now, twenty-three hours a day in isolation, seven days a week. It was as I had felt all along, her abusive husband. He beat her, cut her throat and let her bleed to death. His cousin and one of his drug supplying buddies, helped him dispose of her body. Those two are also calling prison their home.

"So what started as a family's unsolved crime has become our family's life work. Seeing that piece of crap behind bars helped me with my grief for my sister. Channeling one's anger on a useful project is a good way to get over the hurt and sorrow of a loved one's terrible life and death."

Wilamina commented, "Seems like we have ourselves another sister, Tex."

"Sure does, Willy. Maybe we're forming some kind of been -there-done- that kind of team. Jessie, maybe you have some ideas that could help us figure out who tried to kill Lacona, a friend of our friend, Sammy?"

Houston brought Jessie up to date with everything they knew about the attempt so far. Jessie said she'd talk it over with Hunt and believed they might be able to come up with some fresh ideas.

The new friends chatted a while longer and agreed to talk soon.

Jessie said when parting, "Sounds like your friend Sammy has more possible enemies then does her friend, Lacona." She said she'd focus on people in Sammy's life.

"Thanks, Jessie. We'll talk with you soon. Say hi to Hunt for us."

CHAPTER FORTY-NINE

"I think we need to do some spy work on Sammy's ex-girlfriend, Louny Robbins. Sammy gave me their old apartment address so maybe we could drive by and do some sniffing around. We may need to spend all day sitting and watching. What'a you think, Willy?"

"I agree partner. We need to start somewhere. We could check with some neighbors, 'cept I don't know what we'd say or ask. I bet you'll think of somethin', Tex."

"I'm first gonna look in the phone book for this Robbins bitch."

A minute later Houston found what she was looking for in the phone book. "Here, right here it says L. Robbins, the address is the same one Sammy gave us. If we don't have anything on the schedule today Willy, how 'bout we take a drive?"

"Nothing on the book today, tomorrow we have a possible new client coming in the afternoon and we're doing some work at the shelter. Let's take that drive."

The phone rang. Wilamina answered and said hi to Jessie. She listened for a short time then hung up. She relayed the conversation, "She said they will do some hunting on the computer and call us back. She reminded us to be sure to stay out of sight of Ms. Robbins. She also reminded us of the investigator's number one rule - BE EVERYWHERE, BE QUIET AND BE INVISIBLE. That sounds almost impossible for the two of us."

"Willy, I bet she just made that up. No matter, let's bring the usual things. Now we both have binoculars and you've got the camera and the cell phone. Let's get moving."

Three hours later...............

Louny Robbins was apparently living in the left side of the duplex, because there was a ramp going up to the front door. Houston parked the truck at the very end of the street. "Luckily this street is lined with trees and we won't be so noticeable. Even better, the house we parked in front of is falling down. I'm sure no one could be living in it. I'm getting crossed-eye from looking through these glass eyes for so long. Wait, someone's coming out of the front door. That's gotta be her sitting in the wheelchair and some woman is pushing her. Take a picture, Willy. Be sure to get both women."

They watched the woman push Louny to a car. Louny stood up and got in on the passenger side. "Hey Willy, that Louny stood up, she looked pretty shaky, but she didn't need a lot of help to get into the car. You've got the pictures, right? Get one of the car and the plate. I'm gonna follow them, but I'm gonna stay far back."

They followed for only a few minutes, before Louny's car pulled into a MacDonalds drive through line.

"Tex, I gotta go to the ladies room."

"So do I. As soon as they drive off, I'll park. We can go inside, use the restroom and have lunch. We've got some pictures to show to Sammy and Sasha. After lunch we can go to Dr. Blackmore's office, see Sammy and then on to see Sasha at the precinct."

Later the same day..........

Sammy identified the woman in the wheelchair as Louny. The more interesting identification was done by Sasha. Sasha had stared at the photo for some time, then excitedly said, "That could be the Winters woman, the one pushing the wheelchair. I've got to run this picture over to Lacona to look at. She described the woman with a long dark braid, can't be too many with that style of hair. You guys can go with me."

They all jumped into Sasha's car. This time she took a patrol car. They quickly arrived at the hospital and raced to Lacona's room and showed her the photo.

"That looks like her. Same long dark hair pulled into one long braid. Yep, that's her. She's the one who brought her injured dog to the shelter and went crazy," confirmed Lacona.

Sasha's eyes lit up! "We've got something here. This is Mrs. Winters, she's been Louny Robbins physical therapist in the past. Mr. Winters has a record a mile long. He's one nasty dude. I'll take you girls back to your truck. Lorenzo and I have some paperwork to wade through. You two don't need to do anything right now. In fact, stay away from Louny. We just may have enough to come up with a search warrant.

"When are you being discharged, Lacona?"

"Possibly today, but for sure tomorrow. Why?"

"I'm thinking about your safety. Now that we can see Sammy's ex is not totally confined to a wheelchair and has a connection between her and the Winters. We need to play it safe. There are policemen already assigned to watch over you in the hospital 24/7 until you're discharged, then Sammy and the famous Salt and Pepper detectives will be your protectors."

The four continued talking while they waited for the next policeman to show up to take over his shift. Then they headed back to the department in Sasha's car. The two other investigators picked up their car and returned to their home office.

"We're gonna be the like the Three Musketeers, with Sammy, you and I watching over Lacona, " announced Houston.

CHAPTER FIFTY

Detectives Lorenzo and Voss worked feverishly filling out papers, talking to a judge and obtaining the requested search warrants; basically getting all their ducks in a row. The plan was to ask Louny and the Winters if they would come to the police station to answer a few questions. Later the police would do to their house to serve the warrants to search their homes and cars. They planned to interview them separately back at the station. Lacona had also remembered to tell Detective Voss that Mrs. Winters looked like she had been beaten. She was sporting a black eye, swollen cheek and a dark bruise on one arm. The detectives discussed the real possibility that both Louny and Mr. Winters were dangerous! They reminded the officers of this and to make sure they all would be wearing their raid vests which would hopefully protect them.

It was decided the two detectives would split up. Lorenzo with two officers as back up would serve the search warrant to Louny and Voss would serve the same to the Mr. & Mrs. Winters, also accompanied by two officers. Detective Voss was first going to attempt to catch up with Mrs. Winters at her place of employment. She was hoping to see her alone without her husband present.

"Voss, you want to pay Mrs. Winters a friendly-like visit? She might be more comfortable with a female officer away from her home. She is employed at a private facility. Since we know the neighbors have called the police several times on Mr. Winters, it would probably be better to question her away from her home and abusive husband."

"I agree, Lorenzo. I'll call her employer to find out if Winters is there or when she is expected to arrive. I don't think Winters would return a call to our department. She might even disappear."

Later, it would be decided how to best approach Mr. Winters. His employment record was quite erratic. Currently, it was thought he was working as a mechanic at a local Ford place.

Detective Voss called the office where Mrs. Winter's was employed. She spoke with the receptionist and asked about Mrs. Winters. Voss was soon speaking to her directly. The detective made up a story about having heard what a very good physical therapist she was and wondered if she could make an appointment with her directly. She was given an appointment for the day after tomorrow.

The detectives headed out in different directions and agreed to keep each other informed of how all was going. They planned to meet back at the precinct, possibly with the suspects in hand.

Detective Voss decided to just show up at the clinic where Mrs. Winters was employed. Since Mr. Winters' rap sheet contained several domestic calls, in the not so far off past, he was definitely someone to play it safe with.

Detective Voss arrived at the clinic's address. She asked the receptionist if Mrs. Winters was available to speak with her. Voss had changed into jeans, sweatshirt and tennis shoes and drove her own car to the clinic. Her plan was to simply ask for an earlier appointment because she had heard Mrs. Winters was a fantastic physical therapist. The detective gave her name as Miss Gomez.

The receptionist walked back to some other offices and spoke with Mrs. Winters. The therapist walked back to the front desk and invited the supposedly new client to follow her to the rehab area. Once they were seated, Mrs. Winters asked the routine questions. The detective gave a short, made up story about being rear ended by some guy with no insurance. "I can afford therapy, but I can't afford the pain I'm in. I need some serious relief for my neck and back. Dr. Wade has been my family doctor for a number of years, but that was when I lived in another state. I haven't needed to find anyone else here. As luck would have it, I met a woman in the grocery store recently and she told me you had worked miracles for a neighbor of hers. I forget the name, but she said the lady had been wheelchair bound for some time and lately was walking, not real steady yet. I'm hoping you can help me."

The therapist was staring hard at Voss and asked, "Who was this woman you say recommended me?"

"I never caught a name, sorry. I was focused on getting the name of this amazing therapist."

Mrs. Winters scratched her head, picked up her pencil and started asking routine questions. At some point, she took some measurements to see how much limitation the client had in the neck area. Then she had her stand and assume different positions and again wrote down her findings. Voss made different moaning sounds she thought sounded authentic when being asked to move in certain ways.

"Miss Gomez, you are actually in excellent condition. I can show you several exercises that should offer you some relief from the discomfort you say you have. You look like you work out regularly, do you?"

DetectIve Voss thought to herself. *This gal isn't buying it. I've got to go the old fashion route and spring with the truth.* "Mrs. Winters, I'm going to take a chance and be straight with you. First off, I've been around long enough to recognize an abused woman; especially when I can see an outline of a thumb on your neck, inside that big multicolored bruise. I'm a policewoman, a homicide detective. My name is Detective Voss, and I need some information on one of your former clients, Louny Robbins.

"I'm giving it to you straight because there are people's lives in danger, and time is of the essence. It is very possible that your husband and Louny are responsible for the attack on a woman. My guess is your involvement was forced and involuntary. You may have been afraid for your own safety, if you didn't follow their murderous plan.

"I can help you, but you will have to come clean."

Mrs. Winters hands were trembling and her breathing was rapid and shallow. There were small drops of perspiration on her forehead and around her mouth. She kept swallowing hard and looking toward the exit door.

"I can offer you protection. Just say the word. Time is racing by and your input may save lives."

Tears started streaming down Mrs. Winter's cheeks. Her shoulders began to shake uncontrollably. "If they find out I've talked to you, my life is over. I know they'll kill me!"

"I repeat, we can protect you, but you need to talk and talk now. I say again, there are others who may be in danger."

"That Louny is the most vicious woman I've ever known. I don't know who is worst, my husband or her."

The detective asked, "Would you permit me to record our conversation?"

"Might as well. You can read it out loud at my funeral."

CHAPTER FIFTY-ONE

"Thanks." Detective Voss rummaged through her purse, found her tape recorder and began recording. "I have a warrant coming that will protect your license according to the HIPAA laws."

"I don't care about keeping my damn license. I just want to do what's right and save lives." Mrs. Winters spoke into the recorder, "I was Robbin's therapist for about six months. She made surprisingly good improvement. I'll say one thing for her, she was determined. She worked hard and was able to ignore her pain while doing the exercises. She can now get around, not well but I mean she's never going to go dancing. She can take care of her own needs now.

"All during our weekly sessions she ranted on and on about the horrible person who put her in the wheelchair. I really got tired of her nasty mouth and she sounded like a broken record.

"When I got home at night, I'd tell my husband, Donald, about this angry, bitter woman I was working on. One day, he offered to take the Robbins woman and myself on a picnic. I couldn't believe he made such a generous offer. He's never been a thoughtful sort of man. In fact, he's just the opposite. He was like Robbins, always complaining about everything and blaming everyone, even strangers, for his miserable life. Anyway, I put him off for a while and didn't mention a picnic to Robbins. I didn't trust him to stay sober long enough to remember the offer he made. Anyway, he didn't forget and angrily insisted I ask her to go picnicking with us. So I did, reluctantly, and she said yes. It was weeks later that I accidentally found out that Donald knew she had won a law suit and had a fair amount of money.

"I reluctantly packed a lunch and we picked up Robbins and drove to the beach. He, of course, brought plenty of beer, whiskey, and I'm sure he had pills stored in his shirt. He'd swallow anything for a buzz. It's amazing he hasn't yet overdosed and killed himself. I kept hoping. Uh, he's not going to hear this tape is he?"

"What you are doing is going to make sure Donald and Louny will not be able to hurt anyone else again," responded the detective.

Winnie continued, "At the beach, the two of them hit it off. They drank like fools and took whatever junk pills he had. He called it his 'special medicine.' What crap! I believe that day the two of them cooked up some scheme. I don't know what it was, 'cause he told me to take a long walk, way down the beach. I did what he said. I always did what he said, or took a beating. I'm a real nothing. Well, I must have walked for an hour. When I got back, the two of them were laughing, drinking and acting like best buddies.

"We took Robbins home and Donald said to me, 'Bitch, you finally did something right.'" Mrs. Winters started to cry again. She wiped her nose on her sleeve, took a deep breath and told the detective about the dog and how her husband abused it. "I couldn't stand looking at the little pitiful guy and tried to give it to the shelter. I changed my mind, but they wouldn't let me take the dog home. When Donald found out what I had done........ " Her lips quivered, she took another breath and continued, "He beat me so bad I thought this time he was going to kill me. I didn't care anymore, I didn't even try to defend myself. Guess I must have fainted 'cause I woke up later and he was gone.

"It wasn't too long after, that he brought home another little dog. I said nothing. One day the dog was gone, just disappeared. I never asked and Donald said he thought the dog must have run away. In my heart, I knew better. What kind of person am I? I deserved to be beaten. Just want it over with. No more fear or pain, death would be a relief.

"Robbins therapy continued, but at her home, per her request. Donald went with me. I would put her through her routine and when she finished I was told to go sit in the car and wait for him.

"About month ago, Donald told me I was done doing therapy for Robbins. No explanation was given and I sure as hell wasn't going to ask any questions. He's been working in our garage for the last month, not going to work. Just drinking, cussing, taking crap pills and whistling. I was glad to go to work. The only time I've felt safe is when I'm here. Now you say you can keep me safe. Just how are you going to do it that?"

"Mrs. Winters, can I call you Winnie? My first name is Sasha and I want to thank you for your frankness and for your courage. I'm sorry about all the abuse you've endured. Today, that part of your life is over. You're not going home and you certainly are not going to die today; not with the Whitefall police department watching over you. Officers are coming here and will escort you back to the department. You will be in protective custody until we have your husband and Miss Robbins in custody. At some point you'll be able to go back to your house. You'll learn more about that this afternoon.

"Do you think Donald is home at this moment, maybe working in the garage?"

"Probably. I just remembered something I saw this morning before I left to come here. I saw a wad of cash, hundred dollar bills, lots of them and one plane ticket. I quickly got out of there and drove to work. I'm sure he'd be enraged if he knew I saw that money. Driving to work I started thinking about what I had seen. All of a sudden, I got a clear picture. He was leaving and he wasn't going to take me with him. He was going to leave me and not leave me alive. You want to hear something really sick? I was going to go home and let him do whatever. I was just too tired of being hurt and scared and feeling so bad about myself. What a worthless piece of flesh I've let myself become."

"Winnie, starting this very moment, you have become your own hero. You've done the right thing, for the right reason and in time to save yourself and others. Today is the beginning of a new life for you."

The receptionist walked into the room and announced to Mrs. Winters, that her husband was on the phone. Winnie froze in place. The detective answered for her. "She'll be right there.

"Winnie, you have to do one more brave act, you must answer him and sound as normal as you can."

"What if he wants me to come home right now?" holding herself tightly.

"You will say, 'I'm almost finished with a client and will be home in less than an hour. Will that be soon enough?'"

"I'm terrified! He's going to know something's up."

"Winnie, the police have arrived. As soon as you speak to Donald, you will be escorted to the police station, where you will be safe. Donald can no longer hurt you."

"Okay, let's do it," whispered Winnie. She slowly walked to the main desk and picked up the phone. "Hello, Okay," there was a long pause. "I have to finish up with my client. I can be home in less than an hour. Okay, I understand. Bye.

"I did it," said Winnie with a big grin and she hugged the detective. "I hope that bastard never sees the outside of a cell again. He said for me not to say anything to Sue, the receptionist, or anyone, that I'm going home early. He said he has some great news for the both of us. I bet he does. He plans to tell me exactly how he's going to beat me to death. I actually think I'm going to live. How unbelievable is that? This morning, I planned to go home as usual and let him do me in. Now, I'm going to be safe and he's going to be locked up for a very long time."

Winnie was smiling as she walked away with the officers. She had a noticeable bounce in her steps. She grabbed hold of officer Smart's hand, who seemed to understand her need for a little extra assurance.

Detective Voss instructed the receptionist to say nothing about Winnie leaving, to anybody, especially if her husband called back. "You saw nothing, say nothing because lives are at stake."

The receptionist said she understood and was going to close the office, lock up and go home. "I'm glad Winnie is finally going to be away from that nasty man of hers. She's come to work many times with bruises and she's always made some stupid excuse for them. I wanted to help her, but she wouldn't even talk about it. Glad you're helping her now."

"Yes. The real sad part is that women, like Winnie, think they don't deserve to be treated with kindness and respect. I have definitely learned that lesson about anyone who is repeatedly abused. Not on my watch! Not if I can help it!"

CHAPTER FIFTY-TWO

Detective Voss got in her unmarked car, called in for her partner and was told he was out of the office and off the radio. "Okay, I'll leave this message for Detective Lorenzo. Tell him, I'm on my way to the Winters' house. Mr. Winters may be getting ready to leave permanently. I've called for back-up. Two officers will meet me at Winters' place, we'll rendezvous at the south end of his block. Suspect has cash and a one-way plane ticket. Wife is in protective custody."

Detective Voss arrived simultaneously with the other officers at the designated spot down the road from Winters house. She explained the plan. All were wearing protective gear. "This guy is a firecracker. He tortures little dogs and was part of setting a trap to kill a woman. He was probably the shooter. Watch yourselves. He's a user and drinker. He is waiting for his wife to come home from work. She believes he plans to kill her and fly off somewhere." She added that he may be working in the garage.

The three cops discuss their plan and took off walking toward the suspects place. Detective Voss went to the front door, the other officers went to the attached garage. Detective Voss stood to the side of the door and knocked. She knocked several more times, no answer. She planned to tell Mr. Winters that she was a client of his wife. While Mrs. Winters was working on her, she became violently ill. The receptionist called for an ambulance and they took Mrs. Winters to the local emergency room. They tried to cal, but there was no answer, so I volunteered to come here personally to tell you where your wife is. Still no response.

"Mr. Winters are you home? I've got an important message for you from your wife." The detective tried the door, locked. She looked through the living room window and could see a gas can with a pile of newspapers nearby on the floor.

At that same moment she heard a gunshot ring out. She reached for her gun, which she had hidden inside her jean jacket, and struggled to get to it. At that very moment a crazed-appearing man came around the side of the house. He was brandishing a pistol. They saw each other at the exact same moment. He fired just as she had gained access to her own weapon. The detective dropped to her knees and fired off several rounds at the shooter.

Blood appeared on his shirt, he dropped his gun and tried to run across the front lawn, but didn't get far before he collapsed.

Another officer came racing around the corner from the garage area. He was yelling into his cell phone, "Officers down, officers down, need fire department and ambulances."

Smoke was bellowing skyward from the garage and quickly becoming an inferno. Within minutes, the fire department arrived with their truck and medic unit.

A first responder was immediately at Detective Voss's side rendering assistance. There was quite a bit of blood seeping through the front of her pants. She was conscious and pale, pulse slow.

Detective Voss tried to raise up and asked the fireman, "How are the other two officers? Is the suspect down and out?" She grabbed the first responder's arm and practically whispered, "Help them. They're my friends. I'm okay. I'm a cop."

"They're being attended to ma'am. The man on the lawn is unconscious and surrounded by the police. One of the other officers was also wounded. The ambulance is on their way for you both. You're in good hands now. You're going to be just fine."

Detective Voss pulled the responder's face down to hers and with great effort whispered, "There is a gas can and papers in the house. Warn them, a fire........." She didn't finish her sentence. She closed her eyes and was still. The next sound was the blasting of the ambulance siren, speeding away with the two officers. The suspect was transported in a separate ambulance accompanied by three police cars.

CHAPTER FIFTY-THREE

The first responder who had so professionally and thoughtfully attended to Detective Voss approached a police officer at the scene. The name printed on the fireman's uniform was Marsh.

"Excuse me officer, you seem to be the one in charge here." said Marsh.

"Yes I am. Can I help you?" responded Detective Lorenzo.

"I was working on a policewoman. She barely was able to whisper to me that there was a gas can and papers visible in the front room. She seemed very concerned and I assume you are the one who needs to know this info?"

"Thank you, Marsh." reading the name on his uniform. "I'll see to it that it gets looked into immediately. How was Detective Voss doing? How seriously was she wounded? She's my partner and a damn good one." Lorenzo hesitated, took in a deep breath and continued, "She's got to be okay."

"She wanted me to help her fellow officers first. She was coherent, just weak. If I might add, she was the most beautiful cop I've ever rendered emergency care to."

Detective Lorenzo responded, "I'll pass that compliment on to her. My guess is it will embarrass the hell out of her. By the way, she's single. Don't tell her I told you that. She's a better shot than I am."

"I'll remember that detective, and thanks."

Detective Lorenzo passed on the information about the gas can and paper to the officers working the crime scene then took off immediately to get to the hospital where his partner had been taken.

At the hospital.........

The news about Detective Voss getting shot spread quickly. A growing number of friends started showing up at the hospital. They were pacing up and down in the surgery waiting room. Each one with his or her own thoughts. They could have been a group awaiting the news of a baby's birth.

It had been six hours since Sasha had been gunned down. With a smile and a sparkle in his eyes, the surgeon walked briskly into the waiting area. Sasha's parents were immediately by his side. He told them their daughter was doing well. She had tolerated the surgery and was still under the effects of the anesthesia. They asked if they could see her. He suggested they wait for an hour or so, and then the nurse would come for them. Fortunately her folks were in town to visit their daughter, Sasha. Unfortunately she was wounded the day of their arrival.

"How about the rest of us, when could we visit her?" asked Detective Lorenzo?

"It would be best if you could give her until tomorrow morning. She'll be less groggy and more receptive to visitors," responded the doctor.

The following morning.........

Lorenzo, Houston and Wilamina arrived at the hospital. They rode the elevator to the surgical floor and stopped at the nurse's station for directions. They were given the room number and the nurse told them the doctor was with Miss Voss at the moment. She asked them to wait outside her door until the doctor came out.

After a few minutes the doctor came out. He introduced himself and told the anxious group that the patient was doing very well. "The bullet was removed. There was some collateral damage, which could require a second surgery later on. Don't stay with her too long. She is rather heavily medicated and needs her sleep and rest. Her parents already visited her this morning."

"Thanks doc. We won't stay long but could we come back this afternoon and perhaps stay longer?"

"That's fine. Check at the nurse's station when you come back. I'll see her again this afternoon. Don't worry about her. She's young and in great shape. She should be good as new, or close to it in the not so far future."

Detective Lorenzo also inquired about the condition of Officer Pruitt and Mr. Winters.

"The officer was released an hour ago. He received a minor wound and was told to see his own physician for follow-up. Quite a different story on Mr. Winters however. He's in the Intensive Care Unit in critical condition. We have been unable to operate to remove the bullet. A policeman brought his wife here last night. It seems a Detective Lorenzo made the arrangements. Mrs. Winters has signed the necessary papers including the organ donor papers, in case her husband should die."

"Dr. Link, I am Detective Lorenzo. I'm glad Mrs. Winters was able to sign the needed paperwork. I've also made arrangements for a police officer to remain outside his room. The officer will be here within the hour. I understand Mr. Winters is critical at the moment, but the safety of the staff and other patients is a priority."

"I appreciate your protection, Detective. I'll notify the nurses of your precautionary measure, and thank you."

CHAPTER FIFTY-FOUR

Visiting time that same afternoon.......

"Hello ladies," remarked the detective. His smiling eyes landed briefly on Houston. Houston barely made eye contact and awkwardly attempted buttoning her already buttoned blouse. He hugged both women. Obviously taking more time with his arms around Houston.

They found Sasha awake. She was pale, but she quickly smiled when she saw them.

Houston said, "We brought you some flowers and a book by Irma Bombeck. Thought you might need something to laugh at."

"Thanks for the flowers. They're very pretty. You girls didn't steal them from that dear Miss Abigail's garden, did you?"

"Nah, we swiped them from the hospital gift shop. Figured Sark could bail us out if necessary."

"How are you feeling, partner?" asked Sark.

"Like I've been run over by a train overloaded with well-fed livestock. How is Winters doing and what about officer Pruitt?"

"The officer is fine. The bullet barely winged him. He's going to have some paid time off. He's been asking about you."

There was a knock on the door and a young woman announced she was delivering a plant for Sasha Voss.

Wilamina took the plant and thanked the young delivery person. "This is somethin' I've never seen before. What kind of plant is this?" She held it up for them all to look it over.

"That's a Bonsai tree. It's a very old and beautiful one. Who sent it, Willy?" asked Sasha.

She looked around the plant and found a note. "It says, 'To the best looking cop on the force. Your friendly 1st responder, Marsh."

Sark spoke up, "He was quite taken by you, partner. I believe you now have a stalker or perhaps a suitor. Whichever you prefer."

"He probably has a wife, maybe two, and five kids tucked away somewhere," countered Sasha.

Another knock on the door and Dr. Link entered. He said good morning to the threesome and asked to have a few minutes alone with his patient.

The three stepped outside the room and used the time to take a potty and/or a coffee break.

The doctor pulled a chair up next to the bed . "Sasha, you are doing very well, so far. I didn't talk with you long enough this morning because I had an appointment. I need to give you more details about your surgery. The surgery was extensive because of the path of the bullet and the kind of bullet.

You'll be with us for about five more days. Then, if all goes well, you can go home. Rehab therapy should begin about a week later. I understand you are single and have no children."

"That's correct Dr. Link. Why are you bringing that up? What does my marital status or having children have to do with anything?

"That's a fair question and deserves an answer. Within four to six months you should be almost good as new. Meaning you will have your strength and energy back. Your uterus was severely damaged and had to be removed." The doctor paused a moment giving Sasha time to grasp what this meant for her."

She hesitated momentarily then pronounced, "So no womb, no babies."

"That's correct Sasha. You will not be able to get pregnant, but that doesn't eliminate motherhood. There are many options like fostering or adopting. I am sorry. I sincerely hope you will confide in someone. I've met several of your friends and they seem to be a very caring bunch. There is a counseling service located in the hospital if you want it. The nurse will ask you if you would like to talk to one of the counselors or pastors.

"I want to add one last thought with you today. A wise person does not bury their feelings. Much better to bring them out into the open and wear them like a medal of honor with pride. Any questions for me?"

"Not right now, but thank you for your good doctoring. I'm real tired and hurting. Could you please tell my friends to come back tomorrow. I want to sleep now."

"Yes, I will do that. See you later today. Someone will be in soon to get you up and moving a short distance."

"By short, I hope you mean inches."

"Not quite, more like feet. Later."

The doctor stepped out into the hall and relayed Sasha's request to be alone until tomorrow. "Please do return. She can use good friends now."

The three were stunned and started to slowly drift toward the elevator when Wilamina spoke up. "No way, she needs us now. We're going back in that room. You both heard the doc. She needs us."

Wilamina barged right into Sasha's room. Houston and Sark moved more hesitantly.

"What's going on here? I thought I was going to get some rest. Didn't the doctor tell you to come back later?" blasted out Sasha.

"Yes he did, but we're your best friends and know you need us now, not later. Is there something you want to share with us?" Wilamina sat down in the chair next to the bed and took a hold of Sasha's hand.

You could have heard a pin drop for the next few moments. The silence was broken by soft whimpering sounds coming from the patient. Sasha's eyes began to glisten and soon tears flowed down her pale face.

"Dr. Links had to remove my uterus. It was too badly damaged and he couldn't repair it. No mommy stuff for me." She covered her eyes with the bed sheet and cried softly.

"I don't know why that's hitting me so hard, I'm not even married and don't have any prospects. So what's the big deal? I forgot to ask about officer Pruitt and that dick-head Mr. Winters.

Sark responded, "The officer is already home and doing fine. The same can't be said for Winters. He's still critical and in ICU. I'll bring you up to date later. Now it's your time to think about your own healing."

Wilamina got a washcloth wet it under the faucet with warm water and gently removed Sasha's hands from her face. She lowered the sheet and wiped Sasha's face, ever so tenderly. "Yes honey, you've got some tough news there and you'll need to chew on it for some time. We'll go and let you do your crying and chewing alone. But, we'll be back later today and every day until you're discharged and then we'll still be around to give hugs and share your tears."

"Thanks, Willy. I'm already glad I told you guys. I'll do my chewing, as you said, and then I will get on with it, whatever that may be. I just had a flash, now I could really be a ho and not worry about getting pregnant. Not funny, but in a strange sort of way it is. Think of all the money I'd save on birth control." She closed her eyes and thanked her friends, but needed her pain meds. "I'm going to push this button and get some relief. Thanks again my friends. See you later."

Houston and Sark both hugged Sasha gently and Wilamina simply kissed the top of her friend's head. They said their good-byes and walked out, closing the door quietly.

Once on the elevator Sark said, "How about I take you two ladies for a nice dinner. I'm not feeling like I want to go home alone just yet." He winked at Houston and she looked down at her feet and started fiddling with her buttons again.

"I have news to share about Sammy and the Robbins' woman. You're both going to be proud of your ex-cell mate.

Wilamina thought dinner was a great idea and pulled her partner along.

CHAPTER FIFTY-FIVE

Back in time to yesterday evening.........

As soon as Sammy heard about Sasha getting shot she called her friends Houston and Wilamina. Houston relayed the facts of what transpired between Mrs. Winters and Sasha at her place of employment and later at the Winters' home. Mrs. Winters admitted that her husband and Louny Robbins had cooked up the ploy of the injured dog to get Lacona into the woods where Mr. Winters shot her. Sasha and the Mrs. then laid a plan to catch the Mr. at home and arrest him.

"Now Sammy," cautioned Houston, "Let the police do their job. They can take care of Louny. You can be righteously enraged, but remember what you learned and said back in Sharon's group about control and making good choices.

"Yeah, I remember. Thanks Tex. Talk with you later."

Sammy's level of anger was at an all time high as she realized Louny had arranged a hit on her beloved Lacona as a pay back. She drove like a maniac to Louny's duplex. She drove her car right up onto the grass and braked hard at the ramp leading up to Louny's door. She jumped out of the car, flew up to the door. She didn't bother to knock she simply kicked in the door.

Louny wasn't able to move fast enough. Sammy had her by the throat.

"I'm going to kill you! You're pure evil! I should have done this after you tortured and murdered my dogs!"

Louny's arms flailed uselessly, her face turned an odd shade of blue. Sammy was sobbing and screaming all the while her hands were squeezing harder. Suddenly she stopped and dropped her hands to her side. Louny was coughing and gasping for air. Sammy pushed her down onto the floor with one strong hand. She then took out her cell phone and dialed 911. She gave the operator the address and stated that someone is being murdered and to send help. "Tell Detective Lorenzo about this call. Hurry!"

Sammy stood over Louny and pronounced, "You're not worth shit. This time you're going to prison, not me. The inmates you'll be rooming with will know well in advance of your coming and will know your crimes of animal cruelty and human baby torture and killing."

"What the f.... are you talking about?" blurted out Louny. "I never did nothing to no damn baby."

"I know that, but the inmates won't and you know what those women do to baby killers. It won't be pretty or quick, but it will be permanent."

The sirens could be heard outside. Detective Lorenzo ran through the broken door, gun in hand and saw Sammy standing over a woman. "Are you okay Sammy? Everything under control?"

"Yes, Lorenzo. I am under control. I'm really okay this time. Take this piece of crap away."

Louny screeching, "Don't let this maniac near me! She almost killed me! Arrest her! She's an ex-con, crazy and dangerous!"

"Not this time Miss Robbins. You're the one getting the Miranda rights read, and he began......"

Louny Robbins was mirandized, handcuffed, placed in her wheelchair, and carefully put into the back of the patrol car. She could be heard cussing and screaming half way down the block.

CHAPTER FIFTY-SIX

This was "discharge day" for Detective Voss. Earlier it had been decided that her parents would pick her up and take her to her own place. Mr. and Mrs. Voss made plans to stay with her the first week and then other arrangements could be made if Sasha needed more help.

The doctor had just left Sasha's room. He told her she could leave for home anytime after 2 p.m. He requested she see the physical therapist before discharge for further instructions. She called her parents and Detective Lorenzo to give them the discharge news. The detective asked to drop by her room before noon to bring her up to date with department happenings and to talk about how much time she might need before returning to duties. They agreed he should visit around noon time.

Sasha had finished taking a sponge bath with a little assistance from the aid. "I can't wait to take a real shower. Keeping this damn dressing dry isn't easy."

"I know," responded the aid, "but necessary. Be patient. You don't want to get an infection from a wet dressing. Now let me help you get into your own clothes. Your parents brought these by yesterday. I bet you'll feel better just wearing your own clothes and getting out of the fashionable hospital gown."

There was a barely perceptible knock on the room door. "Come in," said Sasha.

Marsh stuck his head halfway through the door. "Is this a good time for a short visit?"

"Yes, Marsh. I'm finally in my own duds. I'm surprised, but glad to see you again or are you here to visit your Bonsai plant?"

"Well maybe I was thinking we could share custody."

Sasha laughed and hesitantly began, "I've had time to really look over the plant. My mother has a deep appreciation of Bonsais. I learned from her it is slow growing and this one looks like it could be more than ten years old. She told me it's obviously been receiving dedicated care and meticulous pruning."

"Actually," responded Marsh, "It was a gift from my aunt twelve years ago. We were close and she had become gravely ill. She wanted me to take care of her beloved plant until she could get better. Sadly, she didn't. I've been the keeper of her treasured plant ever since her death."

"Marsh, I can't accept such a personal, special gift. We are strangers. What would your aunt think about you giving away her treasure to a stranger?"

"She would understand completely and be happy about it. You remind me of her. You have the same hazel eyes and the same strong heart. You don't feel like a stranger to me. Hope I'm not scaring you, but I felt drawn to you the first moment I was at your side after you'd been shot. I'm truly not a weirdo or dangerous. Have your detective partner do a background check on me. I'm as clean as a newborn. Well, that may be an exaggeration, but I'm one of the good guys and not a bad dancer either. After you return home and feel strong enough, I'd like to call you and maybe we could go for coffee, or lunch, or whatever."

Sasha hesitated for a moment and answered, "I'm not quite ready to dance, no wild gyrations yet, but I can have coffee. Don't expect too much too soon. I have some sorting-out-kind of thinking to do. Why don't you give me your phone number and I'll call when I'm in better shape."

He wrote it down and slipped it inside the Bonsai container. "Good-bye for now, I'll wait impatiently for your call."

The next visitor was Lorenzo. "Hi there partner. Bet you're ready to get out of here."

"You better believe it. I'm ready to hear what's been going on, every sordid detail, spare me nothing. I'm sick of only thinking about my pitiful self."

"Okay, here goes. Mrs. Winters is doing great. She has a lawyer now. Another attorney friend of ours, Roco Lagunta, recommended someone he knows well. Winters has been one terrified, abused woman for a long time. I don't think she will have to serve any time for her part of the attempted murder of Lacona. Sammy wants to help her because she made it easier or even possible to apprehend her husband and Miss Robbins.

"It's possible Donald Winters will be taken off life support sometime today or tomorrow. His wife signed all the necessary papers. Hopefully there will be some organs to donate.

"Now for the good report on Sammy. When she learned her ex-partner was the one who planned to murder Lacona, using Mr. Winters as the shooter, and the poor tortured dog as bait, she nearly went crazy. She raced to Robbins's house, kicked in the door, grabbed Robbins by the throat and nearly strangled her to death. She called 911. To make the story shorter.... Sammy managed to get her rage under control and had the pleasure of witnessing the arrest, the rights being verbalized, handcuffing applied and Louny being dragged off screaming profanities. Sammy has a new sense of respect for herself.

"Our department is fairly quiet right now. You take all the time you need to recover completely. How are you doing, really?"

"I guess pretty good. Once in a while I feel like I'm on a roller coaster with my emotions flying up and down. I'm not sorry about Donald Winters. Though I don't care about his dying and that makes me question what kind of person am I? His death will make the world safer, I'm sure. Maybe later I'll feel shitty about shooting and killing somebody, but right now I don't feel any regret.

"Mrs. Winters is a trooper. It took courage for her to do what she did. I'd like to tell her that in person some day."

"She's asked about you every day. Seems to feel guilty about what her husband did to you and to Lacona. I think it would do her some good to get to talk with you. She's living back in her house temporarily, waiting for what's going to happen to her in court. The cruelties that humans do to each other is mind blowing. Houston and Wilamina send their best and told me to tell you they'll call you tomorrow and asked about visiting you."

"I'll call them today after I get settled in at home. I want you and my other friends to meet my parents. I'll figure something out in the next week. By the way, that first responder, Marsh, he's been by and wants to get better acquainted. Now that I'm 'neutered,' I can't see any kind of permanent relationship growing with a guy like him. When do you tell a guy you're sterile? I feel like damaged merchandise. I'm a mess. Never mind answering partner, I'm just having a short-lived pity party. I'll work it out."

"I know you will work it out in your way and in your time. Many guys that aren't worth much would be overjoyed to know you couldn't get pregnant, but the guys that are worth a second look, would say 'so what.' I want you and if we want kids, we will adopt or involve ourselves with children in other ways. Talk with your women friends and maybe even your folks. You have some very special people in your life who care deeply for you;

keep sharing. I hope you know how much I care for you. You have become the first female best friend I've ever had. You'll will never be damaged goods. As far as being a mess, you could do something with your hair." He was grinning as he left the room. Sasha was laughing and looked for her hair brush.

CHAPTER FIFTY-SEVEN

Two weeks later..........

Sasha's parents changed their plans and stayed another week with their daughter. Sasha decided to call Marsh and invite him over to her house to meet her parents before they returned to their home in Oregon. Secretly, she want to see Marsh's reaction to meeting her Japanese mother.

"Hello Marsh, this is Sasha Voss. Am I calling at a bad time?"

"No. Not at all. I'm surprised, but very glad to hear from you."

"I'm wondering if you would like to come to my house for coffee and to meet my parents. They've been nursing me back to health and spoiling me rotten. They're leaving tomorrow morning for Oregon."

"What time do you want me there?"

"How about 3 p.m. or around that time?"

"Great. I'll need an address."

She gave him her address and cell number. "If something comes up, you can call me and cancel."

"I'll not be cancelling Sasha, see you at 3."

She thought to herself, *What am I trying to prove? I'm so selfish, what about my mother's feelings? She is so kind and gentle and worse she will know what I'm doing. I'll call him back and cancel. No, I'll call Willy first.*

"Hi Willy, you got a minute?"

"Sure thing, honey. For you, I've got hours. What's going on? You okay?"

"Yes, everything is okay. Just want to run something by you. I called Marsh, the first responder guy, you know the one who sent the Bonsai?"

"Yes, I remember that beautiful, strange little tree."

"I called him a few minutes ago and asked him to come by my house to meet my parents. They're leaving tomorrow for home and my evil self wants to see Marsh's reaction to my mother being Japanese. I don't know what the hell I'm trying to do here. I'm thinking of calling him back and cancelling. What would you do?"

"Honey, if you're feeling some kind of attraction to him it is okay to find out if he is some kind of racist bastard. And you're about to find out, maybe. You have great parents and I'm so happy Houston and me had the chance to spend some time with them. You asked me what would I do? I would want to know so guess I'd let him come and find out what kind of man he is. You know, the character stuff. Hope you're fireman passes the test. Lorenzo said the guy was okay. Lets us know how it goes soon as he leaves."

"Thanks Willy, I don't trust myself when it comes to men. I made such a lousy choice before. That man hurt me and my folks big time financially and emotionally. I don't want to repeat my ignorance."

"I've been there too, but there comes a time you just got to jump into the river and trust you haven't forgotten how to swim. Go for it girl."

"Thanks, Willy."

3 p.m..........

Sasha's mother, Kim, watched her daughter change outfits three times. Mrs. Voss chuckled to herself and said, "All three outfits look attractive, but this last one brings out the color in your eyes."

Sasha was about to respond to her mother when the doorbell rang. Marsh arrived exactly at 3 p.m. Mr. Voss opened the door and introduced himself and his wife. They both greeted him warmly and shook hands.

"Mrs. Voss, I can definitely see who Sasha inherited her beautiful eyes from. I'm very honored to meet you both."

Sasha stood in the hall staring at the three of them. She rubbed the back of her neck embarrassed by her own nervousness.

Mrs. Voss looked over at her stage-struck daughter and took the initiative to invite Marsh to follow her into the kitchen for coffee and pastries.

As soon as they were all seated, Marsh began, "Mr. and Mrs. Voss I haven't known your daughter for very long. We met under some unusual and stressful circumstances, but I want you to hear how brave, unselfish and professional she was after being shot. You can be proud of her. She is a hero."

Mr. Voss reached across the table and took hold of his daughter's hands, "We have been proud of her since the day of her birth and every day since. She is like her mother, gentle, wise, kind and possess' the heart of a lioness."

Mrs. Voss added, "And she is like her father who is also wise and kind. Sometimes he can be stubborn like a donkey, but a man of honor and respect. He also has the heart of a lion."

Sasha covered her mouth with her hands and a giggle slipped out, "Mother, dad can be stubborn like a mule, not a donkey."

"I like the way your mother coined it better. From now on, I will always refer to my stubborn friends as donkeys." Everyone laughed heartily and nibbled some more on the pastries.

"Your gift of the treasured Bonsai speaks volumes." said Mrs. Voss. "Thank you for taking such professional care of her."

"You're welcome. I was doing the job I love. My mother and aunt's grandmother was born in Japan. She married an American and lived the rest of her life in the U.S. My aunt was influenced greatly by that dear lady. I was adopted when I was one year old. My mother and aunt were very close, in fact, my aunt lived with us after her husband died. She would tell me stories about her grandmother. I learned to love my adopted great grandmother through the stories told to me when I was young.

"Sorry about going on and on. I had a wonderful childhood and I get carried away talking about it."

Sasha appeared trance-like while listening to Marsh's sharing. Her mouth slightly opened with a tear or two falling over her flushed cheeks.

The four visited for a short time longer and then Marsh said his thanks and took his leave.

Mrs. Voss said to her daughter, "That young man has a gentle soul. Did he pass your test, Sasha?"

"What are you talking about, Mother?" Sasha hesitated, blushed and looked away from her parent. "I'm so ashamed, did I hurt you?"

"No dear. You like him and wanted to know if he had prejudices. Now what have you discovered about him and yourself?"

Sasha answered thoughtfully and let the tears start up again. He is a better person than me and so are you. I do like him and I just couldn't bear it if I had chosen again poorly. I don't trust myself to choose wisely."

"Once a lesson is learned, time to move on to new experiences, new adventures," added her mother. She kissed her daughter and said, "Now I'm going to pack, because tomorrow we leave for home and you can have some privacy with your father while you both clean up the kitchen."

Next morning...........

Her parents were gone. Sasha was changing the bed linen and freshening up the bathroom. She spotted a note on the dresser. It read:

'To our daughter,
　　Don't be afraid to take the next step. Love has many nets. Falls, don't break us only make us stronger and wiser!
　　Mom and Dad'

CHAPTER FIFTY-EIGHT

Weeks later..........

"Miss Voss, I couldn't believe it when you called the office and requested me to be your therapist. At first I wondered if you were going to hurt me or thank me," remarked Winnie Winters.

"Please call me Sasha and I'll call you Winnie. I'm pleased you are to be my physical 'terrorist' for the duration. Only kidding. I've often heard a therapist called a 'terrorist' for the pain they inflict by making the recovering person move."

Winnie looked sheepishly and stuttered, "I'm so sorry you were shot. I feel responsible. If I'd had the courage long ago to get away from Donald, you and the other woman and the policeman would have never been hurt. Not to mention the terrible things that happened to those innocent little dogs. All that pain that Donald caused still haunts me. I'm never going to be able to forgive myself."

"Winnie, you've made some poor choices in your life, so have I. I believe we are supposed to learn from our many mistakes and go on. Hopefully not repeating the same stuff. I'm finally learning that lesson myself. Your husband did the deeds. He was the one responsible for the all the cruelties. Now he is gone and I'm the one responsible for his death. My friends tell me I returned fire. I did my job and Donald Winters had to be stopped. My insides are torn up because I have taken the life of another human being.

Willy told me to feel the feelings, chew on them, spit them out and move on. This might be something you could try also.

"It took a ton of courage to do what you did, Winnie. You can now see yourself as your own hero. No sense in looking back, unless you need to remind yourself of a learned lesson.

"Speaking of moving on, how long do you think I will need to have physical therapy? I'd also like to ask what plans you are making for your future?"

"The doctor will have the final word about your therapy, but in the end it's up to how you are feeling. You know your body better than the doctor or me. As to my future, I'm putting the house on the market and I'll probably stay until it is sold. I'm keeping this job. I really like my work and this the town. I've met some nice people, like you and your partner. Sammy and Lacona have also been very kind to me. They're encouraging me to adopt a dog or two, or a cat or three.

"Maybe I'll get a pet after the house is sold, which won't bring much money considering the fire and smoke damage, but I did have home insurance and life insurance on Donald. He insisted we take out a hefty policy on each other. I think now he was probably figuring on doing me in at some point and collecting. How ironic! I'm going to benefit from his death. I plan to do something good with it. One thing, for sure, I'm going to help Lacona financially with her animal shelter. Did you know she adopted both those little dogs that Donald tortured?

"Something good is going to come from the horrible life my husband led. He never told me much about himself, except to say that his mother was a drunk and a weak person. I think he hated all women. He wouldn't say a thing about his father though. One day I asked again about his young life. He got a wild look in his eyes, dropped his pants and showed me some strange scars on the inside of his thighs. He screamed that those were the signs of love from dear dad and mom. He told me never again to ask him anything about his past. He then hit me right in the face, broke my nose and cut my cheek. His words were, 'at least I don't try to hide what I do.'" Winnie started to cry softly. Sasha let her cry. She remained quiet and shed some tears herself for her new friend.

Some time past and Winnie then said, "Can you believe his parents burned him with cigarettes? I don't think he ever showed those scars to anyone before. They're both dead now and I hope it was in a fire. I know that's a terrible thing to say, but how can someone do that to their own kid?"

Sasha responded, "It never ceases to shock and send me into a rage when I hear what horrible things adults can do to kids, animals and each other. Abuse breeds abuse. Some individuals are not able to rise above their childhood abusive experiences and they often pay it forward. Kindness is the only permanent solution I can think of. I'm not sure that our human race will ever be able to attain such a universal trait or behavior. I haven't yet been able to."

"Do you want to set up a therapy schedule and put yourself in my care?"

"Absolutely, Winnie. Let's get it done!"

CHAPTER FIFTY-NINE

Marsh showed up at the Salt and Pepper Agency one morning unannounced.

"Good morning Marsh, greeted Wilamina with bright eyes. "What can I do for you? Maybe a hot cup of coffee and one of my homemade muffins?"

Sounds great, Miss Wilamina. I've been pacing outside your office for some time. I've got to admit, damn this is embarrassing, but I need some advice."

"Honey, the last time I was embarrassed was when I was admitted to Lancer,s Prison. So don't you worry about shocking me. Maybe I just shocked you Marsh." Wilamina lead him upstairs to the kitchen and called out to Houston, "We've got company Tex, Marsh is here."

"Hi Marsh, I'll be right there. I hope everything is okay, is it?"

"Yes ma'am, everything's okay. I know you and Wilamina are good friends with Sasha and I can't figure her out. I don't want to scare her away, but I really like her and would like for us to get to know each other better. I could sure use some suggestions." He briefly looked over at the two women and then quickly stuffed a muffin into his mouth.

Houston responded, "I think Detective Lorenzo could be the better one to ask. He likes you and he works five days a week with

Sasha. Go and have a beer or coffee with him and ask his advice. He's definitely a straight shooter."

"I agree with Tex," added Wilamina. "I think being up front with Sasha is a good way to earn her trust. Give her a call and simply ask for a date. Sasha told Lorenzo she's waiting for a 'cellophane man.' Honesty and openness are real big with her."

The three chatted a little longer. Marsh offered thanks and went on his way. He called back to Wilamina before heading out the door, "One day I'd like to hear about your prison experience."

While driving back to work he decided he'd make a call to Sasha as soon as he could muster up the courage, which he did that evening. He called her and she agreed to go out on a date for Saturday night.

Saturday night..........

Marsh knocked on her door exactly at 6 p.m.. *I can't believe how nervous I am. I've been on a thousand dates before, what the hell is going on with me? I feel like I'm back in high school again. This date feels different, like this is the first one that really matters.*

"Hello Marsh. I'm ready, or did you want to come in for a minute?"

"No, but thanks for asking. We have reservations at the Pelican Roost at the beach. It's about a thirty minute drive. You look great. How are you feeling?"

"Almost like new. I do get tired at the end of the day, but I'm so glad to be back at work for the past three days. I was beginning to feel like an invalid. My only outing has been to therapy and back home again. So I'm happy you called. I needed to get out of the house and do something fun."

Neither one said much on the way to the restaurant except to remark about the weather or the scenery. When they arrived at the restaurant's parking area, Marsh opened the door for her and took her hand and kept it until they were inside and had been seated. Sasha never tried to remove her hand from his. They ordered a drink and gave the waitress their dinner order.

Marsh turned sideways to look Sasha in the eye and said, "I've got to confess, I'm a little nervous, like I was in high school at the prom. I've felt something special about you since our first encounter. There you were wounded, bleeding and you asked me to take care of the other officer first. You were brave, hurting, but thinking of your co-worker first. I couldn't help noticing how beautiful you were, bloody yet beautiful." He stopped talking briefly, took a sip of water and continued, "Sorry, I'm rambling on, but I'm sincere. I'd like for us to get to know each other."

"Marsh, I do like you. I think you are a good man and have a good service heart. You're easy to talk to and pleasing to look at. I would like to see more of you, but I have to tell you something. This may change your mind about seeing me anymore."

Their food arrived and they both simply stared at the attractive meal that had been set before them. They started to eat slowly, silently for a short time. Then Sasha put her fork down and said, "I need you to know that I cannot ever bear children. The bullet damaged my uterus and it was removed. So, no babies for me." She kept her eyes focused on her plate until Marsh spoke.

"I'm sorry you were so seriously wounded, but my feelings for you have nothing to do with having children. You are still the brave, selfless, beautiful policewoman I felt drawn to. If you would take the chance to get to know me, you would find out I'm one hundred percent loyal. I'm a straight shooter and an open book.

"Children are important, but not necessary for my happiness. There are other options like adoption, fostering, or other ways to involve oneself with kids. There are Boys and Girls Clubs, volunteering at Juvenile Hall and more. I've been a Guardian ad

Litem for the past five years and have loved every minute of it. I've never felt a strong need to sire my own offspring. I like other people's kids just fine."

Sasha tried hard not to cry, but lost the battle. The flood gates opened and she let her feelings spill out.

Marsh moved close to her, "I sure hope those are happy tears and not sad tears of good-bye."

Sasha wiped her face with her napkin, "They're definitely happy, relief tears. So what's for dessert? And when does the band start playing? I want to know just how good a dancer you really are."

"You're in for a treat, Sasha. Hope you can keep up." Marsh was grinning from ear to ear.

CHAPTER SIXTY

"Hey Tex, I just finished talking with Chance. He said that the support group at the Grief Clinic has been very helpful. Richard is doing much better, making A's in school and has some friends. They still visit Melody weekly. The doctor told Chance that she probably won't live more than a few months. The cancer seems to be showing up everywhere. It sounds like Richard and Chance are both more at peace with their feelings about Melody. Chance also said that he and Lynn have decided to stay friends and not rush into any kind of romantic relationship for now. They are both still sorting through their grief over the loss of Charlene.

"Thank goodness for our friends at the Grief Clinic. They keep on walking along side those folks being held in the arms of loss and mourning. They're sure a blessing."

"I agree partner, they're the best. What do you say we take a drive to the beach. I'm hankerin' for some great sea food and I want to feel the sand between my toes."

Wilamina responded, "I like your idea. It's time we talk about what's weighing heavy in our hearts. We're looking at some big changes in our lives, aren't we Tex?"

"Yes, my friend. Some wonderful changes. I don't want anything to happen to our detective work. But I do see our living arrangements changing. Sark and me we're talking marriage and so are you and Stoney.

"Winnie Winters has asked me about the possibility of renting our upstairs apartment. We'd keep the office space. You'd be living in Stoney's new house and that's about twenty minutes out of town. That's not far. Sark and I can live in his house or he said, if I wanted we could buy another place. I love his house and it's close to work for him and me.

"I'm sure gonna miss livin' with you. You're the closest I've ever come to havin' a lovin' family."

"Tex, I see it as just growin' our family bigger. Sark and Stoney are two real good men. You and me, we'll always be best friends. Now, add the guys and we'll have two more best friends plus benefits. I like the benefits and I'm not talking about finances." She let out a hearty laugh.

"Right on, Willy. I like the benefits too. I can't believe how wonderful our lives have become. I could almost get religious here, that is almost.

"How about we talk some more about our ideas starting a half way house for newly released inmates? I'm also thinking about the young ones. The kids who land in Juvenile Hall, cuz of rotten parents or poverty or just plain loss of hope. If they got the right kind of help sooner, they wouldn't have to become inmates later on.

What'a you think about getting a group of our friends together and asking for their ideas? We could set up a team. You and me, Sasha, Sammy, Lacona, the Grief Clinic gals and Jessie. Sharon could help from Lancer's and so could the warden. We might even talk to Winnie Winters. She's another one whose been-there done-that."

"I like it plenty, " answered Wilamina with gusto. "We got a bunch of great guys to add to the gang, Stoney, Sark, Tony, Luke, Roco and the Rickels. Maybe even Marsh and Dr. Blackmore would be interested. Nothin' could stop a team made up of such wise and lovin' folks. We could call ourselves The Dream Team!"

"I like the sound of that Willy. Let's go take our shoes off and run through the sand and stuff ourselves with sea food."

They hugged for a long, shed a few tears and off they went to the beach.

CHAPTER SIXTY-ONE

The second annual Picnic..........

The same group of friends that attended the first picnic along with a few new ones, were gathered at the Pelican Park. The new additions were Marsh, the Rickels, Dr. Blackmore and Winnie Winters. An abundance of food dishes were placed on two round tables. The round tables that were brought by Brooksie and Luke were thought to be more conducive to sharing ideas rather than the long, oblong ones.

Houston blew a whistle and announced, "Before we dive in, Willy, our singing religious leader, wants to say something. Go for it, Willy."

"Many things have happened this past year. Most real good and a few not so good. If I'd known that my goin' to prison was gonna to turn my life completely around and bring me more happiness than I thought possible for someone like me, I'd have gone to jail sooner. Tex, Sam, me and even Sasha owe a ton of thanks to many folks. Some of you great folks are here today. My first thanks is to Jesus and the second goes to the rest of you. Don't want to forget, Sharon, the warden and Mela."

Stoney squeezed Wilamina's hand and belted out, "AMEN!" followed by the rest of the group.

After the meal had been eagerly devoured, Houston made another announcement. "Before we start to play our famous kind of football, we would like to have a discussion about some future ideas and goals.

"Willy and me feel the need to reach out to others who are in prison or the younger ones who are headed there. We've been talking about a half-way house for women who are leaving Lancer's and working with kids who are in Juvenile Hall. Would love to get everybody's ideas. Willy even came up with a name for this group, 'The Dream Team.' Everyone here today has a heart for helping others so if we put our ideas together, I bet something good can come from it."

Sark immediately said, "Count me in Tex. I know firsthand, that most times, once a kid lands in Juvenile Hall, the next step may probably be jail."

Luke added, "I've seen some real sad cases of the plight of the foster kids. Many of those kids never had a chance. They don't know the first thing about caring for themselves in a loving way. All they know about is surviving and what it takes. What can a five year old know about hope when their own parents neglect them, starve them, beat them and make life a living hell? I would love to be part of 'The Dream Team' and make a difference for the innocents and for those women who need and deserve a second or may a third chance."

Everyone started talking excitedly and, eagerly giving their ideas voice. Wilamina grabbed Houston's whistle and blew hard. "I can't write down your ideas 'cause you're all talking at the same time. How about later, say in the next week or two, you write down your ideas and then we can come together and share what we've got?"

There was an agreement all around and a date a time was set for the first meeting of "The Dream Team."

Stoney shouted out, "Okay then, let's play football, and if I'm lucky, my Willy will land on top of me, just like the first time we played football!"

Lacona was the last person to speak out, before the game began, "Anyone interested in adopting an adorable kitten or puppy?"

Look for my next book...

SALT AND PEPPER DETECTIVE AGENCY AND THE DREAM TEAM

A mystery novel

Donna Underwood